LAY DOWN
THE LAW

What Reviewers Say About Carsen Taite's Work

It Should be a Crime

"Taite also practices criminal law and she weaves her insider knowledge of the criminal justice system into the love story seamlessly and with excellent timing."—*Curve Magazine*

"This [*It Should be a Crime*] is just Taite's second novel…, but it's as if she has bookshelves full of bestsellers under her belt."
—*Gay List Daily*

Do Not Disturb

"Taite's tale of sexual tension is entertaining in itself, but a number of secondary characters…add substantial color to romantic inevitability"—Richard Labonte, *Book Marks*

Nothing but the Truth

"Author Taite is really a Dallas defense attorney herself, and it's obvious her viewpoint adds considerable realism to her story, making it especially riveting as a mystery. I give it four stars out of five."—Bob Lind, *Echo Magazine*

"As a criminal defense attorney in Dallas, Texas, Carsen Taite knows her way around the court house. …*Nothing But the Truth* is an enjoyable mystery with some hot romance thrown in."—*Just About Write*

"Taite has written an excellent courtroom drama with two interesting women leading the cast of characters. Taite herself is a practicing defense attorney, and her courtroom scenes are clearly based on real knowledge. This should be another winner for Taite."—*Lambda Literary*

The Best Defense

"Real Life defense attorney Carsen Taite polishes her fifth work of lesbian fiction, *The Best Defense*, with the realism she daily encounters in the office and in the courts. And that polish is something that makes *The Best Defense* shine as an excellent read."—*Out & About Newspaper*

Slingshot

"The mean streets of lesbian literature finally have the hard boiled bounty hunter they deserve. It's a slingshot of a ride, bad guys and hot women rolled into one page turning package. I'm looking forward to Luca Bennett's next adventure."—J. M. Redmann, author of the Micky Knight mystery series

Battle Axe

"This second book is satisfying, substantial, and slick. Plus, it has heart and love coupled with Luca's array of weapons and a bad-ass verbal repertoire…I cannot imagine anyone not having a great time riding shotgun through all of Luca's escapades. I recommend hopping on Luca's band wagon and having a blast."—*Rainbow Book Reviews*

"Taite breathes life into her characters with elemental finesse…A great read, told in the vein of a good old detective-type novel filled with criminal elements, thugs, and mobsters that will entertain and amuse."—*Lambda Literary*

Beyond Innocence

"Taite keeps you guessing with delicious delay until the very last minute…Taite's time in the courtroom lends *Beyond Innocence*, a terrific verisimilitude someone not in the profession couldn't impart. And damned if she doesn't make practicing law interesting."—*Out in Print*

"As you would expect, sparks and legal writs fly. What I liked about this book were the shades of grey (no, not the smutty Shades of Grey)—both in the relationship as well as the cases."
—*C-spot Reviews*

Rush

"A simply beautiful interplay of police procedural magic, murder, FBI presence, misguided protective cover-ups, and a superheated love affair…a Gold Star from me and major encouragement for all readers to dive right in and consume this story with gusto!"
—*Rainbow Book Reviews*

Switchblade

"I enjoyed the book and it was a fun read—mystery, action, humor, and a bit of romance. Who could ask for more? If you've read and enjoyed Taite's legal novels, you'll like this. If you've read and enjoyed the two other books in this series, this one will definitely satisfy your Luca fix and I highly recommend picking it up. Highly recommended."—*C Spot Reviews*

"Dallas's intrepid female bounty hunter, Luca Bennett, is back in another adventure. Fantastic! Between her many friends and lovers, her interesting family, her fly by the seat of her pants lifestyle, and a whole host of detractors there is rarely a dull moment."
—*Rainbow Book Reviews*

Courtship

"The political drama is just top-notch. The emotional and sexual tensions are intertwined with great timing and flair. I truly adored this book from beginning to end. Fantabulous!"—*Rainbow Book Reviews*

Visit us at www.boldstrokesbooks.com

By the Author

Truelesbianlove.com

It Should be a Crime

Do Not Disturb

Nothing but the Truth

The Best Defense

Beyond Innocence

Rush

Courtship

The Luca Bennett Mystery Series:

Slingshot

Battle Axe

Switchblade

Lone Star Law Series:

Lay Down the Law

LAY DOWN THE LAW

by

Carsen Taite

2015

LAY DOWN THE LAW

ISBN 13: 978-1-62639-336-3

THIS TRADE PAPERBACK ORIGINAL IS PUBLISHED BY
BOLD STROKES BOOKS, INC.
P.O. BOX 249
VALLEY FALLS, NY 12185

FIRST EDITION: APRIL 2015

CREDITS

EDITOR: CINDY CRESAP
PRODUCTION DESIGN: SUSAN RAMUNDO
COVER DESIGN BY SHERI (GRAPHICARTIST2020@HOTMAIL.COM)

Acknowledgments

I was a junior in high school when the "Who Done It" episode of the popular series *Dallas* (the original version) aired on TV. Unlike the 90 million folks who tuned in to watch, I didn't get to see the show that night. It was Friday night, I was in the high school band, and the Plano Wildcats were battling it out in 5A football. This was before the days of cell phones and instant downloads, but loud shouts revealing the truth about who shot J.R. spread through the stadium full of Friday night light fanatics with as much enthusiasm as "Take State!"

I truly believe the series *Dallas* was so popular because of its bold characters and the colorful canvas of the setting. Big oil, corruption, and dark family secrets kept a nation glued to their televisions week after week for fourteen seasons. So, when Rad and I discussed my plan for a new series, it was a no-brainer to put the lawyer and cops I usually write about smack in the middle of a dynamic Texas setting, complete with ranches and oil and corruption and crime. I look forward to taking these heroines on a wild ride full of twist and turns, and I hope you'll enjoy this first installment enough to hop on board for the rest of the series.

Thanks to all the usual suspects: Rad, Sandy Lowe, and all the rest of the crew at Bold Strokes Books for all the hard work they do to get our stories out into the world. Sheri, thanks for another great cover. Cindy Cresap—my intrepid editor—you're the best. Ever. Ruth Sternglanz, for always being available when I need to brainstorm, thank you! Ashley Bartlett and VK Powell—you two are the best first readers a gal could hope for. You keep me on track, and your willingness to give me insightful critiques under the gun of a deadline always amazes me. I owe you both. Big time. And a big hug to all my fellow BSB authors—you are family.

Lainey, I couldn't have realized this dream without you. I notice everything you do, big and little, to support me, and I appreciate you more than I can ever express.

To my readers—all the notes you write, all the books you buy are fuel to my creative spirit. Thanks for all your support. This story is for you!

Dedication

To Lainey, my fellow dreamer.

CHAPTER ONE

A t first glance everything looked exactly as it had when
she'd left three years before.

Peyton hefted her duffle bag onto her shoulder, handed the
driver a fifty, and declined his offer to traverse the rocky drive up
to the main house. The long walk along the rugged path would
give her just the right amount of time to adjust to the change from
the cement, steel, and bustle of the nation's capital.

A few steps in, sweat beads formed on her forehead, and
Peyton mourned the fall weather she'd left behind. North Texas
would likely be warm for at least another month, maybe more.
She'd need to invest in some cooler clothes. She set down her bag
and rolled up her sleeves while saying a silent thanks that she'd
thought to wear her boots on the plane. She paused and looked
around. The portion of fence she was leaning on was in good shape,
but at least three other sections in plain view needed repair. From
this distance, the house looked the same—large, but unassuming.
Round bales of hay dotted the field to the left, but she didn't see
any cattle out to pasture. No doubt they'd found the nearest shade
tree for a nap, which is what she'd wind up doing if she didn't get
inside soon.

She strode briskly the rest of the way, with mixed feelings
about coming home to the Circle Six Ranch. But now that she was
here, she was anxious to drink in all she'd missed. Land as far as
the eye could see. The crisp, earthy smell of hay and horses. The

sweat of a hard day's work. A week from now, she'd be back in an office, but when the workday was over, she'd come back here to open vistas and a twilight ride on her favorite horse. Much better than a steel and glass apartment building on the Metro line.

As she got closer to the house, she realized it wasn't the same. She surveyed the obvious signs of wear and tear. Nothing major, but she wasn't used to seeing anything out of place on the ranch, which made the peeling paint on the eaves, the overgrown shrubs, and the taped up window on the second floor cause for concern. Before she had a chance to process her feelings, a loud but welcome voice shattered her concentration.

"Peyton Davis, get your butt up here! Did you walk all the way from Washington D.C.?"

Peyton grinned at her mother who stepped down from the porch. People said they looked exactly alike, and she took it as a compliment. Helen Davis was a handsome woman, tall and rangy with rugged good looks. Like Peyton, she was dressed in jeans and boots. She tugged on the duffle bag hanging on Peyton's shoulder.

"I got it, Mom."

"Fine then." She let the bag go. "You're almost late for lunch. Can't be late around here. You do and you won't eat. There's not a restaurant on every corner. You're going to have a lot of things to remember now that you're home. Come in and wash up. You look like you just waded through a dust bowl."

Her rapid-fire speech complete, she turned and walked back into the house, letting the screen door swing shut behind her. Peyton shook her head and followed, taking care to knock some of the dust from her boots before she crossed the threshold into the main house of the Davis family ranch.

When the smell of fresh baked cornbread combined with the leftover scent of breakfast bacon hit her, she knew she was home. Her mouth watered. The package of peanut butter crackers she'd eaten on the plane had long since worn off. She set her bag in the mudroom and followed her nose to the kitchen. She was steps away when strong arms swept her into a huge embrace. She knew who it was without looking.

"Zach, let me go, fool. I'm covered in dust."

Peyton mock struggled, but her younger brother only grinned. "I'll match you, dirt for dirt. I just came in from the north forty. Couldn't let you get to the food before me."

"I should've known this wasn't about you being glad to see me. Hello to you too."

"Seriously, sis. It's great to have you home."

She leaned back and studied his face. As with her mother, it was like looking in a mirror except Zach's usually playful brown eyes were tinged with melancholy. He'd always been the most expressive child in the family, but his mood was rarely serious. Then again, recent events had given all of them more to be serious about. Still, something about his tone signaled his display of affection was about more than the time they'd spent apart. She filed the observation away with the others. She'd pull them out and examine them once she'd had a chance to settle in. "It's great to be back. I want you to catch me up on everything, but right now I'm starving. Are Dad and Neil coming in for lunch?"

"Uh, Dad's here. I think he's already in the kitchen. Come on."

He took off in front of her, but she waited a second, noting that Zach had glossed over the mention of their brother, Neil. She'd have to face him sooner or later, but later would be preferable. Today was a packed day, and she'd need a good meal, one without conflict, to brace for the rest of it.

Jim Davis was already at the head of the table, drinking what she suspected was thick, sweet tea from a large glass. He stood when she approached and pulled her into a hug, not as forceful as Zach's, but every bit as intense. The embrace was tender, but his grip wasn't as strong as she remembered. When he finally pulled back, she searched his eyes for more signs of change. His gaze wasn't quite as clear, his pallor was gray, and he braced an arm against the table. She'd known he was sick, but the reality of it was hard to witness.

"Dad, it's great to see you."

"Good to have you back, Peyton. We have a lot of work to do."

Her mother strode to the table with a large platter of fried chicken, and was followed by an elderly Latina carrying bowls with mashed potatoes and fried okra. "Work talk later," her mother said. "We have to sort out the details for this afternoon." She turned to Peyton. "Fernanda put some go-to-meeting jeans and a few new shirts with your black boots in the closet upstairs. We need to leave at five."

Peyton nodded and shot Fernanda Luna, the family house-keeper, a smile. While she would have much rather spent her first day back in Texas settling in, she knew the family had never missed the annual Cattle Baron's Ball, and her homecoming wasn't a good enough reason to change that. Thank goodness her mother had arranged to have some clothes ready for her, since all she had until the movers arrived on Monday was the clothes on her back and what she'd been able to fit in her duffle bag.

As they settled in to eat, Zach took over the conversation, enthusiastically including her in all the plans he had for the ranch. She heard the words, but she couldn't ignore the cautious undercurrent from her internal ear. The broken rails, the peeling paint, the empty fields. For every thing Zach said he wanted to do, she could think of two others that had been neglected. Where was Neil and why wasn't he taking better care of things?

She studied her dad, trying to get a read on his feelings about all of Zach's plans. He looked back at her, but his eyes were tired, distant. None of this exuberance was coming from him. She chewed her food and her thoughts, slowly, carefully. She wasn't here to tend fields, herd cattle, or raise horses. The ranch wasn't hers, and she shouldn't let its disrepair concern her. She'd decided before she ever got on the plane that she'd find a place to live in the city. Her father's voice interrupted her thoughts.

"Mother, pass me the mashed potatoes."

He was staring directly at her, but he seemed a million miles away. Peyton looked from her father's outstretched hand into his eyes, waiting for him to realize his mistake. One, two, three seconds passed before she finally lifted the bowl and handed it to him, holding his gaze the entire time. When she released the bowl, he smiled and said, "Thanks, Peyton. It's good to have you home."

She cast a look at Zach who seemed to be unduly interested in a chicken thigh and then at her mother who shook her head. Peyton reached for her tea glass and took a long drink of the cool, sweet liquid, escaping into the simple pleasure. She'd drink her drink, eat her dinner, visit the horses, and get ready for the ball. Later, she'd sort through all the things that had changed in her absence.

❖

"It's not supposed to rain."

Lily Gantry turned around at the sound of her best friend Courtney Pearson's voice and pointed at the gathering clouds. "When was the last time the weather here did what it was supposed to?"

"Well, if the bottom falls out, you'll just have a bunch of soaking wet donors. We already got most of their money, so what's the downside?"

"Silent and live auction, bar receipts," Lily ticked the list off on her fingers. "I've already let the convention center go as our in case of rain venue. If it pours, we stand to lose a bunch of money."

"And we've already made a ton for a wonderful cause. In just a few hours, people will start pouring in here, and rain or shine, we'll get them liquored up and they'll start emptying their pockets. Relax."

Lily took a deep breath. This was her first time to chair the annual Cattle Baron's Ball. She'd stepped in at the last minute when the other co-chair had a family emergency, but despite her late entry, she'd made it her personal goal to raise more money for cancer research than any of the years before them. Courtney, her co-chair, seemed more interested in finding an eligible bachelor in the mix of attendees than raising funds, but her charisma was sure to rake in the bucks.

Two hours later, Lily changed into her outfit for the evening and went back outside to check the sky. She heaved a sigh of relief when she saw the clouds had scattered and the dusky night hinted at a cool, comfortable evening. The full moon was in view, and crowds of well-heeled donors started to pour through the gates at South Fork Ranch, ready for one of the biggest events of the year. Now that all the details for the event were in place, her primary job was hostess. She squared her shoulders and headed for the front entrance to greet the hundreds of guests who were arriving to support cancer research and have a Texas-sized good time.

"Shall we?" Courtney hooked arms with her and they walked to the front gate.

They'd barely made it a few steps before Dalton Henry, the chair of the Cattle Baron's Ball board, corralled them. "Ladies, looks like we're in for a record crowd tonight. You sure you're up for it?"

Lily squeezed Courtney's arm before she could snap out a sharp retort in response to Dalton's usual condescension. "We've done everything we can do at this point. Only thing left is to make sure everyone has a good time." She offered her sweetest smile. "You'll help us with that, won't you, Mr. Henry?"

Before he could reply, a big voice interrupted. "Dalton Henry, are you bothering my girl?"

Lily smiled as her father pulled her into a hug, but this time her smile was genuine. "Dad, this dress has to make it through a long evening. Let's try not to wrinkle it to death in the first five minutes. Where's Mom?"

Cyrus Gantry waved his hand in the air. "She found Courtney's mother the minute we got here and I haven't seen her since." He signaled to Dalton. "Dalton, leave these girls be. They'll do you proud. Now why don't you do something important and show me to the bar?"

Courtney pointed behind him. "Isn't that the Davis family?"

"Who?"

"You know they own the Circle Six Ranch. They're long-time supporters and sponsors. Time for me to go schmooze. Mr. Henry, will you wait here? I'm sure they'd love to meet you."

Dalton looked at her father who shrugged and signaled that he was headed to the bar. Lily watched Courtney walk away, her curiosity piqued. She and Courtney had split the duty of gathering sponsors for the event. She'd heard of the Circle Six Ranch, but she'd never met the Davises. She suspected the handsome young man in Courtney's sightline was the primary reason she was interested in giving them a personal greeting.

Their warm embrace proved her right. Even from a distance, Lily could tell Courtney was flirting shamelessly. Just like in high school. If she were interested in men, she might flirt too. He was devilishly attractive.

Lily's glance moved to the couple she assumed were his parents. Mrs. Davis was a taller version of her son—handsome, full of life, but Mr. Davis was hunched and sallow. He looked exhausted. Before she could process her impressions, Courtney and the Davises started walking toward her. As they approached, a woman who'd been standing with them came into view, and Lily locked eyes with her, taking in honey eyes, short waves of brown hair, and a firm jaw. They held each other's glance, and then the woman's face softened slightly and her lips curled into the hint of a smile. Infectious. Lily smiled back, even started to walk across the lawn, drawn to the magnetism of the stranger, but two steps in, she froze.

"Are you okay?" Courtney grasped her arm as she whispered the question in her ear.

Lily could only manage a nod, her gaze still fixed on the woman who'd hung back from the rest of the crowd. While Courtney introduced the Davis clan to Dalton Henry, Lily watched Virginia Taylor, the bane of her existence, casually drape an arm around the tall, mysterious stranger and lean in close. Too close. Lily wanted to look away, but inexplicably she seemed destined to see this play out. All traces of the stranger's smile disappeared as Virginia's body hugged her tight, but the connection between them lingered, and Lily couldn't bear to be the one to break it.

"You look like you've seen a ghost."

Courtney again. Unwilling to risk looking away, Lily grabbed Courtney's arm and willed her to look in the direction she was focused. "Who is that?"

"Where?"

"Over there. With Virginia."

"Are you sure you're okay? You look pale."

"Courtney," Lily growled, willing her to focus.

"Okay, that must be Peyton Davis. She's Zach's older sister. I hear she just got back in town today. Rumor is she left town a few years ago—some kind of falling out with the family. She's been living in D.C. I think she's a lawyer. I hear she's got a new job in Dallas."

"Peyton Davis." Nice name. Lily repeated it silently in her head, several times. She wanted to say it out loud again, but didn't want to seem crazy. Instead she focused on the other details Courtney had provided. A lot of information, but not much substance. Did Peyton know Virginia from when she used to live in Dallas or was she easily charmed by shallow beauty? She decided Peyton must know her. Virginia moved fast, but even she didn't move that fast. Lily watched for a few more seconds, and then decided she didn't care how Peyton knew Virginia, especially since Virginia's pole climbing routine hadn't distracted Peyton from their connection yet. "Introduce me."

"Really?"

Lily broke her connection with Peyton for a quick second, and turned to Courtney. "Yes, please. Now."

"Okay." Courtney whispered something to Zach Davis, who hadn't left her side, and then tugged Lily's arm. "Come on then."

"Wait, she's gone!" Lily glanced in every direction. She'd only looked away for a second, and now it was like the entire silent exchange had been a figment of her imagination. No matter where she looked, she didn't see a single sign of Peyton, and Virginia had disappeared too. Didn't take a rocket scientist to figure out what had happened.

"She has to be here somewhere," Courtney said. "Let's look around."

Lily took a moment to consider before shrugging the idea away. She was here to do a job, not stalk handsome strangers. She and Courtney were supposed to make everyone feel welcome and receptive to parting with their money in the name of cancer research. Time to focus.

"No, the whim has passed. I'm over it. Sorry. Let's get to work." Without waiting for a response, she marched past Dalton who was chatting up the rest of the Davis family and took up a position near the gate to welcome the rest of the guests as they arrived. She cast one look back. No sign of Peyton, but she did catch Courtney giving Zach Davis a very friendly hug before she walked over to join her.

"That was quick," she whispered.

"What are you talking about?"

"You just met the guy and it looks like you have plans for later."

"We might. You should try it sometime."

"Making plans with some guy?"

"No, silly. Being impulsive. Once everyone arrives, take a break and go find Peyton. Better yet, why don't I ask Zach to introduce you?"

Lily nearly burst into flames. "Don't you dare," she hissed. "If you do, I will never speak to you again."

"Cool it, girl. I'm not going to embarrass you, but if you want someone, you've got to take the bull by the horns and go get her."

"Bull, huh? Don't talk to me like I'm a virgin teenager. I'm perfectly capable of getting what I want."

"Sure, honey. The problem is you don't. When are you going to realize you're the best-looking woman in this city and you should take advantage of your assets while you have them? You haven't dated a single woman since you've been back, have you?"

Lily shot her a scathing glance, but Courtney was already back in hostess mode, shaking the hands of newly arrived guests. Didn't matter what Courtney said. She was perfectly capable of attracting another woman and she could do so whenever she wanted. After all, she hadn't been the only one staring across the room. Peyton Davis had been just as interested as she was. At least until Virginia, with her wandering hands and whispered promises, came along. Well, if that was the kind of woman Peyton Davis was attracted to, she was better off not making her acquaintance.

❖

"Come on and dance with me."

Peyton pushed her way out of Virginia Taylor's grasp. "Thanks, but no thanks." She'd let Virginia drag her to the other side of the party supposedly to meet up with some of her friends, but so far it was looking like a ploy to get her alone. Peyton's polite quotient had run out. If she didn't make a break for it now, she'd never get back to her family in the growing crowd, let alone find the dark-haired beauty from earlier.

"Peyton, over here!"

Relieved to hear Zach's voice, she murmured apologies to Virginia, and made her way over to the bar where he stood with a tall blonde. "Where's everyone else?"

"Mom and Dad went to look at the silent auction. Neil's not here yet." He gestured to Courtney. "Peyton, this is Courtney Pearson. Can I get you two something to drink?"

Courtney said, "I'll have a glass of champagne, but when I ask for another, stop me. Technically, I'm working."

Peyton ordered a beer. "What does technically working mean?"

"She's the chair of the whole damn event," Zach said. "She's in charge of everything."

Courtney lifted her glass. "Co-chair." She took a drink and looked pointedly at Peyton. "I couldn't have done it without help from my good friend, Lily Gantry. Have you met her? She was at the front gate when you came in. Dark and mysterious, a real beauty. I can arrange for an introduction if you like."

Peyton spent a moment pondering the question beneath the question before responding. She'd only come here tonight out of a sense of tradition. She'd had absolutely no intention of spending the evening chasing a skirt, no matter how captivated she was by the wearer. She sought to bow out gracefully. "I'm afraid I haven't had the pleasure, but if she's 'technically working' like you, I can meet her some other time."

"I'll have her come by your table. You'll love her."

Peyton nodded her reply while Zach smirked. Time to move along before she wound up the subject of his meddlesome matchmaking. "I should find Mom and Dad. I'll catch up with you both later." She had no idea where her parents were, but being hemmed in at the bar was wearing on her nerves. She offered a slight bow and made her way across the room, giving silent thanks that the event was outside. When the crowd closed in, she could pretend she was at a real ranch, steps from her horse and dozens of winding trails. Her horse. Ranger. She supposed he wasn't really hers anymore and she'd have to get used to that. Still, she planned to make time to ride him tomorrow. Today had been a whirlwind, but tomorrow she could settle into some routine. Take a ride, figure out her next steps.

"You already ditch the rest of the family?"

Peyton recognized the voice of her older brother and she knew he wasn't kidding. "I walked them in. You would know that if you'd shown up with the rest of us."

He took a step in front of her and moved close. Passersby probably thought he was about to hug her, but his low tones delivered only anger. "Don't lecture me on obligations. You have no idea what's been going on here, and if you think you're going to show up and be welcomed like the prodigal daughter, then you're in for a big surprise."

Peyton shook her head. She'd been prepared for Neil to be unhappy with her, but she hadn't planned on such vitriol. No point in responding. Anything she said at this point would be fuel to the fire he'd been tending since before she'd left. She bit back a response and resolved that this week she'd find a place of her own, close to work. She could handle city life a bit longer while she figured out what her future held.

She'd been grateful for the transfer back to her hometown, but it had come through so fast, she hadn't had a chance to make proper plans. Her boss in D.C., Deputy Attorney General Rodriguez, probably thought he was doing her a favor by pushing it through, but the rush meant she hadn't had time to find a place of her own. A place where she wouldn't have to deal with her brother's lingering anger. She faced Neil, knowing what she wanted to say, but also knowing he wasn't ready to hear it. She settled for a conciliatory stance.

"I don't expect anything, but if there's anything you need, I'm here and I'm happy to help."

Neil took a long draw from his beer before answering. "I think you know how you can help best. Stick to your law job and leave the ranching to us."

"Careful, Neil, you sound like the sheriff in an old Western. Next thing you know, you're going to gather the townsfolk and run me out on a rail. Don't worry. It's not my plan to get in your way. Besides, it sounds like Zach has plenty of energy and enthusiasm for the job."

Neil's brow tensed further at the mention of their younger brother. "Zach's a piece of work, but I can handle him. Don't you worry."

She hadn't planned on it, but the strong undertow of anxiety that accompanied his words stuck with her. Before she could examine it further, her biggest distraction of the evening was suddenly at her side. From a distance, Lily Gantry had been beautiful. Up close, she was stunning. Peyton sucked in a breath at the sight of her caramel skin, deep brown eyes, and waves of jet-black hair. But Lily's smile was the winning feature, and Peyton wanted to be the one responsible for her radiance. For now, she returned the smile and held out a hand. "You must be Lily Gantry."

"And you must be Peyton Davis." Lily took her hand. The touch was soft, yet firm. It lingered. "I'm glad to finally meet you."

"My pleasure. I was hoping to make your acquaintance."

"Perfect, then we have something in common, right off the bat."

Neil cleared his throat and Peyton glanced down at her hand, still holding Lily's. She shot Lily a look of regret and gently released her hold. Figured. Neil didn't want her in his life, but he had no problem standing square in the middle of hers. She motioned to him with her now free hand. "And this is my brother, Neil Davis."

"Good to meet you, Neil." Lily's eyes slid back to Peyton's. "I met your other brother, Zach, earlier. Does that complete the collection of Davis siblings or are there more of you?"

"That's all of us."

"And all of you are ranchers?"

Peyton paused and Neil jumped into the break. "Peyton's not a rancher. She's a fancy lawyer. Doubt she's been on a horse in years."

He punctuated his remarks with a smile Peyton knew he didn't feel, but she kept silent and watched as Lily looked between them, obviously trying to gauge whether Neil's words carried true animosity. She knew they did, but he'd injected enough teasing tone to fool a stranger. She had no plans to engage and merely waited for Lily's response.

Again, Lily addressed her directly. "Too bad. I was hoping I might be able to arrange a ride. The Davis quarter horses are reputed to be the best in Texas."

Peyton looked at Neil before she answered and when she did speak her words were deliberate. "Reputation can be deceiving, but our horses are the best. I'd be honored to escort you on a ride."

"Excellent. I'll write down my number and you can call me when you're available." Lily took her hand again, her grip firm and sure, her fingers lingering as she released her hold. "I should get back to work, but I hope you have a wonderful evening."

Seconds later, Lily disappeared into the crowd. Peyton watched her go, watched the light fade with every step Lily took in the opposite direction. She waited until Lily was completely out of sight before turning back to face Neil. His expression was incredulous, and Peyton didn't wait for him to take the first jab.

"Guess I'll need some time with the horses this week. And gee, I hope I remember how to ride."

CHAPTER TWO

No, she hasn't called." Lily placed the phone between her shoulder and ear as she shuffled the papers on her desk. She'd spent Monday morning at the Cattle Baron office sorting through the aftermath of the ball: receipts, donations, lists of auction winners whose money they still needed to collect. More often than she wanted to admit, her thoughts had strayed to memories of Peyton Davis and her electrifying first impression. "Maybe she was just being polite. Besides, her brother Neil acted like she wasn't much of a horsewoman."

"That's not what Zach says," Courtney spoke the words in a conspiratorial whisper. "He says she's an accomplished rider and has won all kinds of awards."

"Maybe that was a long time ago."

"Not that long."

"Aren't you supposed to be making me feel better?"

"Sorry. I guess I'm just saying there are more layers there than you may want to peel your way through."

"Maybe." Lily closed her eyes and conjured Peyton's handsome face. Her strong jawline, gentle eyes, and barely tamed hair. And the killer smile that invited her in, made her believe no one else in the world mattered. She didn't care if Peyton couldn't ride the coin-operated horse at the grocery store, she wanted to see her again, bask in the heat of that radiant smile. "But maybe I'm ready for a little complexity in my life. The last woman I dated was Elsie Gifford, and she's still trying to relive her first cotillion."

"Speaking of high society, are you still going to the mother daughter Junior League lunch this weekend?"

"Damn. I'd almost managed to forget all about it."

"So I'll see you there?"

"I suppose I'll have to show up. Mother is one of the committee chairs. Have I ever mentioned how much I'd love to spend a weekend in jeans instead of dressing up for some affair?"

Courtney laughed. "Guess you should've been born into a different family."

Lily nearly dropped the phone. Courtney was joking, but like any reference to her status, the remark stung. She struggled to summon some levity, but Courtney beat her to the punch.

"Oh, sugar, I'm sorry. I'm a thoughtless bitch. It's Mondays. I hate them and they hate me. Plus, I think they put decaf instead of the hard stuff in my coffee at that dreadful new Starbucks down on Elm…"

Lily let her drone on. She'd wear herself out and the entire topic would be forgotten. Besides, it wasn't as if everyone didn't know she wasn't a true born Gantry. Family photos featuring her brown skin and dark hair alongside her mother's and father's fair complexions were an obvious clue. She was grateful to have been adopted rather than left to languish in the care of the Our Lady of Guadalupe children's home. But the sense of feeling like she didn't quite fit had a way of creeping in. Wealth and all its trappings had always felt suffocating to her. She wondered if her connection to a mother she'd never known, one who hadn't had the resources to feed her new baby, let alone raise her in any way close to the lifestyle the Gantrys' wealth allowed, spurred those feelings. Which brought her back to the topic of the luncheon.

"Tell you what," she interrupted Courtney who hadn't quite wound down yet. "You pick me up on Saturday and I'll forgive all. Mother will already be down at the Adolphus bossing the help around, and I don't want to have to show up on my own and make inane conversation with a bunch of women I haven't seen in years. Deal?"

"Deal." A beeping sounded on the line. "Darn, I have to take this call. I'll call you later and we'll discuss details."

Lily hung up, but not more than a minute later, the phone rang again and she picked it up without looking. "Just can't wait until Saturday to see me can you?"

"Actually, I'd love to see you before then, but I've got a busy week ahead."

The low and slightly rough tones of the unexpected voice startled her, but she had no doubt who spoke the words. She held the phone out from her ear and stared at it as if trying to divine the miracle that had conjured Peyton's call. Placing the phone back against her ear, she wished for composure. "I suppose I should've answered with a simple hello."

"Hello to you too. This is Peyton Davis, by the way."

"I know. I hope you had a good rest of the weekend."

"I did, but I missed seeing you again at the ball."

"Alas, I was in high demand."

"I'm sure you were."

She was flirting wasn't she? The words were flirting, but the tone was straightforward. Lily contemplated her next move, but before she could get the words out, Peyton said, "About Saturday, I was wondering if you would join me for a trail ride. Nothing fancy. Maybe a picnic lunch if that would interest you."

Visions of a red-and-white checkered blanket strewn across a well-worn trail and Peyton Davis in snug 501s and dusty boots robbed her breath. And almost stole her memory. Saturday. Junior League. Lunch. Her mother. No casual picnic on the ranch for her. She'd be sipping tea and eating five-star food while wearing the latest fashion from Neiman's. Damn. "A trail ride and picnic interests me a great deal, but unfortunately, I already have plans for Saturday."

"Oh, I see. That must have been the call you were expecting."

Lily rushed to mend the misunderstanding. "Not exactly. I mean, not like that. I thought you were Courtney. We have a luncheon with our mothers on Saturday. I love my mother, but believe me I'd rather be in the saddle with you."

"Oh you would, would you?"

Peyton laughed, and the sound was rich and full. Contagious. Lily found she was laughing too, and any embarrassment she might have felt about her faux pas quickly vanished in the wake of Peyton's refreshing candor. "How about Sunday?"

"Sunday works. Let's start mid-morning. I'll pack lunch. Should I pick you up?"

"I'll meet you at the ranch." Lily didn't spend a lot of thought on the subject. She only knew she was going to have to explain to her parents why she wasn't joining them for church services and she didn't want to have to explain a date with Peyton at the same time.

She wrote down the directions and they agreed on a time.

"I look forward to seeing you," Peyton said.

"It'll be fun."

"I'll do my best to show you a good time."

Lily hung up the phone already imagining the likelihood of that outcome.

❖

Peyton looked out across the ridge and smiled, happy that Lily had seemed as glad to hear from her as she'd been to make the call. She reached over and stroked Ranger's mane.

"Guess we have a date this weekend, big boy." She laughed when he tossed his head. "I know, not what I was expecting either, but this new adventure is full of surprises." Ranger nickered and shook his head. Peyton laughed at their casual conversation and grasped the reins, ready to head back to the house. As she started to mount her ride, she spotted a large, dark green tractor-trailer truck in the distance. It didn't look like any of the other vehicles she'd seen on the property. She looked closer and saw the faint outline of a logo in white, and she made a mental note to ask Zach about it. She'd ask Neil, but he'd likely bite her head off before she could get a word in. Before she had a foot in the stirrup, her cell phone rang again. Had Lily Gantry changed her mind already? She pulled the phone from her pocket and glanced at the screen—No Caller ID—but instinct told her who it was.

So much for a peaceful end to her morning ride. "Hello?"

"Ms. Davis, I have Mr. Gellar on the line for you."

"I'm ready." She wasn't. She wasn't supposed to meet with her new boss until Monday morning when she reported for duty at the federal building in downtown Dallas. This week was supposed to be about getting settled, including finding a place to live that wasn't in close proximity to her perpetually angry brother.

"Ms. Davis, Hershel Gellar. You enjoying being back in Texas?"

"Yes, sir." He wouldn't give a shit about any equivocation and she didn't know him well enough to confide her true mixed feelings. "And call me Peyton, please."

"And I'm Hershel. We're going to be spending a lot of time together. No sense standing on formalities. Speaking of which, I'm sending over a couple of agents to pick you up. Got something you need to see. They'll explain everything when they get there, say around eleven thirty. Let me know if you need anything else before Monday. We're glad to have you on board."

He was gone before Peyton could utter another word, and she spent a full minute just staring at her phone. Damn. She stroked Ranger's head and urged him to hang tight while she called her realtor to reschedule the planned afternoon of house hunting.

Appointments rescheduled, she rode back to the house, grabbing a few minutes of solitude before her day exploded. Over the course of the last two days, she decided that wherever she chose to live, it needed to be like this. She'd forgotten how much she missed the wide spaces, the open sky, and the fresh air. She may not be in the market for a ranch, but she'd settle for a trailer on a big piece of land before she'd go back to the cement blocks of a bustling downtown.

When she reached the stable, Andy, their long-standing stable manager, was shoveling hay into the stalls. "Hey there, Miss Davis, you have a good ride?"

She dismounted and removed Ranger's bridle. "I did, but it wasn't nearly long enough. How are you doing?"

"Can't complain. I've still got work when plenty don't."

He held out his hand for Ranger's headgear, but she shook her head. "When I can't clean my own tack, set me out to pasture," she said. "Besides, don't you have enough to keep you busy?"

"I suppose I do."

Peyton leaned against the nearest stall. "How are things going around here?"

Andy gave her a wary look. "You should ask Neil. He's had a lot going on lately, but I don't reckon he'd appreciate me running at the mouth, even to you."

Peyton nodded, both aggravated at the tight-lipped response and pleased at Andy's loyalty, however misplaced. She abruptly changed the subject. "You spend much time with Dad lately? How do you think he's holding up?"

Andy stopped shoveling and leaned forward on his pitchfork. "Your father was always a hard-working man. Sometimes the body outlasts the mind, sometimes it's the other way around. Not sure which is worse. I do know he'd much rather be riding a horse than sitting in the house being waited on."

Peyton sighed, not sure whether she'd expected a real answer. She figured she had as much of one as she was going to get from Andy. She made a mental note to carve out some time to talk to her mother about the lapses she'd noticed. She'd expected the physical changes, but not the zoning out, the memory loss.

An hour later, she was showered, dressed, and in the kitchen looking for an early lunch. Head in the fridge, she barely heard her mother enter the room.

"Don't snack. Fernanda's making chicken fried steak."

Peyton emerged from the fridge with a hunk of ham. "Pretty sad I'm going to miss that, but I've got to be somewhere, so I'll just grab a sandwich. Where's the bread?"

"New loaf on the counter." Her mother pointed. "Over there. Where are you off to in such a hurry? Still insisting on buying your own place?"

Peyton found the loaf of homemade bread and cut two generous slices. The ride had made her hungry and she fixed and ate a sandwich in short order. "You know I can't stay here and you know why. And I'm not sure where I'm headed. Some folks from the office are coming out here to pick me up in a few. Apparently, Mr. Gellar thinks it can't wait."

"Hershel Gellar is a blowhard. I'm glad you're home, but I can't believe you're going to work for that man. There's plenty you could do around here, you know."

Peyton fixed her with a hard stare. Her parents and Hershel had all gone to high school together, and they occasionally socialized. She'd never heard her mother speak ill of the man who'd been the United States attorney in this area for the past ten years. "Something you feel like sharing?"

"Nothing you need to worry about. Just remember my words when you start wondering whether it was a good idea to work for him."

"You're full of opinions today."

"I'm always full of opinions. It's the sharing them that doesn't always suit me, but I have some definite opinions about your future. When you get settled in, we'll have a good long talk, but now's not the time."

Peyton took stock. Her mother was never one to mince words. For her to need a ramp up to talk about a particular subject meant it involved a weighty subject. The list of possibilities was short: her dad, Neil, the ranch. None of those subjects could be covered in the few minutes she had until her ride showed up, and her mother had made it clear she wasn't going to spill whatever it was right now anyway. "I'll be home for dinner."

"You will or you won't. I know you have places to be, people to see." She pointed a finger into Peyton's chest. "Just call if you won't make it home for dinner." Her hand moved to Peyton's side, and she patted her with what an onlooker might mistake for affection. "And I hope you've kept up practicing if you're going to carry that thing. Didn't think that's the kind of work you came back to do."

Peyton met her mother's stare. Donning the holster and carrying her Smith and Wesson had been a gut decision spurred by not knowing what in the hell Gellar was sending her out to do. "They've got gun ranges all over the country, not just in Texas. I can shoot as well as I ever could."

"Good." Her mother nodded curtly and turned to the fridge and started pulling out fixings for the midday meal. "Now scatter.

Fernanda's going to want to start cooking in a minute, and she won't be happy if you're in the way."

Peyton strode out of the kitchen and made her way to the front porch, unaffected by her mother's dismissive tone. Her stoicism was mostly an act, the by-product of years living among cowboys who didn't truck with overt displays of feelings. It was impossible not to like her when they were so much alike.

She'd no more settled into one of the rocking chairs on the front porch when a Ford F-150 four-door truck spun into the drive, churning gravel and kicking up clouds of dust. She stayed seated, waiting and watching. The driver's side door opened and a woman jumped out, took two steps, and then stood still, facing the porch. She was tall and rangy and her jet-black hair blew wildly in the wind. She was dressed in jeans, ropers, and a black T-shirt that showed off well-toned muscles. Her eyes were covered by dark shades, but Peyton could tell she was being checked out. Thoroughly. She didn't budge.

Seconds later, the passenger side door opened and a man stepped out. Unlike his driver, he wore a suit and tie. Navy blue and all business. He exchanged a look with the woman and then stepped gingerly across the gravel drive in fancy leather shoes as he made his way to the porch.

He stuck out a hand with a business card. "Agent Dunley, ICE. I'm looking for AUSA Peyton Davis."

Peyton read the card. Agent Elliot Dunley from the Dallas ICE office. If she had to guess, she'd say he'd transferred in from a big city up north, where suits and fancy shoes on field visits were the norm. She glanced at the driver and saw her grimace. Whoever she was, she'd probably been saddled with this guy and would be all too happy to shove him off on someone else.

Peyton handed the card back to Dunley and nodded at the truck. "Who's your friend?"

"What's your name?"

"Answering a question with a question, are you? I guess I'll just go find out for myself." She didn't wait for a response and walked over to the truck and offered a hand to the driver. "I'm Peyton Davis. Did Gellar send you?"

The woman lowered her sunglasses and sized her up. She ignored Peyton's outstretched hand and said, "Yes, he did. Well, me anyway, but he"—she jerked her chin in the direction of Dunley who was still on the porch—"decided to tag along. I'm Dale Nelson, DEA."

"I'm ready to go if you are."

"Let's go. You can fight the asshat"—she flipped a finger at Dunley—"for the front seat."

Dale slid into the driver's seat and started the truck. At the rumble of the engine, Dunley made his way back. Peyton motioned for him to sit in back and she rode shotgun. A few minutes later, they were headed down I-20, driving at a fast clip.

Peyton wanted to know where they were going, but didn't want to let on that she didn't have a single detail about this little field trip. All she did know was that in response to her request to transfer back to Dallas, she'd been selected by the deputy attorney general to head up a special task force investigating business dealings of the Zetas, a faction of the Mexican Cartel. She'd been given only a cursory briefing with promises of more detail on her first day at the office. The only word she'd gotten from Gellar had been a quick welcome e-mail when she'd signed on and his vague phone call this morning.

"So, you moved here from D.C.?"

Peyton saw Dale shake her head at Dunley's question, and she was purposefully cagey in her response. "Back here actually."

"Whose ranch was that we were just at?"

"What division of ICE are you with?"

He didn't miss a beat. "Homeland Security Investigations."

Peyton suppressed a groan. Fresh from Washington, she was all too familiar with the long tentacles of Homeland Security. Practically every federal law enforcement agency had co-opted the name in hopes of garnering additional funding and power, but the amorphous title told her nothing about this guy's position. "What's your role in this investigation?" she asked, bluffing knowledge of the investigation itself.

"He's my stalker." Dale gunned the truck around a slow moving tractor and sped down the road. "You know how it is. U.S.

attorneys with something to prove think they have to make a big show by sending in a suit to watch the folks in the boots and hats."

Peyton made a note of the lack of deference to her new boss in a file to be examined later. Maybe Dale was right, but she'd make that decision on her own. "Where are we headed?"

"Weatherford."

"You assigned to the Fort Worth Division?"

"No," Dale replied.

The one word answer fell flat, but Peyton let it lie. Hershel Gellar's jurisdiction extended to the New Mexico and Oklahoma border, but the district was divvied up into divisions, and AUSAs didn't make a habit of trampling on each other's turf. An unexpected answer to her unspoken question came from the suit.

"Our task force is not confined by division," Dunley pronounced.

"Meaning?"

Dale beat him to the punch. "We can go where we want, do what we want, wherever we want, as long as we stay in the Northern District and catch the bad guys."

"I'm guessing that makes you popular with the locals."

"If we wanted to be popular, chances are we'd be doing something else," Dale said.

Peyton wished Dale would take the damn sunglasses off so she could get a hint as to whether she had a sense of humor. As it was, she was looking at over an hour drive with a straight-laced man and a woman who didn't seem to want her in the car, let alone want to engage in conversation. She pulled out her phone and started flicking through e-mails. Tons of folks apparently hadn't gotten the message that she'd transferred. She fired off a quick message to her former secretary, then shut it down to check out the scenery along the way. Hills, fields, and bales of hay. She drank in the openness of it all and settled back to enjoy the ride.

In just over an hour, they pulled off the highway and started down a two-lane farm road, part paved, part not. Within a few minutes, a barn stretched into sight, aging and decrepit with only a few stripes of brick red paint that had probably once covered the entire building. Peyton counted at least ten cars out front, all from various law enforcement agencies. Dale pulled the truck around the back of the building and parked a few feet from a tractor-trailer. Once the truck was stopped, Peyton reached for the door handle, but Dale stopped her.

"Hang on a sec."

She reached across Peyton and flipped open the glove compartment. After digging through the contents, she produced a couple of bandanas. Peyton shook her head. "You planning to rob a bank?"

"Put it on. Trust me, you'll be glad you did. I doubt your cush little D.C. job prepared you for what you're about to see."

Peyton ignored the insult and watched Dale tie the bandana around her face. She followed suit. She glanced to the backseat where Dunley scrunched down in his seat as if trying not to be seen. Dale followed her gaze and said, "He's already had all he can take. Come on."

Without waiting for a response, Dale jumped out of the truck and strode over to the trailer. Peyton followed a few feet behind, watching the crowd of uniforms make a path for them both. Three steps in, she tugged the bandana from her face because it wasn't doing any good. The stench of death, cloying and bitter, drew her closer even as she wanted to turn around, climb into the truck, and ride back to her family's quiet ranch. But she'd chosen fighting evil over the simpler life of a rancher and she'd already paid a heavy price for her choice. She'd be damned if whatever was in that trailer was going to send her packing. Peyton squared her shoulders and prepared to face the first task of her new job.

Chapter Three

Lily stepped out of the elevator and into the already crowded Tower Club on the top floor of Thanksgiving Tower in downtown Dallas. She glanced around but didn't see her father anywhere in sight.

"Ms. Gantry?"

She turned to the maître d'. "Yes?"

"Mr. Gantry is with Mr. Rawlins in the Cimmaron room. If you'll follow Jasper, he'll show you back."

Lily followed the waiter, reluctantly. She should have known her request to meet her father for lunch to discuss her future with Gantry Oil was too much to ask. Since her return from Germany, he'd stubbornly refused to talk about her career. Well, she was tired of afternoon teas and charity lunches, and it was time to put her education and training to use in the family business. She was determined to pin him down today, whether or not his lawyer was present.

She entered the small, private dining room to find her father and Nester Rawlins clinking heavy crystal glasses with healthy doses of amber liquid, most likely bourbon. They both glanced her way, smiling broadly.

"Sorry to burst in in the middle of your celebration. What's the occasion?" she asked.

Nester stood. "We're just toasting to our good fortune. Today and every day." He raised his glass in her direction. "Join us?"

She read the hint of a challenge and she wasn't about to back down. Turning to Jasper, she said, "Bulliet Rye. Neat." She took a seat between the two men and folded her hands on the table. "What's on the menu, gentlemen?"

They shared a glance and then her father cleared his throat. "Well, honey, I know you wanted to talk about your future, so I invited Nester since he manages the family trust. Whatever you decide to do with your life, the trust will help you do it."

The trust. Definitely not a subject Lily wanted to discuss today or any day. From the time she'd known the value of a dollar, that's all Gantry family members had talked about. The trust was the safeguarded wealth earned by the sweat of prior generations. No one seemed to know its true value, but everyone had an idea of what they would do with it once they came into their share. And during every discussion, people fell silent when she came near, since as her parents' only child, she'd garnered the largest share despite her lack of blood ties to the family name. The funny thing was she'd much rather work to earn her money than have it handed to her in big fat sums. She'd prefer not to burst her daddy's bubble in front of the family lawyer, but there was no better time to hammer her feelings home.

"Daddy, I want to earn my money. I didn't go to school and study with some of the leading pioneers in alternative energy to come back here and get everything handed to me on a silver platter. I wanted to meet with you to discuss my future with Gantry Oil."

Nester leaned back in his chair. "I never figured you to be one for the oil business. Weren't you off learning about all that junk science, the ozone layer and all?"

"You mean renewable energy? Ways we can save the finite resources we have by using sustainable energy sources? If that's junk, I'm full of it." Lily turned to her father. "Don't worry. I have no interest in climbing rigs or showing up at drill sites to boss your roughnecks around. But you can't tell me you spent all your hard-earned dollars for me to get an MBA and an engineering degree to have me waste away planning parties and picking china patterns.

"I have ideas for Gantry Oil that could expand your reach. Why limit yourself to oil when the future is in other forms of energy? With the business model you have in place, you have the perfect platform to diversify." She slid a folder across the table. "The very least you could do is read my proposal for implementing my two latest patents. Investing in wind and solar energy will not only allow you to diversify your portfolio, you can use my methods to improve your drilling efficiency. Take a look at the prospectus. If you and your accountants think it's not a worthy proposition, then I'll shop it elsewhere."

Her father turned to his lawyer and raised his glass. "Didn't I tell you she's a smart one?" His smile was big and broad. "And a pistol too." He picked up the leather-bound folder and quickly thumbed through the pages before shutting it again with a loud pop. "I'll read it first thing when I get back to the office." He paused. "What does your mother have to say about all of this?"

Lily chose that moment to take a taste of her bourbon, savoring the rich oak and spice as she contemplated how to respond. As far as she knew, her mother thought she was out shopping with her friends and would probably faint dead away if she knew Lily was making a play to enter the family business. Well, her mother wasn't exactly the fainting type, but she would be displeased, and sternly so. To her mother, the oil business was only a means to an end, and the dirty details that fueled her way of life were not to be discussed out loud. She'd been beside herself when Lily had first expressed an interest in studying science, fully expecting her to become a teacher or librarian, or some other gentle, more ladylike profession, if she chose to work at all.

She decided on a vague response. "I'm sure mother wants me to be happy."

"Speaking of happy, the reason I asked Nester to join us is that he has some information about the family trust. Now, I know you want to make your own way, but you know as well as I do, that it's a sight easier to do so when you don't have to worry about a roof over your head or where your next meal is coming from."

Lily leaned back in her chair and considered her options. As much as she hated to admit it, he was right. She'd spent the last couple of days tallying the money raised from the Cattle Baron's Ball. All the proceeds weren't in, but so far the event had garnered over four million dollars, all of which would go to the American Cancer Society. For most of the people that attended, their donations were a drop in the bucket compared to their net worth, but cumulatively, the donations would go a long way toward finding a cure for cancer. Wealth, earned or not, could make a difference. Was she really willing to shed her family's riches out of personal pride, or should she use it to make a difference?

"Okay, Nester, I'm all ears. What do you need from me?"

Nester pulled a folder from his briefcase and spread its contents on the table. "It's quite simple, really, and I don't know how we overlooked it." He pushed a piece of paper across the table to her. "Your grandfather's trust provided a codicil that placed a condition on your inheritance. You were supposed to sign your acknowledgement, and the bank has pointed out that we neglected to file the acknowledgment."

"I don't understand. I've had access to the trust for years."

"I know. It's just an administrative error. Easily corrected." Nester tapped the edge of the paper. "Your signature will clear it all up."

Lily pulled the paper closer. Nester's eager encouragement for her to sign signaled she should slow down and actually read the form before she did so. It only took a moment to skim the two paragraphs, but she'd need much more time to digest what she'd just read. She pushed the form away. "This says I have to agree to keep my adoption closed or the terms of the trust will be void."

Nester picked up the paper and looked at it as if the news were a surprise to him. "Why yes, yes it does."

Lily wasn't buying it. She turned to her father. "I don't understand. Why would Grandfather have cared about that?"

Her father shook his head. "I don't know. Of course, he was always concerned about family stability. Maybe he just wanted to make sure you realize that you're a Gantry and nothing or no one can take that away from you."

Lily folded her arms. Cyrus and Rose were her parents. Of that she had no doubt. They'd given her love, acceptance, and opportunities many people could only dream of. She'd been with them since she was only a few days old, placed by the church after her mother died in the hours after her birth. She didn't know her mother's identity, and even if she cared to find out, she wouldn't know where to begin. She said as much.

Her father spoke up for the first time since they'd started on this subject. "I know, dear, which makes this just a formality. We're your family, and apparently, the entire trust, not just your portion, would be placed in jeopardy if we didn't keep to your grandfather's request."

Lily met her father's eyes. He'd never asked her for anything and he'd always been generous to a fault. Granting this request should be simple, easy. She pulled Nester's document back across the table and read the contents one more time. Simple, straightforward. She saw the pen Nester extended, even started to reach for it, but at the last minute, she picked up the paper instead. She folded it in half and reached for her purse and placed it inside. "I appreciate you explaining this to me. I'll read this over again and get back to you soon."

When she looked back up, she sensed a shift in the room. The friendly lunch had an edge to it. She met their incredulous expressions with a smile. "After all, if we've been out of compliance for all this time, a few more days won't hurt. In the meantime, I'll look forward to hearing what you think of my proposal."

She may not be a Gantry by birth, but she'd had a lifetime to learn how the family operated, and she would not be outplayed.

❖

Peyton shook her head. The scene in the back of the trailer was ghastly. She counted at least a dozen bodies, mostly women and children, riddled with bullets and already well on their way to decay. She took her time assessing the scene, imprinting it into her memory. After a few minutes, she turned to Dale and motioned for her to join her several feet away. She could feel the eyes of all the local cops on them both, but no way was she going to have this conversation in front of a big bunch of people she didn't know. She kept her voice quiet and calm. "Tell me what you know."

"This is the third one in as many months. This trailer has seventeen total victims, including the driver. Manifest says the truck is carrying building supplies. Not even sure why there's a manifest at all since it looks like the ride's been scrubbed of all identifying information. My best guess is it's a coyote transport. The last two trucks we found like this, none of the victims were documented."

Although she'd been at main Justice in D.C., Peyton was up to speed when it came to border control issues. Coyotes were hired by families to help them cross the border illegally and get to safety. Their services were in high demand in border states. "Any leads on the coyote?"

"None that pan out. The plates and registration are all bogus."

"Kind of odd to find them this far north."

Dunley stepped into their space. "Actually, it isn't. It's become quite common for illegals to try and get as far from the border as possible before entering society."

Peyton looked at Dale who gave a slight eye roll. She almost joined in, but instead said, "Well, Agent Dunley, nice of you to join us. But isn't it true that coyotes don't usually kill their customers? Do you have any theories?"

"Perhaps they refused to pay."

"Or they saw something they shouldn't," Dale offered. "Each time we've found one of these, we see an associated surge of meth trafficking. I think they're using the immigrants as mules and, once they get the stuff where they want it, they get rid of them."

"They?"

"Zetas. Mexican Mafia. We think Sergio Vargas is running this operation."

"But why even transport the bodies this far? Why not take the drugs from them the minute they cross the border, load it up, and take off? Seems like dragging this many people along is a risky venture."

Dale shook her head. "It's just a theory. I know it needs work. You or Mr. ICE have any better ideas?"

Peyton glanced at Dunley who merely shrugged as if to say there was no understanding the mind of a criminal. Well, he was wrong about that. Certain they were missing a key piece of the story, Peyton started outlining what she wanted done.

"Agent Nelson, I want all these bodies taken directly to the medical examiner in Dallas. You will personally oversee their collection and chain of evidence. Get whatever help you need, whoever you absolutely trust, but from this moment on you're in charge of this scene and all the evidence. The truck will go directly to SWIFS for processing. I want this entire area blocked off and set up a guard. No one gets in or out without your express permission.

"I don't officially start until Monday. If you want to question my orders, call Gellar right now and clear it up, but don't wait because every minute that goes by is a minute we lose in this war. Understood?"

"I think I know how to run an investigation. Done a few before."

Peyton heard the angry tone and filed away the animus and decided to sort it out later. Dunley looked like he'd been struck. "But what about protocol?" he asked. "Local state agencies have jurisdiction over these bodies."

"Not anymore they don't. This is a federal investigation, and according to you, our task force isn't bound by jurisdiction as long as we're in the district. I may add some local folks to the task force if I feel it's necessary, but I'll say who does what and when. Are we clear?"

Dunley nodded.

"Good. Now, ask one of these guys for a car we can take back to Dallas, so we can let Agent Nelson and her crew get to work."

Over an hour later as they approached the city limits, Peyton asked Dunley to drop her off downtown.

"Are you going into the office?"

"No, but I have a few things I need to take care of and, since things are heating up at the job I haven't even started yet, I may as well use this afternoon to get them done."

He seemed relieved to hear she wasn't planning to go to the federal building. A few minutes later, she directed him to pull over at the corner of Ross and Harwood. "Here's good."

He pulled over and she stepped out of the car, but leaned back in before he drove away. "Elliot?"

"Yes?"

"Thanks for the ride. Maybe if you lighten up a bit, don't worry so much about what you're wearing as what you're here to do, you would enjoy this more." She didn't wait for a response before she walked off down the street.

Once his car was out of view, she pulled out her phone and searched for the nearest Wells Fargo, hoping the branch was still open. When she found the location, she headed that way. Dallas had changed a lot while she'd been gone. A shiny red opera house, a bustling park over the freeway, and food trucks on every corner, were all new additions. She strode past the Belo Mansion and the Trammell Crow building and stopped for the light.

"Peyton?"

She turned at the sound of the familiar voice. Lily Gantry was every bit as lovely as the first time she'd laid eyes on her, despite the fact she'd traded boots for heels and a tea length dress. "Lily, what a pleasant surprise."

"Indeed it is. I was just having lunch with my father. What are you up to?"

Peyton flashed to the scene of death and horror she'd just come from and willed the gruesome images from her mind. She could still smell the scent of death and decay, and she hoped like hell it was only a memory, and that she didn't carry it on her clothes. "I'm looking for my bank. I need to buy a car."

Lily grinned. "So, you're really going shopping, but you just don't want to call it that."

"Truth is, I hate shopping. Does that knock me down a few notches in your estimation?"

"Not in the least. Those of us who do enjoy the sport don't need more competition. I'll tell you a secret though."

"I'm dying to hear."

"It's a lot easier to buy a car when you have a car. How did you even get down here? I'm pretty sure the DART bus doesn't go by your family's ranch."

Peyton laughed. "You're right about that. A colleague dropped me off after a...business meeting. I suppose I figured I would take a cab to the closest dealership and find something."

"You are truly an amateur at this sport. The closest dealer to a major city is going to charge you the highest price. Tell you what, my car is parked over there." She pointed to the valet lot behind the art museum. "How about I give you a ride to your bank and then take you to a dealership where I can guarantee you'll get the best deal around? I've had a bad day and I could use a bit of retail therapy, even if it's vicarious."

Peyton kicked a pebble on the sidewalk, conflicted. The idea of spending the rest of the afternoon with the bright and beautiful Lily Gantry was enticing, but not at all what she'd planned. What she should do was the most efficient thing: go to the bank, transfer funds, go to the nearest dealership, and buy something sensible. Lily would only be a distraction, but maybe after what she'd seen today, she deserved a little distraction.

"Sounds like a plan. One thing though."

"Only one?"

Peyton shook her head. "I'll do the negotiating. No special favors. Other than the car ride and your company, of course."

Lily gave her a long, approving look. "Fair enough. I'll take you to the wares, but what you pay for them is your business."

Less than an hour later, they left Peyton's bank and were headed east on Interstate 30 in Lily's Lexus coupe. Peyton looked at her watch.

"You on a timeline?" Lily asked.

"Not really." She should've asked her mom what time they were eating dinner. She could call, but she didn't want to spend time on the phone while she was in the car with Lily.

"Word is you're a lawyer."

"That would be correct."

"What's your specialty?"

"Criminal law. I'm a prosecutor." Peyton braced for Lily's reaction, anticipating either prurient interest or revulsion.

"Ah, a true law woman. Is that what you did before you moved back here?"

"Kind of."

"Let me guess, you could tell me but you'd have to kill me."

"Not quite." Peyton cast about for a change of topic. The last thing she wanted right now was to talk about the details of her job. "What do you do when you're not throwing parties?"

Lily's brow furrowed and Peyton wondered why her supposedly harmless question would evoke such a response. Within seconds, she felt stupid. "Not that putting together large charity balls isn't an enormous endeavor. Our family has supported Cattle Baron's as long as it's been around, and I'm always amazed at how much money the event raises."

"It's okay. The association has a staff. I was just one of the event chairs this year, and I was filling in for someone else, so I didn't even work the whole season. My basic duties involved showing up, shaking hands, and goading people into coughing up extra donations. The full-time staff does all the real work. I'm actually kind of in between jobs right now. I've been out of the country, studying renewable energy sourcing."

"A scientist, a super shopper, and an event planner. Any other talents I should know about?"

Lily's cheeks turned a light shade of red, but her answer was sassy. "Well, in case you hadn't noticed, I'm a hell of a fast driver." She pointed to the right. "Look, we're already here."

She swung the car into the exit lane and then turned into the parking lot of an enormous car lot. Peyton read the name on the marquee, Pearson Motors. "Pearson. That name sounds familiar."

"You remember Courtney Pearson from Cattle Baron's? Hard to miss, she was kinda sweet on your brother."

"Neil?"

"No, Zach. Can't believe you didn't notice."

"Maybe I was a bit distracted."

"I'm going to take that as a compliment." She pulled into a parking space near the entrance of the gigantic building. "Okay, it's time to shop. Don't worry. I'll only offer my opinion if I'm asked."

"I'm sorry. I didn't mean to be so abrupt before." Peyton surveyed the rows and rows of shiny new cars and trucks. "This is a little overwhelming. The last car I bought was from an ad in the paper. Your help would be very welcome. Although I must warn you that energy efficient isn't going to be my first priority. I need something that can handle carrying a load and riding over rough terrain."

"Truck or SUV?"

"I'm open to either."

"What did you drive in D.C.?"

Peyton cocked her head. "Did I tell you I lived in Washington?"

Lily laughed. "Probably not, but surely you weren't gone long enough to forget that for all it's bustling big city appearance, Dallas is really a small town when it comes to knowing other people's business."

"I seem to recall that. D.C. isn't much different. I didn't drive much there, and when I did, I rented a truck. I didn't intend to stay as long as I did so I never got around to buying a car. Used public transit most of the time."

"That'll only get you so far around here."

"Definitely. I had to go out to Weatherford today, and I'm pretty sure the light rail wouldn't have gotten me there and a cab would've set me back plenty."

"What's in Weatherford that captured your attention?"

Peyton wished she could bite back the words. What she'd seen in Weatherford would likely be on the six o'clock news, but she had no desire to talk about it. Not on this fun and carefree errand with the fresh and lively Lily Gantry. "Nothing pleasant. Now, aren't you in charge of helping me find wheels?"

Lily's smile was sunshine. "Yes, I am, although I fear that if I do, I will not have the pleasure of your company on the ride home."

Peyton reached for Lily's hand. "Then we should probably make an adventure of this."

"Why do I have a feeling everything with you is an adventure?"

"Maybe you just like adventure," Peyton said, hoping it was true.

CHAPTER FOUR

The doorbell rang and Lily glanced at her watch. Courtney was right on time. Damn. She'd been hoping she'd be her usual tardy self and she'd have a few more minutes to get ready. This Saturday morning had flown by, likely due to the fact that she was dreading the lunch they were about to attend. Nothing to be done about it now. It was just one more obligation that came with the Gantry name. She grabbed her purse, took one last look in the mirror, and headed downstairs.

Courtney was waiting in the foyer and she drew her into a hug. "Where's your mom?" Lily asked. "Did you forget it's a mother-daughter lunch?"

"In a stroke of luck, she volunteered for your mother's committee and she's already at the hotel. I don't for the life of me know what they're doing. It's not like the folks at the Adolphus haven't thrown a banquet before."

Lily laughed. "They wouldn't be our mothers if they weren't micromanaging every last detail. I'm just glad they didn't make us show up early too."

"Especially since it appears we have some things to dish about," Courtney said. "I'm not sure how mad I should be at you."

"What are you talking about?"

Courtney poked her in the arm. "Don't play dumb with me. It's Saturday. That's five, count 'em, five days since you and Peyton Davis not only had a date, but bought a car together. And you haven't had the decency to pick up the phone and tell me all about it."

"You're crazy. It's true, she bought a truck and I drove her to the dealership—tell your father he's welcome, by the way—but I would hardly call it a date. It was just…I don't know…nice." Lily looked out the window and imagined she could see Peyton driving off in her brand new, midnight blue truck. The whole thing had been surreal, from running into Peyton on the street in downtown Dallas, to accompanying her on what seemed like an impromptu shopping trip for a truck of all things.

"Are you seeing her again?" Courtney asked.

"Tomorrow. I'm meeting her at the ranch and she's taking me riding."

"She's living at the ranch?"

"I suppose. Why?"

"No reason. Zach made it seem like he hoped she would stay, but he wasn't sure she would."

"So, it sounds like I'm not the only one who's seen more of the Davis clan since last weekend."

"We've talked. And we have a date Friday night. He's a doll. Nothing like his older brother Neil who's kind of a jerk."

"Family. You don't get to pick 'em that's for sure."

"Speaking of which, here we are."

Courtney swung her Mercedes sedan into the valet loop at the Adolphus Hotel, nearly taking out a cluster of men in business suits waiting for their cars. Lily shook her head at the doorman who opened her door. Once inside, they made their way to the ballroom where they were greeted by a tall, broad-shouldered woman who had a panicked look in her eyes.

"Ladies, your mothers have been looking everywhere for you." She clutched her chest. "We are shorthanded at the registration table, and they said you would help out. I've been posted here waiting for you to arrive, and I was beginning to wonder if you were going to show up at all—"

"Of course, Mrs. Kaufman." Lily interrupted for fear the woman might have a heart attack detailing the stress of the ordeal. "We're on it." Lily waited until Mrs. Kaufman left before exchanging an eye roll with Courtney. She didn't mind helping, but she did think the drama associated with the request was a bit overdone.

A few minutes later, she and Courtney were busy checking names off the guest list and handing out name tags. It sure beat making small talk with a bunch of women she hardly knew even though she'd grown up with most of them. She was so enmeshed in the routine she barely noticed when Courtney started poking her in the leg.

"Stop it. You're hurting me."

"Don't look now, but trouble's in the house."

Lily looked up from the list in her hand and locked eyes with Virginia Taylor, mere steps away. Scalding memories of Virginia wrapping her body around Peyton at the Cattle Baron's Ball surfaced. "Damn," she muttered under her breath.

"Why hello, Lily. I saw your mother, but I didn't realize you two were close enough to attend this event together."

Virginia reached out her hand, and Lily's good manners dictated she do the same. The shake was strong, borderline bone crushing, but Lily schooled her expression into what she hoped was pleasant indifference and purposely ignored the remark about her mother. "Why, Ginny Taylor, so very nice to see you."

Virginia frowned at Lily's use of the despised nickname, but refrained from voicing her displeasure. Instead, she flipped her hair and waved her mother, a well-kept, vintage version of herself, over to the table. "I'm not sure we're on the list, but I know we have seats reserved since we're the platinum sponsors of the event."

Of course you are. Lily scoured her copy of the list and found their names and table assignments. She relayed the information, hoping they would leave her in peace, but no such luck. Virginia leaned in close and whispered, "Lily, I wonder if I might have a word with you?" She pointed to a space some distance from the registration table. "In private."

Lily looked at Courtney who only shrugged. Lily could think of a thousand things she'd rather do than have a word in private with Virginia Taylor. They'd known each other since high school and, although social status meant they ran in the same circles, Virginia had always done her level best to try to make Lily feel like an outsider. Like she needed any help. Curiosity was the only reason she gave in to Virginia's request.

They'd barely made it across the room before Virginia started in.

"I know you've been gone a while, so you probably missed out on this, but Peyton Davis is off limits."

Whoa. This was way out of left field. "I'm sure I don't have any idea what you're talking about."

"It's one thing for you to be strolling around downtown with her. I'll assume that perhaps you just bumped into each other on the street, but now that you know where things stand, there's no excuse for you to spend time with her." Her eyes narrowed and she fixed Lily with a hard stare. "Do we have an understanding?"

Lily's mind whirred. Peyton sure didn't act like someone who was off the market, Virginia's very public display of affection notwithstanding. Besides, Peyton had just moved back to Texas. Even if she and Virginia were dating, how close could they be? Peyton had asked her out, so she must not think things with Virginia were exclusive. She resolved to ask Peyton about it when she saw her. On their date. A date that was none of Virginia's business. She met Virginia's eyes and offered the only response she could. "I understand you perfectly."

She returned to the registration table, but everyone had scattered to take their seats for the lunch. Courtney waved her over to their table, and Lily gave a silent thanks that the platinum sponsors had their own table far across the room. She'd barely slid into her seat before Courtney asked, "What was that all about?" Before she could offer an explanation, her mother sat down next to her, effectively killing any chance of gossip. Lily turned to greet her mother and counted their differences. Her mother's fair skin versus her own dark tone. Fine, blond waves instead of thick, dark tresses. Lapis blue eyes so unlike her own deep brown ones. Unlike Virginia and her mother who were practically carbon copies of each other, Lily and Rose Gantry were complete opposites in appearance, among other things.

For the first time in a very long time, Lily wondered what her birth mother was like. Did they share the same looks? Did they dream the same dreams? She shook away the thought, certain that the only reason she went there was the information about the trust that had been pawing at her subconscious all week. Despite their differences, Lily loved the woman who had raised her. She was the only mother she'd ever known. Lily leaned over and whispered, "Everything looks amazing."

"Thanks, dear. I appreciate you helping out earlier. I know the hotel catering staff does most of the work, but there are always little details that need to be attended to."

Lily nodded. She'd been raised with constant reminders about how important all those little details were. Don't stare too long, fork on the left side of the plate, don't cross your legs at the table. She'd always resisted complying with the rules, but they were sacrosanct to her mother who insisted the wrong move, however small, could derail her daughter's future, or at least the future she envisioned for her. As they listened to the speaker and ate their dainty lunch, Lily contemplated her future as she saw it. Soon she'd need to have a talk with her mother about what she actually had planned—a career without regard to social status—but today was not the right time or place. Today she would enjoy having a mother who loved her and wanted the best for her, even if they defined best in very different ways.

CHAPTER FIVE

T hat's a beautiful truck, Peyton."
Peyton shut the tailgate and looked back at her mother who, even on a Sunday morning, was dressed to work. There was always something that needed to be done around the ranch, and with her father ill, the bulk of the duties fell to the rest of the family. "I think I might have been a bit impulsive when I bought it."

Her mother shook her head. "Nonsense. Impulsive is not a word I would ever use to describe you. Besides, I don't think you've ever bought a new vehicle before. You deserve to spoil yourself every now and then. You headed somewhere?"

"No, I was just checking out a few features I haven't had a chance to explore since I brought her home."

"You've had a busy week. I thought you were going to have a few days to get settled in before Hershel started working you to the bone."

"Me too, but something came up."

Her mother's eyes pried hard, but she didn't feel like getting into the gruesome details of the case that had dropped into her lap. Agent Nelson had sent along a few preliminary reports from the crime scene analysts, and the early bet was full money on the Zetas as the culprits. The how and why could wait until her official start date tomorrow, but she'd spent a large part of the week sorting through the information they had so far.

Her mother finally broke her gaze. "All right then. I was hoping maybe you and I could take a walk and talk for a few minutes."

Peyton read the shift to serious mode in her mother's eyes. She didn't bother mentioning that Lily Gantry was scheduled to arrive any minute. She didn't want to do anything to break the moment. Maybe now she'd find out what was going on behind the scenes here at the ranch. Throughout the week, she'd sensed troubles in addition to her father's battle with cancer, but she hadn't been able to pinpoint the source of her concern. She took her mother's arm and led her to the path behind the stables. "I'm all ears."

A good hundred yards passed in silence, and Peyton didn't attempt to fill the void. Finally, her mother cleared her throat and said, "I'd like you to stay here at the ranch. For good."

Peyton nodded, not in agreement, but in acknowledgment. She sensed her mother had more to say on the subject.

"Your father isn't himself and Neil has taken over," her mother said. "I must confess I've let him. He needed it…"

Peyton resisted the urge to point out that Neil's needs were rooted in his inexplicable insecurity and would likely never be met, no matter how much everyone around him conceded for his benefit. His jealousy, his needs, were the primary reason she'd left in the first place, but the pain in her mother's eyes told her she already knew all that to be true. "But now?"

"But now Zach is interested in the business, and he needs a proper role model. Neil has made some decisions that could compromise the legacy of this place, and I need your help to rein him in."

"Dad's always been best when it comes to Neil." Peyton watched as her mother glanced away, clearly hiding something. "Dad's condition is worse than you first thought, isn't it?"

Her mother still didn't face her, but she answered, "Early onset Alzheimer's. He knows, most of the time, but sometimes he doesn't. It's made his treatment difficult. He forgets to take his medicine, to eat, but there's no telling him he needs help. If it wasn't for Fernanda helping out…" She took a deep breath. "Neil has stepped up and is doing his best to fill your father's shoes, but his ambition is sometimes misplaced."

Peyton's laugh was humorless. "And you think I'm the one to redirect his ambition? Has it been so long you've forgotten what happened the last time Neil and I were on the opposite side of something?"

It was her mother's turn to laugh. "Frankly, I can't remember the last time you were on the same side of anything." Her face settled back into a somber expression. "Last week Neil signed an agreement with Ray Explorations to let them drill an exploratory well on the back half of the ranch."

"What the hell?" Peyton stopped walking and leaned back against a tree. The revelation triggered a memory. "That explains the trucks I saw earlier in the week. I kept meaning to ask about them." She let the words trail off rather than admit that she hadn't been willing to let anything about the ranch be a priority.

Her mother raised her arms. "I'm mad as hell about it, but I didn't find out until after the fact."

"He knows neither you nor Dad would ever let him drill."

"And now you see why I need your help. With your father's health the way it is, he thinks he's de facto in charge, and he doesn't think he needs to listen to me."

Peyton looked down at her boots, scuffed and dusty even after only a week back on the ranch. This wasn't her fight. She'd made it clear when she left, that she'd moved on and the ranch was Neil's inheritance, his legacy to build or break as he saw fit. "Even if Dad isn't up to telling him no, you still own half this place. Neil can't just act on his own."

"You're right, he can't, but he's stayed on, taken charge. If someone else is going to make the hard decisions about keeping this place running, they need to have more than just a financial stake in the business."

Peyton looked out over the vast acreage and a childhood memory surfaced. She and Neil riding in the far pasture, planning their futures.

"I'll raise the cattle and you'll breed the horses," Neil said. "We'll be the biggest working ranch in north Texas, and buyers will line up to buy our stock. We can compete to see who gets to be in charge."

"Why can't we just run the place together?"

"Because someone has to be in charge to get things done. That's what Joe Taylor says."

"You shouldn't pay so much attention to folks like him. He doesn't know jack about running a ranch. His family makes their money tearing up land, not respecting it."

"Well, they're rich, aren't they?"

"Rich isn't all about money." Peyton pointed to the ridge. *"All of this? It's worth more than every penny the Taylors have in their fat bank accounts. And it's all ours."*

Neil delivered a mock salute. "You're right, sis. And that's why I'll always be one step behind you."

The bright light of childhood dreams fades for a reason. As they'd grown older, she and Neil had grown apart. His obsession with the ranch had fueled one-sided jealousy, ugly and dark. Peyton had turned to other pursuits, college, law school, hoping one day Neil would realize they made a better team than opponents, but nothing changed. Her father, pleased at Neil's apparent devotion, seemed to miss the fact his oldest had steadily eased out of the operations, but their mother watched, silent, but knowing. Only when Peyton decided to take the transfer to D.C. had she expressed her dismay at Peyton's choice.

"I should've insisted you stay."

Peyton touched her mother's arm. "It wouldn't have made a difference."

"If there's one thing you have in common with Neil it's that you're both stubborn. I wish that trait had skipped a generation."

"At least we come by it honestly."

"True." She sighed. "When your father's condition started, we met with Roscoe."

Peyton smiled at the reference to the family lawyer. He'd written one of her recommendation letters to law school. "How's Roscoe?"

"He's good. He agreed with us that it would be best if your father went ahead and signed papers. Papers that would give someone else the right to make decisions on his behalf."

Peyton held her breath, waiting for her mother's next words, knowing they would be important, dreading what they might mean.

"He gave you power of attorney along with me. Between us, we're in charge of all the decisions having to do with the ranch, if we choose to be. I've been waiting for you to come home so we can discuss things, but it's time to take over and let Neil know that he's not in charge anymore."

A childhood dream fulfilled, but would it be an adult nightmare? Peyton could see the resolve in her mother's eyes and knew she hadn't made the decision to go against Neil lightly. But she hadn't come home to take over control of the ranch. She'd come home to work the career path she'd chosen and, although it hadn't been her first choice, she'd made a commitment and that commitment was even more important after the horror she'd witnessed this week. Her mother had clearly thought this through, but she needed time to process. Time to sort out her feelings.

Tire wheels crunching the gravel drive interrupted her thoughts, and she turned to look. Lily Gantry's Lexus. Then Lily Gantry, tall and pretty, but dressed to ride in well-worn denim and not new boots. She looked at her watch. She hadn't forgotten, but her mother's news had thrown her off kilter. Thankfully, she'd gotten out to the barn early to get the horses ready, but she would've preferred a little more time to make sure everything was just right before Lily arrived. Shouldn't surprise her—nothing since she'd been back had gone according to plan.

❖

Lily stepped out of the car and hesitated just a minute before walking over to join Peyton and her mother who were standing by the barn. As she approached, the air was thick with stony silence.

She glanced back at her car, suddenly uneasy. It had been almost a week since she'd spoken to Peyton. Maybe she should've called to make sure their date was still on.

"Good morning," she called out.

Like sun through the clouds, both of their expressions morphed from serious to welcoming, and Peyton walked over to meet her. She took Peyton's offered arm and whispered, "If you're in the middle of something, we can do this another time."

Peyton's smile erased all doubt. "Not a chance. I've been looking forward to seeing you all week." She gestured to Helen Davis whose welcoming expression held a hint of surprise. "Mom, I'd like you to meet Lily Gantry."

Lily held out her hand. "Mrs. Davis, it's good to see you. I don't know if you remember, but I met you at the fall luncheon," she said, referring to one of the events leading up to the Cattle Baron's Ball.

"Of course I remember." Helen looked down at her boots and laughed. She pulled Lily's outstretched hand into her warm grasp. "It's not every day I change into a fancy dress and do lunch. It's good to see you again. How are your parents?"

"They're good, thank you for asking." She noticed out of the corner of her eye that Peyton was watching this exchange with a curious expression, but before she could say anything, Helen chimed in with an invitation for lunch.

Peyton spoke first. "Actually, Mom, Lily and I are going for a ride and Fernanda packed a lunch for us."

"Oh, did she? Well, girls, have a wonderful time. It's a beautiful day to enjoy the ranch." Without another word, Helen strode back to the house, her confident gait and strong bearing almost a carbon copy of Peyton's.

"Sorry about that."

Lily shook her head. "I'm the one who should be sorry. I'm pretty sure I interrupted something important."

"Please believe me when I say that spending this morning with you is the only thing I want to be doing. Now, the big question is what's your comfort level?"

"Excuse me?"

"Horses. I should've asked before how comfortable you are on the back of a horse."

How refreshing to meet someone who wasn't already well-versed in everything about her. She resisted the urge to outline her personal pedigree, settling for a simple, "I'm up for whatever you have in mind."

"Perfect."

Lily followed Peyton to the stables where two beautiful horses were saddled and waiting, one a sorrel mare and the other a stunning black stallion. Peyton gestured toward the mare.

"Lily, meet Destiny."

Lily reached up to stroke her new friend's muzzle and Destiny nuzzled her hand. Destiny stood about fifteen hands high, average for a quarter horse.

"She's fourteen," Peyton said. "And Ranger here is her son."

Lily watched Peyton stroke the taller black beauty. Ranger reared his head and spoke his pleasure. "He loves you. He must have missed you when you were in D.C."

Something, pain maybe, clouded Peyton's eyes, and Lily wished she could take back the casual remark. But as quickly as the look had appeared, it was gone, replaced by an easy smile.

"We've enjoyed getting reacquainted, haven't we, Ranger?" Peyton motioned to Destiny. "I gave it my best guess, but the stirrups probably need to be adjusted. How about I help you up?"

Lily looked at Peyton's outstretched hand and resisted the urge to insist she could mount the horse and deal with any adjustments herself. She was so used to people in her life underestimating her, she had to be careful not to attribute her assumptions to Peyton. She took the offered hand and then watched while Peyton fit the stirrups to her boots. She might not need the help, but she had to admit she enjoyed watching Peyton's strong, sure hands at work.

"Feel right?"

"Feels perfect," Lily replied.

"I'll go grab our lunch if you want to take her around the ring and get a feel for how she handles."

Peyton vanished into the barn and Lily leaned down to whisper to her mount. "Hey, Destiny, want to show me around?" She used the reins to guide Destiny around the building and into the open corral. From there, she let Destiny lead the way as they first walked and then galloped around the outer circle. After a few quick laps, Lily pulled up on the reins and Destiny trotted to a stop. As her hoofbeats faded, Lily was greeted by applause. She met Peyton's eyes and grinned. "She's a sweet ride."

"And you're a skilled rider."

"It's been a while since I've spent much time in the saddle, but I guess it's like riding a bike."

Peyton nodded and Lily watched as she mounted Ranger and rode over to meet them. "Ready to see the ranch?" Peyton asked.

"Definitely."

Peyton led the way, her pace brisk, but easy. Every so often, she'd stop to point out a landmark. An old mill, a rushing creek, a campsite complete with benches and fire pits. At the campsite, she slowed Ranger to a walk.

"Is it time for lunch?" Lily asked.

Peyton pointed to a spot in the distance. "Actually, I'd like to take you to my favorite spot. It's about a mile in that direction. Care to let the horses run?"

Lily heard the challenge beneath the question and grinned. "Absolutely."

Peyton nudged Ranger and she was off, with Lily close behind. She gave it a good shot, but she had no chance against the younger, more powerful horse. Seconds later, she pulled Destiny to a halt and peered out over the ridge where Peyton had led them. She gasped. "Breathtaking."

"Yes."

Lily glanced at Peyton who seemed to be in a trance, and she settled in to enjoy the moment with her. A few moments of silence passed and then she sensed Peyton stir. She must have been transfixed as well, because Peyton was standing beside her, offering her hand. As she dismounted, they were standing close. Very close. She stared into Peyton's eyes and saw they were no longer looking off in the distance, but were focused only on her. If she leaned forward just a few inches, she'd be close enough to kiss.

"Are you hungry?"

Lily smiled, resisting the urge to make a suggestive remark. As attracted as she was to this enigmatic woman, she sensed a kiss would have to be the result of a slow burn, or the flame would extinguish before they had a chance for real heat. She answered honestly. "I'm starving."

The red-and-white checkered spread, napkins, and delicious fried chicken drew her focus away from her desire to kiss Peyton. Partly. As they ate, she focused on conversation to calm her raging hormones. "How long has your family owned this ranch?"

"Six generations, for the land anyway. It's been different things throughout the years, but for the last hundred years, horses have always been at the heart of it. My great-great-grandmother bought her first horse at an auction in Dallas."

"Grand*mother*?"

Peyton grinned. "Yep. My great-great-grandfather died in a gunfight in his thirties, leaving her with six kids, all daughters."

"Let me guess, that's how the ranch got its name?"

"Yep. The deed to Circle Six stayed in his name, but it was her family money that had made the purchase, and she used the rest of her savings to hire help to get the place up and running. As her children grew up, they all stayed and took on various jobs around the ranch. Since then, the property has been passed down from daughter to daughter. My grandmother passed a few years ago, but she's the one who was responsible for perfecting the quarter horses we raise."

"Your mother's mother?"

"Yes. You sound surprised."

Lily shook her head. "I suppose I am, a little. It's a little unusual for property to pass down to the women in the family."

"True. Just so happens the women in my family seem to be the heartier sex."

Peyton's eyes clouded over again. Was it pain? Was it sadness? Lily didn't know, but she desperately wanted whatever it was to go away, to resume their friendly banter. Peyton was so completely unlike the women she lunched with yesterday. With the exception of Courtney, every one of them would defer to the men in their lives in all things business, content to spend their lives shopping and attending fancy lunches on their husbands' dime. Peyton wouldn't put up with their nonsense. Nonsense. The word caused Lily to think of Virginia Taylor and her admonition to steer clear of Peyton. She hadn't taken Virginia seriously, but she was curious about what prompted yesterday's confrontation. The question was did she really want to know more about Virginia's connection to Peyton or did she want to enjoy the rest of the afternoon?

She quickly decided on the latter. "My mother believes women are supposed to be the gentler sex, or at least pretend to be. She was horrified when I was a child that all I ever wanted to do was play outdoors and do all the things the neighborhood boys did."

"I don't recall meeting either of your parents at Cattle Baron's."

"You'd remember if you had. My dad is one of those larger-than-life men who takes over a room whenever he walks in. My mother's name is Rose and it suits her perfectly—strong, but sometimes thorny."

"They raised a beautiful daughter."

Lily felt the heat of a blush. "You are very sweet."

"It's the truth."

"Thank you. And I didn't mean to speak ill of either of my parents. They adopted me just days after I was born and have always treated me as if I was blood."

"They probably love you just as much as if you were related by blood. How could they not?" Peyton handed her another one of the amazing maple pecan cookies from the basket. "Do you know anything about your birth parents?"

"I know they were both from Mexico, but other than that, not much." Lily looked at the cookie, but the turn in conversation was starting to make her lose her appetite. The trust waiver Nester had asked her to sign was sitting in her desk drawer at home where she'd managed to ignore it for most of the week. Soon she would need to make a decision about whether she would sign it and cut off any possibility that she might find out more about her family of origin.

"Are you okay?" Peyton asked.

"I'm sorry. Don't get me wrong. I'm very grateful to have been adopted into such a wonderful family, but sometimes I wonder what my life would have been like…"

Peyton reached over and grasped her hand. "Let's steer this conversation to lighter things. I'm thinking favorite books, movies, you know, stuff like that."

Lily smiled with relief. "That would be perfect."

"I do have one very important question I need to ask, though."

Peyton's expression became deadly serious and Lily braced herself. "Go for it."

"Are you going to eat that cookie? Because, if you're not, then…"

Lily laughed and broke the cookie in two. As Peyton reached to take her half, their fingers touched and lingered, sending warm tendrils of attraction through her entire body.

An hour later, full of food and talk, they rode back to the stables. Lily couldn't remember a better day. She felt vigorous and alive.

"You look content," Peyton said as she led the horses into the barn.

"Content? No, it's more than that. I feel invigorated."

"You should ride more often. Don't think I didn't notice how well you handled yourself on Destiny."

Lily felt a slow blush curl up her cheeks. "I used to compete. Dressage. This…this was different."

Peyton stepped close. Close enough to touch, close enough to feel. "Tell me."

Lily took a deep breath. "Running full out, racing you to the ridge. It was out of control, unpredictable. Completely at odds with all my competitive training."

"Is that a bad thing?"

Lily looked up and met Peyton's eyes. "Not in the least. I liked it. In fact, I liked it a lot."

Peyton smiled. "Good, because I'd like to see more of you."

"I was hoping you'd say that."

CHAPTER SIX

Peyton parked her truck in the lot down the street from the Earl Cabell Federal Building in downtown Dallas and walked the short distance to her new office. Once she passed through security, she rode the elevator to the third floor and gave her name to the receptionist at the window.

"Peyton Davis. I'm here to see Hershel Gellar."

The woman took her ID and pointed at a clipboard. Peyton signed her name, not bothering to explain that she was here to work. This first time, she'd have to jump through hoops, but from here on out, she'd have access without having to wade through bureaucracy. She settled into a chair and spent her time rereading the reports the office had e-mailed to her the night before.

The vehicle identification number had been scraped clean, and the forensics team was still processing all the evidence they'd gathered in an attempt to identify the owner of the truck. None of the occupants had been identified yet.

The clues were sparse, but the overall situation wasn't an unfamiliar one. Uneducated, poor laborers in Mexico spent years raising enough money to hire a coyote to help them cross the border. Some made it, some didn't. Some got here only to be sent back, poorer and less hopeful than when they arrived. But failure usually didn't equate to winding up slaughtered before they ever had a chance to breathe the fresh air of freedom.

"Miss Davis?"

Peyton looked up at the woman who'd called her name. She too wore a navy blue suit, but hers was a more stylish cut with a skirt that showed a healthy amount of leg and heels that made her look like her petite frame might come tumbling down at any moment. Peyton figured she was around thirty years old, probably one of the younger assistant United States attorneys in the office. She stood and held out her hand. "That's me."

The woman's grip was strong and sure. "Great to meet you. I'm Bianca Cruz. Mr. Gellar asked me to show you around before the task force meeting at ten." She handed Peyton a badge. "This one's temporary. You'll get your full credentials by the end of the week." She started walking. "We're getting set up for a meeting, but I'll show you the space and give you a couple of minutes to settle in."

They walked to the end of the hallway. When Bianca stopped, Peyton pulled up short behind her, waiting while Bianca swung open the door and strode inside. Peyton paused in the threshold to survey the enormous room. It held a massive oak desk, leather chairs, a couch, and a seating area over in the corner. When Bianca turned around, Peyton asked, "Where's Mr. Gellar?"

"He's in the conference room."

"And we're in his office because?" Peyton tried to telegraph her confusion without outright saying anything.

"Oh, wait, you thought…No, this is your office. Mr. Gellar's office is the corner office, down the hall." She started pointing out features. "The computer system's up and running, but IT will be by later today to get you set up to log on to the network and give you a PACER ID. Kitchen and break room are just around the corner, and there's a pretty decent cafeteria on the sixth floor. You can also use the sixth floor as a crossover to get to the elevator banks that lead to the courtrooms, but I'll take you over this afternoon for arraignments so you can get a feel for the place. The secretaries stocked you up, but if you need any supplies, just let them know." She stopped only long enough to glance at her watch. "Meeting starts in thirty minutes. I'll come back for you in about twenty."

Before Peyton could respond, Bianca had whirled out of the room with the same speed at which she spoke. Amazing, considering the stilts she was wearing. "Thanks," Peyton said to the empty doorway.

Alone, she shut the door and took a few minutes to survey her new office. From the cramped quarters she was used to in D.C., the spacious room was a serious upgrade. Gellar's office must be enormous. Several familiar looking boxes were in the corner, and she recognized her handwriting. She'd arranged for everything from her D.C. office to be sent directly here. The small collection of framed certificates and mementos would barely make a dent in the large space.

The ringing desk phone interrupted her thoughts. She picked up the handset. "Davis, here."

"Ms. Davis, I have a call for you on one."

"Thanks." She was surprised to be getting an outside call within moments of her official start. She punched the button to take the call. "This is Peyton."

"I told the receptionist I want to turn myself in, and she said you were the one I needed to talk to. Is this a good time?"

Peyton laughed at the flirty good cheer in Lily's voice. After spending last night and this morning preparing for her first day at the new office, yesterday's ride seemed like it had happened in the distant past. Lily's call was a pleasant surprise.

Surprise. She sat forward. "Not that it's not great to hear from you, but how did you know I was here?"

"Mad detecting skills."

"Is that so?"

"Well, more a case of accidental detective. I called your mother this morning to ask her a question about your family's donation to Cattle Baron's and she mentioned you were starting your new job this morning. I interrogated her and she gave you up. U.S. Attorney, huh?"

"Assistant U.S. attorney. Big difference."

"Didn't sound that way to your mother. She sounded like she couldn't be more proud."

"She's my mother. Consider the source." The words were a rote reaction. Peyton believed her mother had sounded proud because that's what mothers were expected to be. Whether she really was or not was an entirely different story. She'd be more proud if Peyton were seated on a horse, running the fence line at the ranch.

"I'm trying to schedule an appointment downtown for this afternoon. I don't suppose you'll be free for lunch on your first day?"

Peyton heard a knock on the door. "Hang on just a second." She placed a hand over the phone and called out, "Come in."

Bianca stuck her head in the door and mouthed, "It's time." Peyton nodded and Bianca shut the door. "Lily?"

"Yes?"

"I'm afraid it's going to be a little crazy around here today. How about I call you this evening and we can make plans for something a little more relaxed than lunch?"

"Why, AUSA Davis, that sounds like a perfect plan."

After Peyton hung up the phone, she waited a few minutes before meeting Bianca at the door. Today would be full of new people, new procedures, new information, but the thing she looked forward to the most was making plans with the new interest in her life.

Lily placed the envelope containing the trust waiver on the conference room table and glared at it. She hadn't signed it yet and wasn't sure she would. This trip to the Bradley & Casey law firm would be a key factor in her decision.

She pushed the envelope aside and pulled out her cell phone. No new texts or e-mails had arrived since she last checked. Her call log showed her morning call to Peyton, and she saved the number into the contact she'd already created for Peyton in her phone. No sense pretending. She wanted to see her again and soon. She'd been disappointed they couldn't meet for lunch, but she completely understood that Peyton needed to be focused for her first day on the job. She pledged to wait patiently for Peyton's promised call.

Before she put her phone away, the entry for the call she'd placed to Peyton's mother this morning caught her eye. She'd dreaded making the call, but Helen Davis acted like the fact that her bank had returned the check for the Davis family's donation to Cattle Baron's was nothing to be concerned about. It was a large donation. Maybe the bank had flagged the account to check for fraud. Helen said she'd talk to the bank and get replacement funds to the charity by the end of the week. Lily had considered mentioning it to Peyton, but she hadn't wanted to waste their precious few minutes of conversation on what was probably a silly accounting error.

The door to the conference room opened, and in strode a tall, elegant woman with waves of auburn hair and friendly emerald green eyes. Lily stood and they shook hands.

"Good morning," the woman said. "I'm Morgan Bradley and you must be Lily Gantry. Nice to meet you." She motioned for Lily to sit and settled into a chair.

"Nice to meet you too. I appreciate you seeing me on short notice."

Morgan smiled. "Happens a lot in my line of work. Tell me what I can do to help you."

Lily pushed the envelope across the table, glad to be rid of the offensive piece of paper, even if the respite was only temporary. "I need to know if this would hold up in court."

She watched as Morgan Bradley scanned the document. Morgan had come highly recommended by one of Courtney's friends, Aimee Howard. Lily knew plenty of lawyers, but they were all big firm types, sure to have connections or conflicts with Gantry family business. She wanted to explore her options, but she wasn't willing to disclose family secrets to get answers. Morgan and her partner had their own small boutique firm and, although they were well known for their work defending high profile defendants, they wouldn't run in the same stuffy, gossipy circles as Nester and his cronies.

Morgan set the paper down and took a sip of water. Her eyes were kind, but her words were hesitant. "You do realize that my specialty is criminal defense? I think the last time I had to learn anything about estate law, it was because one of my clients was accused of killing his mother to inherit her pristine 1927 Model T."

Lily nodded. "I know. I just thought maybe you could point me in the right direction." She fixed Morgan with a stare. "Discretion is crucial." Surely, Morgan knew who she was, who her family was.

Her serious look signaled she got it. "I understand." She stood. "Wait here for just a minute."

When Morgan left, Lily took a moment to survey the conference room. Accolades for the firm decorated the walls, but they were interspersed with soft touches like original paintings by a well-known local artist and a beautiful vase of Gerbera daisies. She felt welcome and safe here, not at all like she needed to be on guard against the sharks her family usually dealt with.

A few minutes later, the door opened and Morgan entered with another woman. "Lily, this is Erica Osten. She recently joined our office. In her former life, she practiced with one of the foremost estate and trust firms in Austin."

Lily sized up the new lawyer. Erica looked young, but she decided that might be due to the enthusiastic look in her eyes and not her actual age. She was short, but not petite. Sturdy, like a bulldog. Oh well, she had to trust someone to give her the answers she needed. She met Morgan's questioning look and nodded. Morgan and Erica sat at the table.

"Morgan gave me an idea of what you're looking for," Erica said. "Do you have a copy of the original trust?"

"Not with me, but I'm sure I can get one." Lily ignored the voice in her head that told her it might be more difficult than she was making out. "I should've known you would want to see that as well."

Erica reached for the paper on the table between them. "Not a problem. I imagine being asked to sign away your rights robbed you of good sense."

Morgan cleared her throat and Erica shook her head. "Sorry about that," she said. "I've been told a lack of tact is my biggest weakness."

"There are worse things," Lily said. Erica's honesty was refreshing. How different from the teams of attorneys that kowtowed to her father, always scared to say the wrong thing and risk him hiring a new firm to spend all his money. "I've always known I was adopted. It was kind of hard to hide the fact since I look nothing like my lily white parents, name notwithstanding." She laughed at the irony and was pleased to see Morgan and Erica laugh with her.

"My parents love me and they've given me everything I've needed or wanted. I've never felt like anything other than a Gantry, but the last few years, I've had nagging thoughts that I might like to know more about my own heritage. My mother died giving birth to me, and she told the nuns my father had been killed several months before I was born, but surely there are others, cousins, aunts, uncles."

"Have you taken any steps to find out more?" Morgan asked.

"No, although the possibility has always been in the back of my mind. And then this request took me completely off guard." She leaned in. "Make no mistake, there's nothing I wouldn't do for the Gantrys, but the knowledge I may have other family out there has always tugged at me. Even if I decided not to do anything about it, the decision should be mine, not to be made under duress."

"Perfectly reasonable," Morgan said. "Erica, what do you think?"

"Restrictive covenants like this are not unusual, but they are often challenged and with a great measure of success, but often at great cost. Any idea why this is just now coming up? I assume you've had access to the trust for some time now?"

"Is that your way of saying I look old?" Lily watched Erica's frown and then laughed to ease the tension. "I'm kidding. You're right. I do think the timing is random, but I can't think of any reason to think it's particularly strange. I've been away since college and only recently returned to Dallas. Maybe it was just easier to wait until I moved back home to get me to sign the papers."

Erica's frown didn't dissipate, and Lily started to question her own logic. She'd had access to her portion of the trust for several years, although she hadn't touched a dime. If she had access to the money, surely the family lawyers could have arranged a way for her to sign what Nester and her father now insisted was necessary paperwork. "I don't know. Maybe I'm making too much of this. I don't care about the money, but it's not just me that could be affected if I don't sign."

Morgan reached a hand across the table and squeezed her arm. "Lily, what do you want?"

Lily met her eyes and saw strength and kindness reflected there. She didn't have a clue what she wanted, but she did know that she wasn't ready to close any doors. "I suppose I just want to know I have options."

"Then I suggest we give you some. Erica, what should we do next?" Morgan turned to her associate and Lily followed her glance, hopeful.

Erica made a couple of notes on her pad and then placed both hands on the table. "First thing I'll need is a copy of the original trust. Shouldn't be difficult for you to get since you're a beneficiary. Once I have that, I'll be in a better position to assess your options."

"Thank you. I'll get the paperwork to you this week." Mission accomplished, Lily pushed back from the table and stood. "I appreciate your time."

Erica stood and shook her hand, but Morgan remained seated. In response to Lily's questioning glance, she said, "Maybe while you're here, we should talk about the other part of this."

"Excuse me?" Lily was genuinely confused until she realized Morgan was probably talking about payment of fees. She'd just assumed she would be billed. "Oh, I'm sorry." She reached into her purse. "Is a personal check okay?"

Morgan shook her head and smiled. "No, no. This was a simple consult. You don't owe us anything unless we determine we can actually help you. And that's what I wanted to talk about. We have a couple of very accomplished private investigators on call. If you'd like to find your mother's relatives, we can help you."

Lily reached out a hand to steady herself against the table. She hadn't come here with the intention of starting down a path to her past, but she had to admit she'd always been curious. More than curious, she'd always harbored hope that someday, someone who looked like her would show up on her doorstep and announce they'd been looking for her all this time. She and this person would embrace and then spend hours talking about memories missed and future plans to stay in each other's lives. Realistic? Probably not, but having the possibility dangled in front of her was sorely tempting. Should she give in?

❖

Hershel Gellar spent way too much time talking about the good work of the task force. His eyes lit up and his voice got faster as he all but salivated at the opportunity to take down the Cartel, or at least the branch that had wormed its way into the regular lives of the good citizens of North Texas. About halfway through his self-serving speech, Peyton glanced around the room, assessing her team. Dale, dressed in jeans and boots was seated next to Agent Dunley. On the other side of the table, Bianca was flanked by ATF Agent Mary Lovelace, and Raphael Martinez, a Texas Ranger. They all looked bored by Hershel's speech. Later she'd be leading them, but today was about reporting in on their work so far and charting a direction for the future.

Finally, Hershel left the room, apparently satisfied his cheerleading skills had done their work. Peyton didn't assume his place at the front of the room, she didn't even stand, but she did take command.

"Okay, we've got a lot of work ahead of us. Luckily, we have a lot of resources. I know you all have other pending cases on your plate, but I'm counting on every one of you to make our work your first priority. Do I have your commitment?"

She fixed each one of them with a stare and returned their nods with one of her own. "Let's get started. Dale, any new developments on the trailer?"

Dale didn't meet her eyes, but she addressed the rest of the group. "Matter of fact, I got a report this morning. The trailer's been reported stolen."

"Who reported it?" Peyton asked. The last information she had was that the trailer had been scrubbed of identifying information, and they'd decided it wasn't likely they were going to find out who owned it.

"Rose Construction. Rose is an outfit out of El Paso. They specialize in building oil rigs." Dale looked around the room. "Anyone want to guess the name of their parent company?"

Dale's comment was met with smiles and nods from everyone in the room, but Peyton shook her head, left out of the inside joke. "Anyone care to fill me in?"

Bianca spoke up. "We just started working on an angle last month. It's in the early stages, and I imagine it'll take a while for the forensics team to run it down, but we think we have a good lead on how the Zetas are laundering their money."

Peyton shook her head. "That was clear as mud. Who really owns the trailer and what do they have to do with the Zetas?"

"Rose Construction is a division of Gantry Oil. The FBI has been investigating Cyrus Gantry's company on the sly for a while based on a tip from someone on the inside who claims he may be defrauding investors. But lately we've come to think the fraud might run deeper than that—maybe the funny financials are a result of the company funneling money from the Zetas' drug and gun sales."

Bianca was still talking, but Peyton heard only a strong buzz that had started the moment she'd heard the name Cyrus Gantry. Peyton stared down at her notes. She'd written and circled the words Rose, Cyrus, and Gantry. If she had any thoughts that Bianca was talking about a different Cyrus Gantry, the name Rose stopped her cold. She could hear Lily's voice as clear as if she were standing right there in the room. *My mother's name is Rose and it suits her perfectly—strong, but sometimes thorny.*

She looked up and realized Bianca was no longer talking. The room was quiet and everyone was looking at anything but her, like they didn't want to draw attention to the fact she'd checked out of the conversation. The last thing she needed was to exhibit any weakness. She'd figure out the implications of what Bianca had said later, but now it was time to grasp the reins and see where this lead. She stood.

"I'd like a report from everyone by end of day on what you've been working on. Include any linked cases. As for the trailer, it doesn't make sense the company would report it stolen if they were involved, especially since someone went to great lengths to make sure we couldn't identify it. Either they didn't know it was being used to transport illegals or they're trying to cover up their involvement. We need to find out which one it is and find out right away." She turned to Bianca. "Come with me."

She stalked off to her office, Bianca walking behind her. She'd wanted to spend some time with Bianca this afternoon and get some insights on the rest of the team members, especially Dale Nelson who treated her with thinly-veiled contempt, but the bomb Bianca had just dropped sent her spinning in a different direction. She waited until they were both inside with the door shut before speaking. "I assume Mr. Gellar knows your theory about the connection between Gantry and the Zetas?"

Bianca ducked her head. "He knows we're looking at Gantry for fraud. The other part is still in the early stages. I've been working on it with one of the agents in the FBI fraud unit, but I didn't want to bother Mr. Gellar with it until we had something more concrete."

Peyton's blood boiled. "But you thought it was okay to blurt it out in front of a bunch of agents looking for blood? It's one thing to look into a little white-collar crime, but you're saying one of the most successful businessmen in Dallas may be in bed with a bunch of drug-dealing, murdering thugs. You ready to have that rumor show up on the front page of tomorrow's paper?"

Bianca's face was bright red. Peyton took a breath and considered whether she'd gone too far, motivated by the possibility that Lily's father was a target in a heinous crime. Her next words were gentler, but measured.

"I promise we will follow up on every lead, no matter where it takes us, but if there's one thing I've learned after a few years in Beltway, it's to have all your ducks in a row before you come out shooting. Now, go and get me whatever you've got to back up your theory."

Peyton walked behind her desk, sat down, and picked up the phone. Bianca took the signal and left, shutting the door behind her. As soon as it was closed, Peyton took a deep breath while she tried to stave off the nagging feeling of dread brought on by all the talk of Lily's family business. She punched in the numbers and waited for the call to connect. "It's Peyton. We need to talk."

LAY DOWN THE LAW

CHAPTER SEVEN

L ily checked her watch. Eight o'clock and still no call from
Peyton.

"You have a hot date?" Courtney asked.

"Afraid not. Just you, me, and a thousand thank-you notes."

They'd met at the Cattle Baron offices with a couple of
interns to begin the task of handwriting thank-you notes to all of
the donors for the event. They'd been at it for hours, and the time
crawled by as Lily hoped, with every passing moment, that a call
from Peyton would break the monotony.

"Anything to do with Zach's gorgeous sister? I heard she took
you horseback riding yesterday."

"Who says we live in a big city? You'd think the way word
gets around that we lived in the sticks."

Before Courtney could fire off a reply, Lily's cell phone
skittered across the table and she pounced on it. "Hello?" When
Nester started talking, she sagged.

"I was hoping I could come by and pick up the signed
document we discussed last week," he said.

"I'm not at home right now," she replied, stalling for time
since she wasn't prepared with a ready excuse for the delay.
"You're working late."

"Always do. How about tomorrow? I'll buy you lunch at the
club."

The last thing she wanted to do was share a meal with Nester where she'd have to spend at least two hours and several bourbons listening to him drone on about how much he did for the family. As she contemplated her options, she heard the beeping that signaled she was receiving another call. She pulled the phone away from her ear, but the listing read No Caller ID. Hoping it was Peyton, she rushed to get Nester off the phone. "I'd rather come to the office. I'll call you tomorrow when I have a better idea about my schedule. Okay?"

"I look forward to seeing you tomorrow," he said.

Lily hung up the phone and quickly switched to the incoming call, but she was too late. She stared at the phone display for a few seconds, willing a message to appear.

"Your phone not working?" Courtney asked.

"Not well enough to screen out the people I don't want to talk to. Can you believe that was my father's lawyer? He's hustling me to sign some paperwork and doesn't understand why I would want to actually read it first."

"Any reason you're still staring at the phone?"

Buzz. Her phone lit up to signal a new voice mail. Lily held up a hand to Courtney while she listened to the message.

"Lily, hi, this is Peyton. Sorry I didn't call earlier. It's been a really busy day and a few urgent things came up that are going to keep me busy for a while. I'll call you when things break free. Have a good week."

Lily played it twice to make sure she hadn't missed anything, like the part where Peyton didn't give her a complete brush-off. The second time was just as brusque as the first. She clicked off the line and tossed her phone into her purse.

"What's up?" Courtney placed an arm around her. "You look like someone stole your lunch money."

"Hardly. Guess I just misjudged a situation." Foolish. That's what she'd been. Foolish to get excited about Peyton and the possibilities, none of which had been promised. Maybe Peyton really was busy with work, but her terse tone hadn't matched her casual, "Hey, I'll call you later," words. Her message had definitely been a don't call me, I'll call you or I won't. Lily could take a hint.

Courtney knew her well enough not to push, and Lily wasn't sure what she would say anyway. *Peyton Davis swept me off my feet and now she wants to sweep me under the rug.* Silly that she even cared since they barely knew each other, but the brush-off stung partly because it called her instincts into question and mostly because it just plain hurt.

Well, she didn't need another woman to make her feel good about herself. She could take care of herself just fine. And maybe it was time to start taking some steps in that direction.

"Hey, Courtney, didn't you say you know a good realtor?"

"Sure. She has an office in Highland Park. It's a boutique agency. She has access to lots of properties before they even go on the market. You thinking about finding your own place so soon?"

Lily reflected on the last week. Lunch with her well meaning, but controlling father. Social bullying by her mother. Placing too much hope in a couple of encounters with a beautiful, but unavailable woman. She needed some space, and finding her own place would be one step in the right direction. "Yes, I am."

Peyton clicked off the call. As much as she'd hated leaving such a vague message, she'd been relieved Lily hadn't actually answered the phone, as it saved her from having to answer questions she wasn't prepared to answer. She stared at the phone for a moment before finally deciding to turn off the ringer. Still not convinced she'd done the right thing, she slid into a seat and waved the bartender over. "Two drafts, whatever's local." When he left, she turned to face her brother. Zach was smiling like a kid in a candy store. "What?"

"Nothing. I was just surprised to get your call. Out on the town on a Monday night. What's the occasion, sis?"

"Just wanted to talk, is all. We haven't had time to catch up."

"Neil keeps me pretty busy. I had to slip away tonight before he could start in on everything he wants me to do in the morning."

"What's he got you doing?"

"A little bit of everything." He stopped while the bartender placed two frosty mugs in front of them. Lifting a glass, he offered a toast. "To good times, now that the whole family is back together again."

Peyton raised her glass, but she didn't return his smile. Their family might be physically back in the same place, but they were a long way from being back together again. She'd barely spoken to Neil since the night of Cattle Baron's and, after her mother's proclamation the day before, she knew tougher times were ahead. "I heard he's had a couple of prospectors out on the property looking to drill."

Zach stared into his drink. His silence was telling. "You think we should drill?" she asked.

Zach pushed his beer aside. "I don't know. Neil says it's better, more reliable money than the horses. And with Dad…Well, someone's got to do something to make sure we stay afloat."

"Afloat? What are you talking about?"

Zach's eyes widened, like he was scared he'd said too much. Peyton knew him well. "Zach, if you don't tell me I'm going to have to ask Mom and Dad. With everything that's going on, don't you think it would be best if I heard it from you?"

Shoulders slumped, he started talking. "A new ranch opened up near Decatur. Run by a woman who moved here from the valley and she's breeding champion bloodlines. Her horses won the Futurity the last two years running. Everyone's using them for breeding, and anyone who wants a winner thinks they have to get it there. Our business has fallen off, and we just can't keep up. Mom's never been interested in all the newfangled breeding methods no matter how much Neil tried to convince her, and Dad, well, he's in no position to make any decisions."

"Watch yourself," Peyton said.

"Come on, Peyton, you can see it for yourself. We'll be lucky if he sees the year out. Anyway, Neil's just doing what he can to keep things going. If we can bridge this rough spot with some oil money, what's the harm?"

Peyton shook her head. Drilling on the ranch wouldn't be illegal, and it wouldn't violate the terms of her mother's inheritance, but it did go against everything her family had ever stood for. The land that housed them was to be respected. They'd take from it only what they needed and cherish and protect the rest. No matter what an oil company promised, digging wells, building rigs, and driving tankers on and off the property would do damage and fly in the face of the legacy they'd worked hard to keep. But that wasn't her only concern. She tried to remember the name of the company her mother had mentioned.

"Zach, what do you know about the company Neil signed with?"

"Some outfit out of Odessa. Ray Explorations. I don't know anything about them."

Peyton breathed a sigh of relief. If he'd said Gantry Oil, she would've marched back to the ranch that night and insisted Neil rescind his agreement. Bad enough she had to dismiss any possibility of pursuing anything with Lily Gantry because of what Bianca had told her, but if her own family was involved with the Gantrys, she wasn't sure what she'd do. Still, something needed to be done about Neil's headstrong willingness to sell out the family legacy. She'd told her mother she needed time to think about her suggestion that they assume control over the day-to-day operation of the ranch, but time was apparently running out. She'd taken this new job to be closer to home, but she'd never intended to be an attorney and rancher both. Surely she'd have to sacrifice one for the other. She owed an allegiance to her family, but what about those dead souls who'd been gunned down when all they'd wanted was a taste of freedom? Didn't she owe it to them to finish what she'd started?

A few hours later, Peyton sat at the desk in her old room at the ranch, typing notes into her laptop in an attempt to clear her mind of all the must-dos that cluttered her thoughts. She stretched and yawned, relieved to finally feel the promise of a good night's sleep. She reached to close the lid of her laptop, but a tickling urge stopped her. She opened a Web browser and typed in the name of the oil company Neil had contracted with to dig the exploratory well.

The first page of the search engine revealed ten results, some press, some corporate listings on sites like Dun and Bradstreet. Peyton clicked through them all, pushing past ads and sponsored links, unsure what she was looking for, but wanting to be diligent, wanting to be wrong. After an hour of tunneling, she found what she hadn't wanted to unearth. Ray Explorations was a partially owned subsidiary of Gantry Oil, but that wasn't the kicker. Ray also happened to be Lily Gantry's middle name.

Peyton shut the laptop without reading another word. She'd seen enough to know she had a problem. If Bianca Cruz was right and Cyrus Gantry was in bed with the Cartel, trouble was brewing and she was smack in the middle of it.

CHAPTER EIGHT

Peyton walked into the toolshed beside the barn and found Neil rummaging through a toolbox. He barely glanced her way as he spoke. "You're up early."

"I need to talk to you and you're kind of hard to catch." She'd tried to corner him around the ranch over the last week, but between her schedule and his elusiveness, she hadn't managed to snag a minute alone with him.

"Oh, I'm around. I'm all over this place. There's a lot of work to do in case you haven't noticed."

"I noticed." She hadn't wanted to start this conversation on an acrimonious note, but there didn't seem to be a choice when it came to him. She searched for a topic they could agree on before she got into the real reason she'd gotten up before dawn to try to talk to him. "Dad doesn't seem to be improving."

Neil tossed a hammer onto the workbench and turned toward her. "He's dying, Peyton. What did you expect?"

She kept her tone low and even. "Don't be a jackass. Mom says the doctors have some hope this new round of treatment will help."

"You're all fooling yourselves. He's doped up on painkillers so of course he feels better, but he's declining more every day. You'd have a little more perspective if you'd been around to see him the past few years."

She didn't bother pointing out that she'd been home for holidays and the occasional rare vacation. He would know that if he hadn't made himself scarce whenever she visited. "I'm here now and I want to help out."

"You can help by staying out of my way. I've got it handled."

"That's exactly what I want to talk to you about. Did you have Roscoe go over the papers you signed with Ray Explorations?"

He shook his head. "Didn't need to. Lawyers only get in the way of real deal making. I looked the owner of the company in the eye and shook his hand. That's how real men do deals."

"Is that so? You shook hands with Cyrus Gantry?"

"What are you talking about?"

"Ray Explorations is a subsidiary of Gantry Oil. You signed an agreement that puts us in business with Cyrus Gantry."

Neil's eyes signaled surprise, but he recovered quickly. "According to Zach, you're sweet on Cyrus's daughter, so that should make you pretty happy. Of course, if I'd known I was doing you a favor, I might've reconsidered."

Peyton didn't bother pointing out Neil had made his dubious business decision before she'd even met Lily Gantry. She didn't want to mention Lily at all, and she sure hadn't planned to talk to him about anything to do with her investigation into Gantry Oil. She took a different tack. "You know Grandma would be rolling over in her grave if she knew there was drilling on the ranch."

"Times change. The horses aren't paying the rent, but Mom won't give them up. I'm doing my part to keep the place afloat. What are you doing to help out?"

"That's between me and Mom, but I'll tell you right now, there won't be any drilling on the Circle Six."

"Says you."

"Says me and a court order if you force me to get one. Did you know Dad signed a power of attorney and appointed me to handle his affairs? That means Mom and I are the only ones authorized to make decisions about the ranch, and that includes signing contracts with oil companies."

Neil didn't recover as quickly from his surprise this time, and his tone turned nastier. "Bullshit. You can't come back here after all this time and tell me how to run this place. Dad's been sick and Mom has no business sense. If it wasn't for me, this entire place would have already gone under."

Peyton stepped close until she was right up in his space. "Don't you disrespect the rest of this family. Dad loves this land more than you ever will, and if he were in any condition to realize what you were doing, he'd be the first to put a stop to it. Mom has plenty of business sense, but apparently she's been trying to make up for the fact you never had a birthright to this place by giving you way too much latitude. And what about Zach? From what I can see, he helps out plenty. You're not the only one who has a stake in the future of this place."

"Zach is dumber than I thought if he thinks any of his work will amount to something. You'll just swoop in and take it all from him."

"I've never wanted to take anything from you. Can't you see that?"

"No. You may have Zach fooled, but I saw firsthand how entitled you think you are."

Anger burned in Peyton's belly. She wanted to punch Neil in the face, anything to stop the steady stream of vitriol, but she knew it would accomplish nothing except to put an even bigger wall between them. She backed up until she was no longer standing right on top of him and raised her hands to signal she was done fighting.

"Look, I don't want to fight with you. I've never wanted to fight with you, and I've never wanted to take what's yours. There was a time we both shared the same dream, and we can do that again. We can make this ranch the finest in the county without selling out to make a fast buck. But it will only happen if we do it together."

She watched closely to see if her words were having any affect on him, but his jaw was tight and his expression sullen. In the face of his silence, she issued an ultimatum. "Here's the deal. You have until the end of the week to get out of the contract with Ray Explorations. I don't care how you do it as long as we don't get sued for nonperformance."

"And if I don't?"

"Then I'll intervene and take you to court. You had no right to sign that contract and everyone will know it. You do what I ask and you can stay in charge, help make the ranch great again. You fight me and your days here are numbered."

Neil picked up the hammer and hefted it in his hand. For a second it looked like he was going to say something, but suddenly he lifted it in the air and slammed it onto the workbench. Peyton flinched at the sound, but she didn't move. His temper would get him into trouble, but she wasn't about to give him the benefit of thinking he'd scared her. Even if he did.

She left him stewing in the shed and walked back to the house. Although she'd started a habit of skipping Fernanda's big breakfasts in favor of getting to the office early, Peyton decided to make an exception today. When she walked into the kitchen, her father was already seated at the table, propped up in his chair with a couple of pillows and a plate of half-eaten pancakes in front of him. Fernanda fussed over the both of them.

"Good morning, Miss Peyton. Mr. Davis just finished his breakfast, but I'll get you some coffee straight away. Mrs. Davis is with Mr. Zach on the back porch and they'll be right in. Pancakes sound good to you?"

Peyton's stomach rumbled. "Pancakes sound heavenly. Especially yours. Thanks, Fernanda."

"Make sure she gets lots of syrup," her father said. Fernanda smiled indulgently and assured him she would.

"Thanks, Dad. How are you feeling?" Peyton braced for the answer. His skin was gray, and he was hunched in his chair, and she didn't expect a positive response.

"I'm doing well. Lots more hay to bale in the lower pasture. And that fence along the northern boundary won't fix itself. It's going to be a busy day."

She couldn't quite tell if he meant he thought he was going to do the work or if he was asking for her help. She started to reply, but Zach, who'd just entered the room with her mother, shook his head and held a finger over his lips. He placed a hand on her father's shoulder and leaned down to gently whisper, "Hey, Dad, sounds like you have a big day planned for us. Why don't we help you out to the porch and you can make a list while I grab a bite to eat?"

Peyton took the hint and rose to help Zach guide their dad to the porch. It was another unseasonably warm November day, but her father clutched a blanket around his middle as soon as he eased into his rocking chair. He looked small and frail, and all she could think about was protecting him and the rest of her family from the dangers Neil had invited into this, their safe haven. By staying away to keep the peace, she'd missed making memories with the rest of her family. She bent down and kissed him on the cheek. Neil was right about one thing—their father was dying, and she'd be damned if she was going to let his final days be ruined by Neil's recklessness.

Back in the kitchen, she told Zach and her mother about the ultimatum she'd given to Neil.

While her mother nodded her head in approval, Zach asked, "But, sis, I'm pretty sure all he's doing is getting a survey done. He won't do anything else without a family vote."

"I wish I could believe that, but after talking to him this morning, I think he's hell-bent on finding oil. The company he hired, Ray Explorations, is owned by Gantry Oil. I can't share everything with you right now, but in addition to not wanting to violate the land, I have a good reason for not wanting to do business with Cyrus Gantry. I need you to trust me on this. I gave Neil until the end of the week to get out of his deal with Gantry, but if he doesn't then I plan to go see Roscoe and do whatever's necessary to take control. Do I have your support?"

Zach glanced at the door as if he thought Neil might come strolling in. Peyton understood he was torn. After all, Neil had been here on the ranch and they'd been working side by side for the past few years. No doubt the bond between her brothers was strong, and she had no desire to come between them, but she would do whatever she had to do to keep her entire family safe and their legacy intact. She reached over and grabbed his hand, but it was her mother who sealed the deal.

"Zach," her mother said. "I need you to listen to Peyton. I love Neil, but he's not seeing things clearly."

He met Peyton's eyes and she saw reluctant acceptance. "Okay."

She squeezed his hand and made a silent vow to earn back his trust.

❖

Lily stood in front of the law office, squared her shoulders, and pushed through the doors. She held a thick envelope in an iron grip, ready to do battle.

"Do you have an appointment?" the receptionist asked.

"Yes. Lily Gantry, and I'm a few minutes early for a ten o'clock."

She walked around the waiting area, too keyed up to sit. It had taken her almost a week to make this decision, and now that she had, she couldn't wait to get started. First thing this morning, she'd driven downtown to the opulent offices of Nester's law firm, knowing full well he had a breakfast meeting with her father.

The receptionist at Nester's firm hadn't even asked if she had an appointment. As a Gantry, she had carte blanche to drop in at any time. The young woman had offered her coffee and then rushed off to find an associate who could assist Ms. Gantry with the urgent matter she wished to discuss.

Lily had bet on the odds that the associate assigned to help her would be male, and she wasn't wrong. Counting on young male hormones to win out over discretion, she implored eager Brice to help her with an urgent matter. Twenty minutes later, she walked out with a copy of her grandfather's trust securely in her grasp.

"Lily?"

She turned to see Morgan standing behind her. She thrust the envelope at her. "I was able to get a copy of the trust document, but I haven't had a chance to look it over. I also put together everything I know about my birth. I'm ready to find my mother's family. Are you ready to help me?"

Morgan smiled. "Of course. Follow me." She led the way back into the suite of offices. They stopped in front of Erica's door. "Erica will talk to you about the trust and I'll go set up a meeting with one of our investigators. I'll see you in about an hour, okay?"

Lily nodded. Now that she was here, committed, she was certain this was the right thing to do.

Erica looked like she was in the middle of a paper tornado, but nothing about the haphazard piles of paper scattered throughout her office seemed to faze her. Lily, on the other hand, couldn't look at anything else. Erica had appeared to be so put together when they'd last met. How good could she be at sorting through her family's complicated dealings if she couldn't keep her office organized?

"They say a messy desk is the sign of genius."

Lily was only slightly embarrassed at being so easy to read. "They do, do they? Looks like you might be a little too busy to help me."

Erica pushed her glasses up her nose and shook her head. "This is how I work. The law is a puzzle and the facts are the puzzle pieces. I have to spread them all out and spend time looking at them to see where they all fit." She held out her hand. "You brought documents for me to review?"

It took Lily a minute to recover from Erica's abrupt change in topic, but she handed over the envelope. "My family doesn't know I have this copy. I got it from an associate at the lawyer's office this morning."

Erica was already thumbing through the pages and merely muttered "uh-huh" without looking up. Lily started counting ceiling tiles to avoid spying at the papers lining Erica's desk, certain to be full of secrets about other people's families, other people's eccentricities. To keep from eavesdropping, she reflected on the only family she knew.

Her grandfather, Rufus Gantry, had been kind to her, always treating her as if she'd been born a Gantry. His kindness was especially welcome since others in the Gantry family had made it clear her lack of pedigree meant she shouldn't be entitled to share the inheritance he'd left behind. As the oldest son, her father Cyrus had taken Rufus's place at the helm of Gantry Oil Enterprises when he died. His brother, Brock, and his children were left with lesser holdings, none of which would ever give them complete power over the family business. While her cousins lived a lavish lifestyle on their portion of the inheritance, Lily hadn't made a single withdrawal from the trust fund she'd received access to on her twenty-fifth birthday, which meant the well-invested fund had almost doubled in worth over the last five years.

"You haven't withdrawn any of the money?" Erica asked.

"No. After my graduate work in Germany at the University of Oldenburg's program on renewable energy, I worked with a cooperative developing new methods of harnessing wind power. I developed a patent during my time there and, as part of my agreement with the cooperative, I licensed it back to them at a reduced rate. Even with the discount, the royalties I've earned have been more than enough to pay my living expenses."

"So you've had access to the trust for five years and they're just now asking you to sign away your rights?"

Lily met Erica's gaze and saw disbelief. "It's odd, I know, but it's not the only eccentric thing my family's ever done."

"Is that so?"

"My grandfather held a contest between his two sons to see who would get married first."

"A contest?"

"It was simple, really. Produce a valid marriage license, a notarized prenup, and the first one to make it through a full year of wedded bliss earned a seat on the board."

"I'm guessing your dad won?"

"He doesn't like to lose."

"How did your mother feel about being a trophy wife?"

There was that bluntness again. Part of her found Erica's candor refreshing. She'd often wondered whether her parents had fallen in love before or after the wedding. She had no real evidence to tell either way, but she did know they were genuinely affectionate toward each other, and she'd always assumed her mother wouldn't have married just for money. Maybe she was naive, but there was the matter of the prenup. "My mother is a practical woman."

"Bet they didn't wait five years after the wedding to have her sign the prenup." Erica looked down at the trust document. "Your father's lawyer is Nester Rawlins. Would he have handled the prenup too?"

"Why does that matter?" Lily was confused about how her questions about the trust had turned into an examination of her parents' marriage.

"On its face, it doesn't, but if Nester has handled previous family dealings like the prenuptial agreement, then he's aware of the importance of timely notice and the possibility of waiver."

Lily shook her head. "You're speaking a different language. English, please."

Erica smiled. "Sorry. Look, your mother would've signed a prenup before she got married, you know, so she could have the opportunity to choose whether she wanted to make that a condition of the marriage. Follow me?"

"Yes, but—"

"If there were going to be conditions on you receiving access to your trust fund, you should have been advised about those before you were given access. Waiting five years to impose restrictions isn't reasonable, it isn't fair, and it probably constitutes a waiver of their right to ask you to sign away your rights."

"Got it. You're saying they waited too long to ask me to sign."

"Oh, they can ask all right, but if they try to take away your access because you won't sign, then we have a good chance of keeping them from doing so."

It was on the tip of Lily's tongue to say she didn't care about the money. She didn't, at least not for herself, but there was so much good she could do with it. More good than if the money fell into other hands. "What's the worst case scenario?"

"You refuse to sign the addendum, you actually violate the terms by looking for your mother's family, and you lose access to the funds."

"But then where does the money go?"

Erica picked up the hefty document and thumbed through the pages. "Here it is. The money would revert to the estate, and Lance and Darla Gantry inherit your portion of the trust. Are they your cousins?"

Lily was impressed at Erica's quick command of the bulky legal document. "Yes. They're insufferable. The money would be gone in less than a year."

Erica set the papers down. "What do you want to do?"

Lily looked back up at the ceiling, pretending to consider her options, but she knew she'd made up her mind before she'd walked in this morning. "I want you to prepare for the fallout. I'm going to find my mother's family and I'm going to keep my trust fund."

CHAPTER NINE

Peyton sat in the first row behind the railing and watched Bianca at work on the morning docket. Most of the proceedings were simple detention hearings, but in her experience, how someone handled the basics told her all she needed to know about their abilities. This morning's docket had been loaded with a series of defendants arrested as part of a large methamphetamine ring over the weekend. She'd carefully studied the pretrial reports for each of the defendants and settled on the one about to stand before the judge as the best bet for what she had planned.

"Your Honor," Bianca said from the podium in the well of the courtroom. "Section 3142(e)(3)(A) provides a rebuttal presumption that in a controlled substances case such as this, where the defendant faces a potential maximum sentence of ten years, she should be detained pending trial. The defense has offered family testimony and evidence of the defendant's commendable work history, but nothing they have presented is sufficient to overcome the presumption. Therefore, we respectfully ask that Ms. Chavez be held without bond pending trial." Bianca finished speaking and waited for the judge to make eye contact. When he finally looked in their direction, it was Peyton he locked eyes with first.

"Ms. Cruz, Do you have co-counsel with you today?"

Peyton stood but waited for Bianca to answer the question since it had been directed at her.

"Your Honor, this is AUSA Peyton Davis. She just transferred in from our D.C. office and will be working with me on cases handled by the task force."

Judge Nivens pushed his glasses up his nose. "Thank you, counselor. Ms. Davis, it's good to see you. It's been a long time."

Peyton saw Bianca's curious glance out of the corner of her eye, but she focused on the judge. She hadn't mentioned to Bianca that she'd clerked at this courthouse years ago, just out of law school. Except for the judges and a few of the U.S. marshals, there were very few folks left from her stint as a judicial clerk. "It's good to see you too, Judge, and it's nice to be back in a warmer climate."

"I imagine," he said and then without taking a breath, he turned to the defense table. "Carmen Chavez, having heard the evidence today, I find there is probable cause to support the charges, and I am ordering you to remain in the custody of the U.S. marshals service pending trial."

Peyton listened while he read the familiar litany of information about pretrial deadlines. This was the final detention hearing of the morning, and they'd saved it for last for good reason. While the bailiff took Carmen to the small holding cell next door to the courtroom, Peyton waited for Bianca, and then they walked over to the public defender. Dominic Fowler was explaining to the defendant's family what would happen over the next few months. She'd watched him handle six detention hearings that afternoon, and she knew all she needed to. He'd been doing this for a while, and he treated each proceeding with rote indifference. He had made a feeble effort in Carmen's case, but probably only because her mother had cried on his shoulder. She couldn't really blame him. The law wasn't on his side in these cases, and his time would be better spent working out a deal or getting ready for trial rather than trying to keep his client free for now.

He turned to them after the family left. "When can I expect discovery?"

Bianca looked at Peyton who nodded. "I can get you copies of what we have in the next few days, but maybe we can shortcut the process."

"You making an offer already? You haven't even arrested everyone involved."

"Maybe your client could help with that."

He started gathering his files. "Fat chance. Did you see her? She works in an office. This bust was a fluke. If she was involved at all, it was minimal. Just because you guys can indict everyone even remotely connected with a drug ring, doesn't mean the little people know the major players."

Peyton responded. "Sure, that's usually the case, but not this time." She stuck out a hand. "Peyton Davis, nice to meet you. We've asked the marshals to hold your client. Think we could talk to her before she heads back to the jail?"

Dominic stared at her hand for a moment before accepting the gesture. "I think the family's considering hiring a lawyer."

"Be a shame if they spent a bunch of money to accomplish nothing better. I really think she'd like to hear what we have to say. What do you think?"

He looked down at the stack of files in his arms and then at his watch. "What the hell, my afternoon's already shot. But you talk; she listens. No questions until I have a chance to meet with her alone. Understood?"

Peyton nodded. "Understood."

There was one tiny room in the holdover that allowed for a contact visit. The three attorneys bunched into the space and Peyton asked the marshal to remove Carmen's handcuffs. She waited until he left the room to start talking.

"Ms. Chavez, my name is Peyton Davis, and you remember Bianca Cruz from the courtroom." Carmen nodded and Peyton continued. "You understand you're charged with conspiracy to deliver methamphetamine, enough to merit a sentence of around twenty years?" She nodded again. "What I want to make sure you understand is that we don't have to prove you delivered the drugs. In fact, I know you didn't."

Finally, Carmen met her eyes. Peyton saw fear, terror even. This young, well-kept girl wasn't a drug dealer. Based on the report from pretrial services, she didn't even use drugs. Peyton suspected she knew what had driven Carmen to crime, and she was about to exploit that weakness. "What I do know is that you set up this buy and that's enough to send you to prison for twenty years." She paused to let the information sink in. "Some people think there's such a thing as parole, like you do a few years and get out early. We don't have that in the federal system. The most you can hope for is a little time off for good behavior. Even if you're an exemplary inmate, you will do at least eighty-five percent of your time."

"Why are you telling me all this?"

"I want you to know exactly what you're facing when we convict you, and we will convict you. This week, I plan to deliver tapes to your attorney. You're on these tapes, calls made from your cell phone, to one of the top captains of the Zetas." She leaned in close. "Everyone thinks you're sweet and innocent. You work in an office, you have a child. You dress right, you don't do drugs. From the outside looking in, you're a model citizen. But I'm not on the outside looking in. I'm right in the middle of it and I know better."

Dominic cleared his throat and spoke. "Did you bring us in here to berate my client? If so, this is a waste of time."

Peyton never took her eyes off Carmen and was impressed that she didn't shy away from the stare. "Truth is, I need your help, and if you give it to me, I'll go to bat for you."

"I don't know anything."

Peyton shook her head. "No one calls Arturo Vargas directly for a drug buy. There's a chain of command, and if word reaches Arturo, it doesn't come through a phone line. You are connected to him somehow. That connection could be the thing that breaks you or the thing that sets you free. Your choice."

Carmen hung her head. Peyton shot a look at Bianca who apparently took it as a sign to take up the thread.

"Carmen," Bianca said. "I know what it's like to have a child who relies on you for everything. What will happen to your son if you go to prison for the next twenty years?"

"And what will happen to him if she rats out the largest drug cartel in Texas?" Dominic said.

Bianca spoke directly to Carmen. "We can protect you. Do you really think that even if you don't cooperate, he will believe you didn't talk?"

Dominic stood up. "Now that you've started asking questions, this meeting is over. You want to talk to my client, you call me." He was two steps toward the door before Carmen spoke.

"Wait."

Peyton motioned to Bianca not to react. If Carmen was going to cooperate, really cooperate, it had to be her decision or at the very least she had to think it was her decision. Truth was, she didn't have much of a choice in the matter. Federal drug laws, especially when conspiracy was alleged, were so easy to prove and federal juries so conservative, they could probably charge and convict Carmen's minor children just for being in the same room as their mother when she called Arturo.

Dominic shrugged and sat back down. "Carmen, you have no obligation to speak to them and I strongly advise you not to until we've seen the evidence."

Peyton saw Bianca open her mouth to speak, and she deliberately dropped a pad of paper on the floor to ward her off. She could imagine Bianca wanted to point out that, as a party to the crime, Carmen already knew what the evidence was and knew she was damned. Pointing that out would be overkill. When she'd been a new prosecutor, she'd made similar mistakes, showboating instead of reeling her catch in, nice and slow. They had to let Carmen feel she had some control or she'd resist the line they had just thrown her.

Silent seconds ticked away before Carmen finally spoke, and when she did, her voice was low and quiet. "I need to know my children will be safe."

Peyton nodded. "I understand."

"And my mother. She will take care of them."

"It's our plan to keep you all safe."

"Your plans mean nothing to the Vargases."

"It's not unreasonable to be scared of them," Peyton said, "but that will never stop me."

"Then you are crazy, because they will kill you."

Peyton wanted to laugh, but there was a grain of truth in Carmen's words that couldn't be denied. "If their power is so great, you won't be safe in prison. Maybe despite my threats, the judge will go easy on you. You think Sergio and Arturo will believe you didn't talk to get a good deal? Then you'll be all on your own." She leaned closer. "I have a feeling you've been all on your own for a while now. Your father's in prison, your brothers are dead, the father of your children only shows up when it's convenient. Let us help you. All we ask is that you help us in return."

Carmen's eyes widened as Peyton recited the litany of personal detail, and Peyton prayed she would see the light.

"I need more than your spoken word. I need your promise in writing that no harm will come to my family."

Peyton hated this part. She looked up at Dominic and then over at Bianca. When she finally turned back to Carmen and opened her mouth to speak, she heard Bianca's voice.

"You have our word. Whatever it takes."

Peyton rose, the only thing on her mind now was getting out of the holdover and giving Bianca a piece of her mind. She calmed her temper long enough to shake Carmen's hand and tell Dominic they would be in touch. She strode back into the now empty courtroom and up the aisle to the double doors in the rear. She could hear Bianca huffing behind her, but she didn't slow down.

"Peyton, wait!"

She stopped and turned slowly as Bianca finally caught up with her.

"Where are you going?"

Peyton looked at her watch. "I have an appointment." She waited, hoping Bianca might use a touch of self-reflection to hit on exactly why she was pissed.

"I thought we could talk, you know, plan how to approach this."

"By this, do you mean the way you promised that young woman nothing would happen to her or her family when you know full well you have no control over that?"

"It wasn't like you hadn't already led her to believe that."

"Maybe, but there's a fine line between outlining the probabilities and making promises you know you can't keep. You as much as told her she'd have full protection. I'm not in a position to make that guarantee which means no way are you. We have a chain of command. I don't know who was running this team before me, but from now on, every decision has to go through me. Understood?"

Bianca's expression was stubborn, sullen, but she nodded her tacit understanding.

"Great. I'll be back in a couple of hours. Let's meet then and go over strategy. Have whoever's available from the team join us." Peyton didn't wait for a reply before she turned and walked to the bank of elevators leading directly to the ground floor. When she burst through the doors of the building, she pulled out her cell phone and dialed the number she'd programmed in earlier that morning.

"Virginia, it's Peyton. You ready for lunch?"

❖

"Lily?"

Lily looked up into sapphire blue eyes. "Yes."

The blonde with the eyes stuck her hand out. "I'm Skye Keaton. Morgan set up the appointment. I hope you haven't been waiting long."

"No, not at all," Lily said. "Not like the Adolphus is a bad place to wait."

"You're right about that. You hungry?"

"Starving." Lily's meeting with Erica had run longer than they had expected, and she'd had to push out her meeting with this private investigator. Skye had suggested they conduct their business over lunch and suggested the Aldophus. Lily wondered at the choice. With so many restaurants in Dallas, it seemed odd to meet at a hotel.

Skye seemed to catch her looking. "You mind if we eat at the Rodeo?" she said, referring to the more casual eatery located at the opposite end of the hotel. "They have amazing hamburgers."

Within moments, they were settled in. Skye placed her order without looking at the menu and Lily followed suit with a simple, "I'll have what she's having." When the waiter left, she asked, "Come here often?"

"I hate to admit this, but I'm double-booked. I'm on a surveillance job. I have someone relieving me right now, but I wanted to stay close."

"Let me guess, husband cheating on wife or vice versa?"

Skye shook her head. "If you hire me, part of what you pay me for is discretion."

"That's a good thing. If the rest of my family found out what I'm up to, it would be sure to cause an uproar."

"Morgan told me you want to locate your mother's family and that's about it. I told her I'd rather hear the rest directly from you."

"It's fairly simple, really, since I don't know much. My birth mother died within moments of my birth." She pulled a copy of her birth certificate from her bag and handed it to Skye. "This should give you a starting point."

Skye gave the document a once-over. "No father is listed."

Lily heard the many questions contained in Skye's simple statement. "I'm told she knew who he was, but he was killed before they could be married. You can't list an unmarried father without a signed Acknowledgment of Paternity."

"Any clues about his identity?"

Lily shook her head. "Not much to go on there. The only lead I can think of is the church that handled my adoption, Our Lady of Guadalupe. Apparently, they took me in because my birth mother and father, I mean, her boyfriend, were both dead." The terms never seemed to fit. Her mother was Rose and her father was Cyrus. She'd never known these other people, and maybe it was a mistake to think that finding out more about them would give her some kind of closure. She looked up to meet Skye's questioning gaze. "I think I may be wasting your time."

The waiter showed up with their drinks, saving her from more embarrassing proclamations. When he left, Skye spoke first.

"Here's the deal. You're not wasting my time. I'm on a stakeout and I've got to eat sometime. May as well have company."

She smiled. "I understand where you're coming from. You love your parents, the people who raised you, and you're worried that looking for these blood-relative strangers would somehow diminish those feelings."

Lily raised her glass in a toast. "So far, you're spot on. I'm just not sure I can reconcile this strong pull to know more about my past, about my roots, with how I feel about the only family I've ever known."

"What if you hold off on all that for now? Let me see what I can find out, and if I'm able to find some of your other family, then you can decide what you want to do with that information. Sometimes just knowing is the thing that matters."

"You may be right. Kind of reminds me of something my father always says—don't borrow trouble. I suppose I can just wait and see."

"Sounds like a good plan."

The waiter delivered their food, and between bites of burgers and fries, Skye asked her more questions about her family, the ones she knew and the ones she didn't. When the check finally came, Lily felt like she'd been through the ringer.

Skye started to reach for the bill at the same time that Lily did, and Lily's hand wound up on top of hers. She moved her hand quickly away, self-conscious at the unintended touch. At that moment, she heard a throat clear and looked up into a familiar face.

"Hello, Lily."

Peyton was looking down at the table where her hand had just touched Skye's, and Lily could swear she detected a hint of jealousy in her eyes. Fine by her. Peyton was the one who'd blown her off. If she was jealous, it was her own damn fault.

"Hello, Peyton. I haven't heard from you in a while. I hope you're doing well."

A slight blush reddened Peyton's cheeks. "I'm fine. And you?"

"Oh, I couldn't be better." She watched as Peyton gave Skye a pointed glance. "Peyton Davis, meet Skye Keaton." She watched as Skye reached out a hand, catching Peyton off guard, certainly a rare event. Peyton's expression was curious, but Lily wasn't about to let Peyton know the striking blonde was an employee and not a date.

"Nice to meet you," said Skye.

"You too." Peyton didn't move, and Lily was almost tempted to ask if she wanted to join them. As mad as she was at Peyton's radio silence over the last week, she missed the moments they'd shared. Had it only been her imagination that Peyton had enjoyed her company too?

"Peyton, I've got us a table."

Lily didn't need to look past Peyton's shoulder to see who was speaking. She'd know that voice anywhere, especially since the last time she'd heard it, the speaker had warned her away from Peyton. Well trained in Southern charm, Lily buried her discomfort beneath a broad smile. "Hi there, Virginia. I was just talking to Peyton. I hope you don't mind." She smiled even brighter when she saw Virginia's glaring eyes.

But Virginia was trained in Southern combat too, and she slid an arm around Peyton and smiled brightly at Skye. "Oh, hi, Lily." She offered a hand to Skye. "Where have you been keeping this gorgeous woman?"

Skye shifted in her seat as she looked around at the three of them. Feeling a tad bit guilty at including Skye in the game, Lily shrugged her answer. Skye looked at her watch. "I didn't realize what time it was. You all mind if I step away to make a call?"

Peyton moved over and Skye slid out of the booth and walked away. Virginia leaned down and faux whispered to Lily. "She's a keeper. Trust me, I know one when I see one." She cast a pointed look at Peyton and then tugged at her arm. "Come on, sugar, I'm starving."

Peyton sidestepped Virginia's clawing grasp. "I'll be right there."

Virginia pouted but walked to a table across the room.

Lily watched her go. "You should hurry. Your date looks like she might die without you."

"Your date seems nice."

"My date is none of your business."

Peyton raised her hands in mock surrender. "Sorry." She put her hands down. "I really am sorry. I should've talked to you in person."

"It's not like you owe me anything. We barely know each other."

"I wanted to get to know you."

"What stopped you?"

Peyton glanced over her shoulder. Lily couldn't tell if she was looking for Virginia or Skye. She tried not to care. Peyton obviously hadn't thought much of the time they'd spent together, so why should she? "Go, have lunch with Virginia. It's clear you already know exactly what you want and I'm not it."

Peyton backed up a step, shaking her head. "It's not that simple."

"Yes, it is. If you think it isn't then we're better off with you over there and me..." Lily floundered for just a moment. "I was doing fine before I met you, and while I enjoyed the time we spent together, it wasn't life-altering." She employed her most dismissive tone. "Enjoy your lunch."

After a few seconds of hesitation, Peyton turned and walked the length of the restaurant to where Virginia waited. Lily tried not to watch, but she couldn't help it. If Peyton wanted the likes of Virginia Taylor, then she didn't know her at all.

"Everything okay here?" Skye took her seat.

"Sorry about that."

"I sense a little history."

"Just a little. Not enough to merit the display I just put on. Please forgive me."

Skye smiled. "No hard feelings. I won't tell my wife you were using me to make someone jealous."

Lily cocked her head. "Is there anything that doesn't get past you?"

"Not much. She likes you too, you know."

"Who? Peyton?" She shook her head. "I'm afraid you're wrong about that, but I'm going to hire you anyway. Can you start right away?"

"Absolutely."

Maybe this project was exactly what she needed to distract her from Peyton Davis. As she and Skye left the restaurant, she shot one last look in Peyton's direction. Peyton was staring right at her while Virginia chattered on about something. Lily raised her eyebrows, but Peyton merely shook her head, telling her all she needed to know. She left the building and left behind any lingering hope that she'd have a chance to get closer to Peyton.

❖

Peyton did her best to appear interested in Virginia's ramblings, but it was hard. Seeing Lily had been completely unexpected, and she'd been caught off guard. Poor planning on her part. She should've expected she'd run into Lily at some point, and she should have had some excuse to offer for her caddish behavior. Something less specific than my office is investigating your family business for possible money laundering.

If she could've figured out a way to do so gracefully, she would have begged off lunch, but she needed Virginia's help. If she could get it. She'd invited her to lunch to get information, but so far she hadn't had a chance to wedge a question into the conversation.

"How well do you even know her?"

Peyton looked up, certain she'd missed at least a paragraph or two in the Virginia Taylor show. "What?"

Virginia dropped her voice to a whisper. "You do know Lily isn't a real Gantry, don't you? I mean, you only have to see her with the rest of her family to tell."

"It's pretty clear she's adopted, but that's really none of our business. Have you always been so shallow?"

"I thought you liked my honesty."

"There's honesty and then there's mean."

Virginia shrugged. "Always the virtuous one, aren't you? I would've thought a few years in the big city would have jaded you."

"When it comes to gossip, D.C. is smaller than Dallas, but you know I've never been prone to gossip."

"Precisely the reason I've been wondering why you wanted to see me."

Peyton faked a smile. "Maybe I just wanted to have lunch with an old friend of the family."

"Try again. I called you a dozen times after you left, even sent flowers to your new office. All I got was a thank you card in the mail. No note, just, 'Thanks for the flowers, Peyton.' Is that how you brush off all your 'old friends'?"

"I'm sorry you thought I was rude, but you're lucky I responded at all. Things were bad enough with Neil. There was no point in making it worse." She didn't expect Virginia to get it, but then again she'd never given her a chance and that wasn't really fair either.

Peyton flashed back to the week before she'd accepted the offer from the attorney general's office in D.C. She'd never intended to take the job, but things had gotten increasingly heated between her and Neil since their parents had finally revealed the family tradition of passing the ranch down through the women in the family. The tradition wasn't a legally binding part of her great-grandmother's bequest, but none of her progeny had broken the trend. Her mother and father had explained the history in a family meeting called when they found out Peyton had been offered the position in Washington. Peyton knew they'd expected her to say no to the job and stay put in Texas, working the law while overseeing her inheritance. How had they not foreseen how their news would affect their oldest son who, despite his professed childhood dreams to share the responsibilities of the ranch with his sister, secretly harbored fantasies of being the master of the Circle Six all on his own? Peyton's up-and-coming career as a prosecutor likely reinforced his belief.

When Neil discovered that the family plan involved Peyton gaining full ownership of the ranch and that he'd only ever be a hired hand, his fury was uncontainable. He'd always been prone to temper tantrums, but Peyton had never seen him so angry. She tried to assure him with promises that she'd never let family tradition displace him or his family. He and his heirs could run the ranch, live on the land, share in all the profits—she'd never leave him or any of her family to want for anything.

"But I'll still have nothing to show for it. The ranch will always be yours."

"Ours. Screw tradition. I'll have papers drawn up tomorrow. We'll split the shares. You, me, and Zach."

"You would do that?"

"Of course. You're my brother."

"What about Mom? What will she think?"

"Have you met our mother? Sentiment is not a word in her vocabulary. She won't care. I get why the tradition was important once, but we of the weaker sex no longer need the protection. If anyone will get that, she will."

For the first time in days, the light returned to Neil's eyes. "Stay here and run it with me. Like we talked about, you know, when we were kids. Virginia and I will be married soon. I want you to be around when we have kids of our own, help me teach them to ride."

But the shiny new job in Washington had beckoned. The position with the attorney general's office was a coup for a young lawyer, and it would place her well up on the ladder to success. On the other hand, there were things about the move that didn't appeal to her at all. Cold winters, complicated politics, cramped quarters. Neil's urgings were tempting. She could find a job here, stay with her family under wide-open skies.

She looked into her brother's hopeful eyes. They'd grown apart, and maybe that had been more her fault than she'd realized or wanted to admit. Family meant unconditional love, unflinching loyalty. Neil was reaching out, and she owed him at least a meeting in the middle. "I'll think it over."

"How is Neil?"

Peyton shook off the yoke of musings about the past and faced Virginia. "The same. What did you expect?" Virginia flinched, and

Peyton was instantly sorry for her harsh tone. She softened her next words. "When's the last time you spoke to him?"

"That night. He wasn't interested in anything I had to say. I returned the ring via messenger since he wouldn't return any of my calls. I'm certain your parents hate me and would be happy if I never showed back up in any of your lives."

Peyton would never forget that night. She'd never seen Neil in such a dark place, but when he'd walked into Peyton's room and found Virginia half-naked on the bed, she could hear him come unhinged. A second later, when Peyton emerged from the shower dressed only in a towel, it had been fuel on the fire.

The night had started innocently enough, a simple dinner at the ranch with the family. It had been Neil's idea, part of his campaign to convince Peyton to stay in Texas.

Virginia had always been an outrageous flirt. Neil even joked about how no man was safe from the siren call of his beautiful fiancée, but tonight her efforts were laser-focused on Peyton.

Every time Neil's back was turned, Virginia ramped up her efforts until smiles and nods escalated into a hand on a thigh under the dinner table and fingers trailing along her neck in a dark corner. At first, the attention was only annoying, but it quickly became dangerous. When Virginia tried to ply her with a glass of wine, Peyton gripped her arm so suddenly, the wine spilled down her shirt. Thankful for a reason to excuse herself from the evening's events, Peyton went up to her room to change, deciding to shower away the scent of the encounter. When she finished her shower, she entered the room only to find Virginia hustling to cover her naked body and Neil looking apoplectic.

She'd left for D.C. a few days later, the decision made easy by the icy coldness that grew from Neil's certainty that she'd once again tried to take everything he'd ever wanted.

Peyton forced her mind back to the present, but the past pushed in. "Why did you do it?"

"You're kidding, right?" Virginia took a sip of her iced tea. "I loved Neil, but you...you have this quality about you that's undeniably attractive. It's like you're outside the circle, unattainable. It makes people crazy, makes them want to do crazy things to get you to notice. I guess I thought I would see if I could get you to notice me before you left for Washington."

"I've always noticed you, but you belonged to Neil."

"I don't belong to anyone."

"You know what I mean. Not belong, but you'd agreed to marry him. Don't act like that's nothing."

"Maybe it was just too confining. Neil's always been the steady guy who would never leave the ranch, who would always do what's expected. You were the exciting one. You went off to law school. You had prospects. You were the catch, the rising star. That kind of shine is irresistible."

"I hope I never gave you the impression there was anything between us."

"If you had, I probably wouldn't have made a move. It was your unavailability that made me want you. And then you showed up back here out of the blue. Is it any wonder I couldn't keep my hands off you at Cattle Baron's? No woman in her right mind could."

Not true. Lily Gantry obviously didn't find her lack of availability attractive. It had only made her angry. How could she inspire such different reactions from two different women? *Because you only care about one of them.*

But it didn't matter if she cared about Lily. Professionally, she had no choice but to keep her distance, and that same professionalism led her back to the real reason she'd asked Virginia to lunch. "I need you to tell me everything you know about the oil business."

CHAPTER TEN

Tuesday morning, Peyton sat in her office, organizing her notes. Virginia's information about the oil business had filled in a lot of the holes in her knowledge. The Taylor family had been long-time competitors of the Gantrys for North Texas's oil and gas market, and meeting with Virginia had knocked two items off her list: helping with the case and learning more about what Neil might have planned for the future of the ranch. She began to wonder if Neil had first started thinking about drilling during the time he dated Virginia. He'd probably envisioned merging their family businesses into an empire, which only added to the ways his breakup with Virginia had dashed his hopes. Peyton shook her head. She couldn't be blamed for Neil's assumptions. His jealousy had always been just below the surface of their seemingly happy relationship.

God, she hoped Neil made the right decision and found a way to extricate himself from the contract, but if he didn't, her path was clear. She had a responsibility to the rest of her family, not to mention the legacy of fortitude the ranch symbolized. Deep in her soul, she'd harbored dreams of deeding the ranch to her own daughter.

She looked back at her notes, attempting to focus on the agenda she'd come up with for the task force. As far as she could tell, before she'd gotten here they'd spent their time reacting to whatever new action the Zetas dreamed up. It was time to go on offense.

"Peyton? Mind if I come in?" Bianca stood in her doorway, posture timid, eyes looking everywhere except directly at her.

She waved. "Sure. I could use your help."

Bianca look surprised, but walked into the room and took a seat in front of her desk. "I just got a call from Dominic Fowler. Carmen Chavez wants to talk."

"That was fast. I figured she'd have to stew for a while before she came around. You should go see her this afternoon before she changes her mind."

Bianca fumbled with the papers in her hand. "Actually, she only wants to talk to you. She thinks you have an in with the judge."

Peyton set her notes aside. "I guess it doesn't hurt to let her think that for now, but I'll make it clear that I can't make any concrete promises at this point." She searched Bianca's face, trying to read her expression. "You're upset."

"Yes, I mean no. I mean…well, never mind."

"It's okay. You're pissed because I chewed you out about making promises you might not be able to keep and now the witness wants to talk to me because she assumes I can move mountains for her. You get the difference, right?"

Bianca hesitated before nodding, which told Peyton she wasn't really on board. "The difference is she made an assumption about me based on my interaction with the judge in court."

"So, it's okay with you if we lie, as long as it's indirect."

"How long have you been doing this?"

"This? Being a lawyer or working at the U.S. attorney's office?"

"Both. Give me the short version of your résumé."

"I graduated from Georgetown and then did one year as a judicial clerk. Two years as a litigator with Harper Whitney, including six months as a lawyer on loan to the Tarrant County D.A.'s office. I've been here for the last three years."

"Impressive."

Bianca rolled her eyes and Peyton laughed. "I mean it, but here's the thing. This is all I've ever done, so I have some nuggets of experience to share with you. You can let the fact that I'm in charge piss you off, or you can choose to learn from the mistakes I've made in the past. Your choice."

Bianca didn't say anything at first, and Peyton let her have a moment to think, since thinking before acting was one of the key things she wanted her to learn. When Bianca finally did speak, her words took Peyton off guard.

"Why did you come back here?" She frowned. "Sorry, that didn't come out right. I mean, word is you were an up-and-comer at the AG's office. Why come back to Dallas when you could make a name for yourself at main Justice?"

Peyton steepled her fingers while she contemplated how much to share. This conversation, right now, could be the key to her relationship with the team. She needed to make an ally if she was going to get them all to work together instead of running off in different directions. She didn't have to share her life story, but a little honesty wouldn't hurt. "Dallas is home for me. I have family here, and I need my family as much as they need me." She paused and then turned the tables on the younger attorney. "You went off to Georgetown. Why did you come back?"

"Same as you, I guess. I have connections here. Staying away was never really an option."

Peyton caught the undercurrent of implicit meaning, but now was not the time to pry. "Then let's both make the most of the time we're here. Get someone from pretrial services to order Carmen over from the jail under the guise of a routine check-in. Make sure nothing about the request references that we want to see her. Find a marshal you trust who can let us know when she's here and we'll go see her. Together."

"Do you want to include one of the agents?"

Peyton took a moment to consider. Normal debriefs would include one or two case agents who usually took on the role of good or bad cop, depending on the situation. It would probably make sense to include Dale at this point, but she hesitated. Dale had made it pretty clear she didn't like her. She didn't need to be liked, but if they were going to conduct an interview together, it would help to at least be able to read each other. No, she'd leave her out for now and make this afternoon more of a bonding exercise with Bianca. "How about we keep this between us for now? If we feel like Carmen has something solid to offer, we can bring the agents in for a second debrief. Sound good?"

Bianca smiled wide. "Sounds perfect."

Several hours later, they were seated around a table with Carmen and Dominic. Peyton opened the conversation. "Thanks for agreeing to talk to us." She pushed a paper across the table. "This is a document I gave to your attorney for you both to sign. Have you read it?"

Carmen nodded.

"I want to make sure you understand that I haven't made any specific promises and I'm not going to at this time. I'll listen to what you have to say. If you're truthful and if your information is helpful then I will do what I can for you, but I'm not making any guarantees in advance. Do you understand?"

Carmen nodded again.

Peyton looked at Dominic who nodded as well. She knew he'd been around long enough to adequately explain to his client the Queen for a Day agreement. Basically, the form said Carmen got a free pass for whatever she told them in this meeting—they couldn't use it to prosecute her. If she ever denied she'd said these things, they could use her statement to impeach her testimony, but otherwise it was off limits. Peyton liked to make absolutely sure witnesses knew exactly what they were getting into before they started talking. "Do you have any questions?" Carmen shook her head. "Do you want to sign the agreement and talk to us?"

Carmen flashed a quick glance at her attorney and then pulled the paper closer and signed her name. Peyton reached over and signed her name as well. "I'll get a copy of this to your attorney. This will likely be the first of several meetings. I'm here with Ms. Cruz today, but in the future, I may include some of the case agents who were involved in investigating this matter." She slid the paper into a folder and then launched her first question before Carmen could settle in. "When did you first meet Arturo Vargas?"

"I've never met him."

Peyton heard a chair scrape and, without looking, she knew Bianca had leaned forward in her chair ready to lunge. She cleared her throat and drummed her fingers on the table. Carmen remained defiantly silent, and finally, Peyton reached into her briefcase and pulled out a manila envelope. She handed it to Carmen's attorney but never took her eyes off Carmen.

"I've just given your attorney an initial set of discovery. Taped conversations. Between you and Arturo Vargas. Would you like to change your answer?"

Dominic leaned over and whispered something in Carmen's ear, and then listened to what his client had to say before responding on her behalf. "Without actually listening to these tapes, we don't have any way to respond to the allegations that Ms. Chavez is on them, let alone whether or not she was talking to Arturo Vargas, but my client insists she never met Mr. Vargas."

"Let's not pretend we need to call him *Mister* Vargas." Peyton let her voice rise a bit to convey she was deadly serious. "He and his brother Sergio are ruthless killers who make their money getting children hooked on dangerous drugs. They're Zetas, Mexican Cartel, and they will never deserve or receive respect from me, including addressing them by anything other than Defendants One and Two in an indictment designed to send them away for the rest of their lives."

Peyton took her tone down a notch with her next remarks. "If your client would like to be named in the same indictment, all she has to do is keep lying."

"I never met him!" Carmen shouted the words, and Dominic placed a hand on her arm to calm her down. She settled back into her chair, but her expression was sullen.

Peyton rolled a hand to keep her talking. "I'm listening."

"I called the number. I talked to the man on the other end, but I didn't know who it was." She lowered her eyes and whispered, "Not for sure."

Peyton decided not to get bogged down in the details for now. "Where did you get the phone number?"

"From my father."

"What's his name?"

"My father?"

Peyton shot a look at Bianca who looked like she was about to boil over with frustration. "Carmen, this is going to go a lot more smoothly if you will just assume that I'm going to want to know everything. If I have to drag every detail out of you, it's going to be painful for both of us and not at all helpful to your case. Why don't you start by telling me your father's name, when he gave you the phone number, and why."

"His name is Enrique Chavez and he's at Allred," she said, referring to one of the Texas prison units. "He called and said he needed me to do him a favor. He said it was for the family."

"Was it a collect, prison call?"

"No. I thought it was strange and I even asked him about it. He said he got a cell phone from someone else in there."

Cell phones in prison, usually brought in by corrupt guards, had gotten out of control. The feds had managed to crack down on the epidemic, but the state prison system, where the guards had less pay and benefits, was a breeding ground for corruption. "What was the favor?"

"He gave me a phone number. Told me to call and talk to the person on the other end. He told me exactly what to say. Said to do whatever was asked, that we would make some money that he needed for his appeal, and his actions would help pay a debt. He said if I did this, the family would be safe." She looked up from her monotone story and met Peyton's eyes. "I have a little boy."

"Did someone threaten your boy?"

"He didn't say so, not right out, but he kept saying we needed to do this to be safe."

"You say he told you exactly what to say, tell me more about that."

"I wrote it down and memorized it. I was supposed to call the number and talk to them about car repairs."

Peyton mentally checked off a box on her list. The taped calls were all about automotive repair, each word part of a carefully crafted code for drug buys. Since the operation was run out of a body shop, the plan was brilliant.

"But you knew you weren't really calling about car repairs, right?"

Carmen looked at Dominic who nodded for her to answer. "Yes, I knew."

"Why did you think you were calling?"

"To buy drugs. Crystal."

"I appreciate your honesty. Now, describe the call."

Carmen described how she called several times to arrange the buy. She didn't know for sure who she was talking to, but she was passed along to several different people, which led Peyton to believe she was being passed up the chain of command. Carmen's father, Enrique Chavez, was doing time on a drug distribution charge, and he had been a top lieutenant of the Zetas on the outside. No doubt he was still doing their bidding even while he did time for them. But why involve his daughter?

"How many times have you done favors like this for your father?"

Carmen shook her head vigorously. "Never before."

"I find that hard to believe. Your father gave you direct access to a very powerful man. Why would he do that if he didn't know he could trust you to get the job done?"

"Who else was he going to ask? My brothers are either dead or in jail. My mother is too scared of him to even visit the prison. I'm the only one he has left. In the eyes of the law, he is a horrible person, but he was always good to me. He loves me."

Could her motivation be as simple as a daughter's love for her father? Had that love driven Carmen to put everything she'd worked for at risk? Was that so hard to believe? Wouldn't she do anything for her own family?

Of course she would, but she'd make better choices because she'd been raised to do so. Carmen had been raised by gangsters. It was amazing she'd achieved what she had, but she might always be limited by loyalty to blood relatives who were nothing more than thugs.

Was Lily just as loyal to her family? She didn't have blood to unite her to her father's empire, but maybe being adopted by rich and successful parents made her ties to their fortunes stronger. She tried to imagine Lily sitting in Carmen's place, but the thoughts didn't compute.

Peyton looked closely at Carmen and saw no signs of deception, only resignation. What she'd done had been misguided, but it was entirely possible this was indeed the first time she'd broken the law, her actions motivated by a sense of duty. If she was a pro at this, she'd be much better at gaming the system by giving up something more helpful than a vague understanding of the dangerousness of the Vargas brothers. Time to stop wondering and put Carmen to the test.

"Are you willing to make contact with Arturo again?"

Dominic stopped his client from answering and said, "You can't be serious. First of all, I'm sure he's the first named defendant in the indictment you're presenting to the grand jury. Second, you're asking her to put her life and the lives of her family in jeopardy to essentially do your job. No way."

"Maybe you're right," Peyton said. "But like I said before, her life is already in jeopardy and her liberty is too. I'm not stupid. I'm not asking her to call him on the phone. I have a different idea and I need to run it by someone else, but I need to know up front if your client is willing to cooperate."

She turned her attention back to Carmen. "All I need you to do for now is keep an open mind and keep your mouth closed. Everything you say, every phone call you make, every letter you write, you should assume someone is seeing and hearing every word. Do you understand?"

Carmen nodded.

Peyton stood up. "I'll be in touch." She looked at Bianca who began scooping her things into a bag before they left together. Bianca waited until they were back in Peyton's office before saying a word.

"Did you get what you needed from her?"

Peyton motioned for her to take a seat. "Not yet. I have an idea, and it might be a little crazy, but hear me out." She watched as Bianca scooted forward in her chair. "Wasn't there another woman arrested during this sting?"

"Yes, Carolyn Guzman. She wasn't part of the same drug buy as Carmen, but she was arrested in one of the meth houses that was covered by the warrant."

"Wife of one of the other defendants?"

"That's what Dale said. Her husband's one of Arturo's top guys."

"Is she being held at Lew Sterrett?" Peyton referred to the Dallas County Jail. The local federal detention center didn't have a wing for female inmates, so they contracted with local counties to house them pending trial.

"I think so, but I'd have to check with the marshals service to be sure. What do you have in mind?"

"What if Carmen told Carolyn that she needs to get in touch with Arturo? That she found out who tipped the cops off about the bust and needs to get him that information. Surely, if Carolyn's married to one of Arturo's lieutenants, she'd have the means to get the word out. Do you think that might make Arturo come crawling out of the woodwork?"

"Maybe. Or he might just send one of his other lieutenants to get the information."

"True, but somehow someone has to get the word back to him, and he may want to come out of hiding to take revenge on whoever set him up. If we play this right, we can set the perfect trap."

"It's risky," Bianca said, her tone cautious like she didn't want to squelch her boss's idea even if she thought it was crazy. "How would we control the situation?"

"What if we put someone in with Carmen, undercover, to keep an eye on her and make sure she sets the bait?"

"I guess we could talk to Dale about it. Maybe she knows an agent who could go in."

Peyton started to say she didn't need Dale's permission, but Bianca was right. Since Dale was the lead DEA agent on the force, running the idea by her was the right thing to do, but she doubted Dale would be receptive to the plan, especially if it came from her. "Maybe you should talk to her about it. I don't think she likes me very much."

"She'll come around."

"I'm not really concerned about being liked, only respected. I get the impression she doesn't have a high opinion of lawyers. Then again, you've worked with her for a while, so you might have better luck. She must not hate all lawyers."

Bianca didn't respond, and Peyton saw her face cloud over. "What? Did I say something wrong?"

"Uh, no. It's just…You don't know do you?"

"Know what?"

"Did Mr. Gellar not tell you about your predecessor?"

Peyton shook her head. "Not really. He said the spot had opened up. I guess I just assumed someone had either retired or transferred out of the division." Bianca's face was gray now and she wasn't making eye contact. "Spill."

"The position's been open for almost a year, but they've had trouble filling it. AUSA Maria Escobar ran the task force for two years. She prosecuted half a dozen Zetas out of a big bust in Seagoville. The day after the trial, she was gunned down in front of her house."

"Holy shit." Rage burned Peyton's insides. Rage at the act of violence against a top official in the justice system. Rage they had found out where she lived. Rage that no one had told her.

She gripped the desk and forced deep, slow breaths. So, no one had told her. Would it have made a difference if they had? She still would have taken the job, probably even been more motivated to do so. She looked at Bianca whose face still held a ghostly pallor. "That's horrible, but what does this have to do with Agent Nelson?"

"Maria was Dale's wife."

CHAPTER ELEVEN

The bar at the Adolphus was lined with men in suits, and several offered to buy Lily a drink despite the fact she had a full glass in front of her. She wished she'd chosen somewhere else to meet her father, but she'd spent a large part of the day downtown, wandering through museums and shops, her eyes searching for distraction while her mind was on the move.

What she needed to do was find a job. Her personal savings were running short, and she held out little hope her father would come through with funding on her alternative energy project, especially after he heard what she had to say tonight.

She'd told herself she'd picked this bar because it was close to his offices, but maybe she'd subconsciously chosen this place because of its proximity to the courthouse and the fact she'd run into Peyton nearby yesterday. If so, she was an idiot and the sooner she accepted that fact, the sooner she could move on.

"You staying at the hotel?"

Lily looked up at a man towering over her, smiling like he'd already sealed the deal. She started to answer, but a deep voice beat her to it.

"Move along, sir. That's my daughter you're trying to pick up."

Lily gave the stranger an apologetic glance as he backed away. As he beat a path to the other end of the bar, she said, "Hi, Dad. Good thing I'm not interested in any of the present company since no one's coming anywhere near me now."

He grabbed her into a big hug and then looked around. "I don't see anyone here good enough for my daughter."

The word daughter reminded Lily why she was here. Best to get this over with as quickly as possible. She stood up. "Let's get a table. I need to talk to you."

They moved to a table in the lounge and her father started the conversation. "I'm always glad to hear from you, but you sounded serious on the phone, and you look pretty serious now. I'm sorry I couldn't get here sooner. I got stuck in a meeting. Is everything okay?"

Lily looked into his eyes and saw genuine concern. Guilt washed through her as she contemplated the reason she'd asked him here. "Everything's fine. I'm sorry to drag you from the office. I just wanted to talk to you about something I need."

He reached across the table and scooped her hand into his. "You didn't drag me away. I'm the first to admit, I'm always thinking about business, but I'd do anything for you. Don't you know that?"

Lily took a deep breath, knowing she was about to put his declaration to the test. "I want to talk to you about the trust."

"Good. As much as I think it's nice that you're exploring your other options with these fancy new energy ideas, I don't want you to think you have to. That money is yours to spend as you wish. You don't need to work to live in the lifestyle we've raised you."

Lily took the plunge. "I'm not signing the waiver."

His brow furrowed and he shook his head like he hadn't heard her correctly. "What?"

"The waiver that Nester gave me last week. I'm not signing it."

"I don't understand."

"Dad, I love you. I love Mom, and you two will always be my true family, but there's a part of me that wants to know more about my heritage." She took a drink of her bourbon and mustered the courage to carry on. "Look at me. I'm not like you. My brown skin means I have connections to a different culture, and based on what I know about my entry into this world, a completely different way of life. Does that make sense to you?"

His face turned bright red, and Lily recognized the signs of an impending explosion. She looked around the bar, hoping he would realize this wasn't the place to express his anger. A few minutes passed in silence as they both contemplated their next moves while drinking. Finally, he broke the silence.

"It doesn't make sense. No matter how many times I turn it over in my mind. You're my daughter. You will always be my daughter. You came into our home within days of being born, and we're the only parents you've ever known. Why you would want to go looking for something that doesn't exist, I can't even begin to imagine."

"I can't explain it," Lily said, wishing she could. "You've always treated me as if I were blood, but my whole life, all anyone has to do is look at us together to know I'm different, and I have to admit, it has affected me on some level. Maybe I want to know more about my blood heritage to know more about myself. It may not make sense, but I feel compelled to see what I can find."

He glanced around and then placed a hand on her arm and whispered, "Lily, I promise you, there's nothing to find. The nuns assured us that your mother was your only living relative. I just don't want you to get your hopes up. I'm sure some shady investigator would be willing to take your money and make you promises, but there's nothing there."

He patted her arm and talked on like the subject was closed. "I have something for you to focus on instead. Nester and I reviewed your prospectus, and I think it has promise. He'll work on drawing up a contract, but I'd like to start moving forward on the Gantry Alternative Energy Plan. Why don't we set up a time for you to meet with the operations team in the next couple of weeks? You can do one of those fancy presentations and talk to them about implementation. By then, Nester's folks should have a solid contract for us to sign and we can get to work. How does that sound?"

"That sounds amazing." Lily injected the requisite amount of enthusiasm in her voice because he expected it, but she knew his maneuver was a designed distraction meant to direct her focus in a different direction. No sense balking now. Better to use the next few weeks expending all her energy before Nester showed up with a contract to trade for her signature on the trust agreement.

Apparently satisfied he'd mollified her for now, he stood. "Will you be home for dinner tonight?"

"Actually, I have a few errands to run, so I'll grab something while I'm out. Give my love to Mother."

He gave her a hug. "We're so happy to have you back at home. Your mother and I love you very much."

By way of answer, she returned the embrace. She knew his words were true, but she felt pressure to be the obedient daughter who lived with her parents and didn't disrupt the status quo. All of that was about to change.

She waited until he was gone before pulling out her phone to check and see if Skye had contacted her. No messages, but she couldn't help but feel the pressure of time. Maybe she should see what she could learn on her own. As she contemplated how she would go about that, she was so engrossed in her thoughts that she didn't notice a presence behind her until she heard a familiar voice.

"Are you living here now?"

She looked up into Peyton's eyes and saw a teasing glimmer. "I suppose I could ask you the same thing."

Peyton waved behind her. "It's close to the office and it's been one of those days."

Lily raised her glass. "I hear that. May I buy you a drink?" The words tumbled out before she could stop them, and when she saw Peyton glance around furtively, she wished she could reel the words back in. "Sorry, not really sure where that came from. I guess I should've asked if you were here to meet someone." She didn't try to hide the edge in her voice as she remembered the particular someone Peyton had been here with before.

"I take it you and Virginia aren't friends."

"You're very observant. Must be an asset in your line of work."

Peyton raised her arms. "Guilty as charged. If it makes a difference, my meeting with Virginia was purely business."

"I'm not sure it matters. You've made it perfectly clear there is nothing between us." Lily wished she could just melt into the floor. She should've said hello to Peyton and nothing more. Would've been a fairly easy task on the phone, but in person, Peyton's warm eyes and the sizzling attraction between them thwarted her ability to remain cool. She'd made a fool of herself by mentioning the obvious, and now all she wanted was for Peyton to leave and spare her further embarrassment. Instead, Peyton settled into the chair across from her and her heart betrayed her by pounding faster at the prospect Peyton might be staying.

"How about I buy *you* a drink?" Peyton asked.

Lily looked down at the empty glass in her hand. She should get up and leave. She had enough going on right now, and she didn't need the complication of a woman who didn't know what she wanted. Peyton might think that having lunch with Virginia was just business, but Virginia's warning to her to stay away from Peyton had been laced with threats that were purely personal. Peyton was complicated, apparently unavailable, and elusive. There were plenty of single, available, and desirable women in Dallas, but like a moth to a flame, she was drawn to this one. She held out her glass. "Bulliet Rye. Neat."

Peyton took the glass and strode to the bar where she ordered Lily a refill while she contemplated what in the hell she was doing. She'd worked late and she should be tired, but after Bianca's bombshell about Dale's wife, she'd been too keyed up to go home and sleep. After an afternoon spent researching everything she could find out about Maria Escobar's murder, she was agitated and hungry. Unable to find anything else open near the courthouse, she'd come to the hotel with plans to find something to eat and a drink to take the edge off. Instead, she had practically run over Cyrus Gantry as he left the hotel. But the biggest surprise had been running into Lily here at the bar. She should walk out now, get in her truck, and drive to the ranch, but after the day she'd had, the prospect of having a drink with a family member of a potential suspect seemed more inviting than facing her own family members and the secrets they were hiding.

She picked up the drinks and turned back to Lily's table, once again stunned at how unassumingly beautiful she was. How completely unlike Virginia who wielded the power of her good looks to gain whatever advantage she could. Lily met her eyes, and Peyton read the many unspoken questions. Questions she had asked herself. What was she doing here? Why had she broken things off and so abruptly at that? What was next? The last one was the biggest. She didn't have an answer, but she strode over to the table, ready to find out.

"They usually aren't so slow here," Lily said as she brought the glass to her lips and took a healthy swallow.

"I'm afraid it was me. I wasn't sure what I would say to you, so I stalled at the bar."

"Maybe there's nothing to say. I think I'm pretty clear on where things stand. I must say I didn't figure Virginia to be your type."

Peyton played the words over, but she didn't hear any notes of jealously. No, it was more like an undercurrent of distaste. For her? For Virginia? Hard to tell. "She's not my type. Like I said before, we had a business meeting."

Lily's laugh held no humor. "Virginia has only one type of business that I'm aware of and it's gossip. I suppose if you want to know exactly who's sleeping with who, she's your source." She cocked her head. "I didn't take you for the gossiping type."

She could protest, but what was the point? Gossip was part of the reason she'd met with Virginia, no matter what the cover story had been. She'd learned plenty about the oil business in general, but the nuggets of information she'd taken away about Cyrus Gantry and his desire to dominate the business were the more valuable insights. But how did Lily figure in? She wasn't a blood relative, but she was still family with all the access and privilege being a Gantry afforded her.

She looked up from her drink into Lily's eyes, a dozen questions reflected in the dark brown depths. She wished she could take her hand, lead her away. Far away from the courthouse, the investigation, the prying eyes that were already infiltrating her family's business dealings. If she'd stayed home, followed the family plan, and become a rancher, she wouldn't be in this position. Her mother's plea for her to help with the ranch rang in her ears. All she had to do was walk away from this life and return to the one she'd been born to and she would be free to indulge her strong attraction to Lily Gantry. The temptation was strong, but she couldn't see her way to it.

What she could do was be as honest as she could without jeopardizing her unit's investigation, and that meant making sure their exchange was limited to personal matters, nothing more. One pressing question rose to the top. "I'm not a gossip, but I am a curious person. Who was the blonde you were with at lunch? A date?"

"Not a date."

Peyton couldn't help but persist. "That's vague."

Lily shook her head. "Please, ask me anything else."

Shelving the topic for later, Peyton asked, "Tell me more about the kind of work you do."

"Really?" Lily narrowed her eyes. "I have to say that's the last thing I expected you to ask. You actually want to hear my spiel about alternative energy?"

"Sure." Peyton would have listened to Lily read calculus equations if it meant she got to be near her, hear her voice.

"Most people are bored silly at the prospect."

"I'm not most people."

"That fact has not gotten past me." Lily took a drink. "Tell you what. Why don't you tell me why you became a prosecutor and I'll tell you all about my career goals?"

"Not an interesting story."

"How about I decide if it's interesting or not?"

Peyton looked around the room, sizing up the exit options. She had come here to relax, not to get into a mini version of her career journey. But the fact was she didn't want to leave. She wanted to sit here and pretend, even if it was just for a few minutes, that she and Lily were on a second date and that a third was in the offing. She turned her focus back to Lily and the earnest curiosity in her eyes. Talking to her was so easy. Maybe she could pretend a few minutes longer. "There's not enough justice in the world."

"Excuse me?"

"You asked me why I became a prosecutor and I'm telling you. There's not enough justice in the world. Too much money, too much power sits squarely in the hands of people who don't care about hurting those less fortunate, the planet, and future."

"Wow. That's a heavy statement."

"Do you disagree?"

"Not necessarily. I do think there are people with money and power who work to make the world a better place, but I agree, many don't. I'm just not sure I'd assign criminal motives to the latter group."

"I didn't say rich people are criminals. Actually, I think having tough laws and strong prosecutors willing to hold people accountable helps keep people in line."

"Interesting."

"What?"

"It's just..." Lily stared hard before shaking her head. "Nothing."

"Not fair."

"Well, your little speech just now was a very general statement, but my initial impression was this was a very personal issue. Was there a particular incident that motivated you to choose a life as a crime fighter?"

Peyton listened close, but she didn't hear any sarcasm in Lily's words. Crime fighter. She'd never thought of herself in those terms, and the superhero moniker seemed inappropriate. Any crime fighting she'd done had been as part of a team, not as a single caped crusader. She considered answering Lily's question, but she ducked it instead. She looked down at her drink as she said, "I answered your question, now it's time for you to answer mine. Tell me about your calling."

Lily stared a while longer, as if by the sheer force of her gaze she could force Peyton to reveal deep secrets. Peyton met her gaze with a smile designed to conceal. Finally, Lily gave in. "Tell me what you want to know."

Peyton jumped right in. "It's no secret that your family is in the oil business. Big Oil is not overly fond of alternative fuel sources, so what was the attraction for you?"

"The planet. Future generations. My unborn children." Lily grinned. "If you're looking for a more mercenary reason, the truth is I think alternative energy is good business. All that stuff underground isn't going to last forever."

"How does your family feel about it?"

"Good question. Mother doesn't like to talk business, so when I bring up the subject, she feigns a headache or just changes the subject. Dad, on the other hand, has surprised me."

"How so?" Peyton couldn't help but lean in, ready to glean whatever information she could about Cyrus Gantry.

"I gave him a prospectus—my ideas about how Gantry Oil could expand their market share and shore up additional business by diversifying into more sustainable fuel sources. Frankly, I expected him to promise to read it and then never say another word about it, but he told me tonight he's got a meeting lined up with some investors to discuss my plans."

Dread shuddered its way down Peyton's spine. She'd known it was possible that Lily was entwined in the family business, but she'd hoped her only role was daughter, not business partner. Any thoughts that this meeting could possibly turn into something besides two acquaintances exchanging hellos promptly faded. She swallowed the last of her bourbon and set the glass on the table as Lily's words replayed in her mind like tiny hammers nailing shut the door on their future. "Wait, you said he told you this tonight?"

"Yes. He left just before you came in. You probably passed each other in the lobby." Lily placed her hand on Peyton's arm. "Are you okay? You look like you've seen a ghost."

Peyton mustered all the self-control she could find, certain she appeared to be acting foolish. If she'd been here seconds earlier, she would've seen Cyrus Gantry plotting business decisions with his only daughter, the heir to the Gantry fortune. *You wouldn't have stopped to chat then, would you?*

Her thought was interrupted by her cell phone buzzing in her pocket. She started to ignore it, but a nagging sensation prompted her to drag it out and stare at the screen. She recognized the number, but couldn't quite place it. She punched the button to answer. "Davis."

"It's Nelson. You said to call if we found anything about the trailer. We did."

Peyton kept her eyes on Lily. "Where?"

"I'll show you. I'll pick you up."

"No, I'll meet you. Where are you?"

"I'm where you are. In the lobby. I'll wait here while you wrap things up."

Dale disconnected and Peyton stared at the phone, slowly realizing Dale knew exactly where she was and who she was with.

"Something wrong?"

Peyton looked up at Lily, reading only friendly curiosity and a touch of concern in her voice. She shook her head. "No, nothing's wrong, but I have to go."

"Duty calls?"

"Something like that."

"I'm sorry you have to go."

"What?"

"I enjoyed talking to you. I've enjoyed every time I've talked to you. I think you're a very interesting woman, Peyton Davis, and I regret we never had the opportunity for that second date."

"Third."

"Pardon?"

"First date was buying a truck, second date was horseback riding. We never had a third date." Peyton had no idea what she was thinking, but the mild flirtation wouldn't stop. She didn't want it to.

"Third then. You know my number if you'd care to remedy that."

Wasn't going to happen, but Peyton couldn't bring herself to say the words. But there was something she wanted to say, something she felt compelled to share. "Lily, don't go into business with your father. Find other investors. Investors not connected with Gantry Oil."

"I don't understand." Lily grabbed Peyton's hand. "What aren't you telling me?"

Peyton looked down and watched as her fingers curled into Lily's. The touch was tender, but searing and she didn't want to let go, but she took a deep breath and broke the connection. "I can't talk to you about this, but for some reason I can't explain, I trust you enough to tell you not to take this step." Peyton edged away from the table. "Now, it's up to you to decide if you trust me enough to take my advice."

As hard it was, as much as she didn't want to, she forced herself to turn and walk away.

CHAPTER TWELVE

Peyton resisted the urge to look back as she walked directly to the valet entrance and out to the sidewalk in front of the hotel. She'd purposefully avoided the lobby, having decided that if Dale Nelson was worth anything as a detective she could find her out here. Truth was she was angry Dale had followed her and she planned to clear the air the minute she saw her.

But first she needed a minute. A minute away from Lily's intoxicating presence. A minute away from the heady way Lily's attention drew her in and made her forget her obligations.

The minute passed quickly, and suddenly Dale appeared at her side. Peyton preempted her questions with one of her own. "Where's your truck?"

Dale pointed to a spot near the front of the valet line. "I didn't know how long you'd be, so I asked them to hold me a spot."

"Badge goes a long way when it comes to favors."

Dale shrugged. "I know a guy who works here." She walked over to the valet stand, retrieved her keys, and waved Peyton over. Peyton climbed into the truck, but waited until they were several blocks away before engaging. She didn't pull any punches. "If you want to follow me around, why don't you let me know? I'll make sure to walk real slow and talk real loud so you can get all the intel you need. Or you could just ask me what I'm doing if you're so damn curious."

"I didn't take you as the kind to make assumptions," Dale said.

"I'm not."

"Then think it through, counselor. I wasn't following you. In fact, you were one of the last people I expected to see tonight."

It only took a second for her words to click, and Peyton wished she could reel back her angry words and start this conversation over again. Of course, Dale had been tailing the Gantrys, not her, but that still left an unanswered question. Which Gantry had she been after? Only one way to find out. "Do you really think Lily Gantry has anything to do with her family's business?"

"No telling."

"Are you always this cagey or is it just me?"

Dale pulled to a stop at a red light and looked over at her. "I don't know you very well."

"Well, if you want to get to know me, you're going about it the wrong way." Peyton considered her next words carefully. "I imagine it's not easy accepting anyone in this position."

Dale shook her head. The light changed and she drove through the intersection. They rode for several miles in silence, and Peyton began to wonder if Dale would ever speak to her again. After a few worthless minutes spent mentally kicking herself for making a thinly veiled reference to Dale's wife, she tried to figure out where they were headed. They'd left downtown and were headed east on I-30, the exact opposite direction from where the trailer had been abandoned days ago. Anxious for new information, she did her best to bide her time, not wanting to engage Dale in conversation until she was ready. She tried to imagine what it must have been like for Dale to work so closely with someone she'd pledged her life to, let alone lose that person in a horrific act of violence she'd been powerless to control.

Her mind flashed to Lily. Was her father really associated with the Zetas? If so, he was putting his daughter's life in grave danger. Those men held nothing sacred, and they exploited the very things everyone else held dear.

"I don't have to accept you to work with you." Dale's low-voiced comment burst into her thoughts. There was no anger, only indifference. That was okay.

She didn't need Dale to like her. All she needed was for her to do her job. Sure, it would be easier if they developed some sort of camaraderie. She had a ton of questions about her predecessor, and Dale was in the best position to answer them all, but she'd have to get her answers elsewhere. Best thing to do right now was change the subject. "Where are we headed?"

"Warehouse in Mesquite. It's down the street from the body shop where the Vargas brothers ran their operation. Care to guess who owns it?"

Peyton didn't bother answering. No sense bringing up the Gantry name and opening the door to a conversation about what she was doing at the hotel with Lily. Instead she asked, "You have a warrant?"

"Not yet. I hear there's a small crew that works at night. Figured you and I could see if anything's going on down there, maybe see if any of the workers care to talk."

"And you think it's a good idea for one cop and an unarmed lawyer to pay a visit to a crew of drug dealers?"

Dale laughed. "There's an extra gun in the glove box if you want one. And I'm not stupid. Mesquite PD has two cars parked at the place for backup. Besides, I'm talking about two guys, max, that check in supplies for one of the Gantry subsidiaries. We'll ask them if they've noticed anything going on at the shop down the way and get an opportunity to sniff around Gantry's place while we're talking to them. Maybe develop a little probable cause to take to Judge Nivens. Word is he's a friend of yours."

"You need better intel. I don't need to be friends with a judge to get a warrant if I have the law on my side." She took a moment to consider Dale's seemingly not very well thought out plan. She started to point out that poking around at a Gantry facility was likely to tip both Gantry and the Vargases off that the feds suspected a connection between them. But maybe that's what Dale was after.

It wasn't necessarily a bad idea. It might shake things up and cause one of them to do something stupid. *As long as they're the ones doing something stupid.* "If we see evidence we can use, that's great, but I'm telling you right now any investigation I'm involved in better be by the book. I refuse to get sandbagged by a defense motion to toss out evidence. If you're used to doing things a different way, turn around right now. Are we clear?"

Dale kept both hands on the wheel, but she turned and faced Peyton with a piercing glare. Several seconds passed before she over-enunciated her answer. "We couldn't be more clear."

The rest of the ride passed in silence. About twenty minutes later, they pulled into the dimly lit parking lot in front of a row of large metal warehouses. There were no signs of life in any of the warehouses save the one on the end, farthest from the highway, and a flickering light by the front entrance was the only clue work might be happening inside.

Dale stopped the truck about a hundred feet from the entrance and turned toward Peyton. "You want that gun, now's the time to get it."

"Why do I feel like I'm about to walk into a shit storm?"

Dale lifted one shoulder. "Look, you had a point earlier. I don't know you, but you don't know me either. Gellar gave strict instructions you were to be included in all task force work, even if it meant tagging along in the field. I have a gut feeling if we go in there now, talk to the grunts who're stuck on the night shift, we might see or hear something we can use later. I'm smart enough not to do this alone, but I was also smart enough not to bring Dunley with me. I could tell you were carrying when we went out last week, so I figure you know how to handle yourself. Now, are you up for this?"

Peyton listened carefully while Dale talked, appreciating her candor. All the years she'd spent studying, carefully preparing arguments, and prosecuting high paid execs who stole from both the rich and poor had been fulfilling, but the adrenaline high she was experiencing right now was a powerful, driving force. The still vivid memory of all those dead bodies in the trailer only fueled the fire. She reached into the glove compartment and drew out the gun, pulled back the slide, and then checked the clip. "I'm definitely up for this."

She walked beside Dale, taking her lead from her. Dale stopped a few feet from her truck, consulted her phone, and then led the way over to a nondescript sedan parked near the warehouse next to the one they were here to check out. As they drew closer, the driver's side window lowered and a large bearded man leaned out and looked them over.

"Slow night?" Dale asked.

"Slow enough."

Dale bent down and looked inside. As she exchanged a few words with the occupants, Peyton noted a slender blond woman seated in the passenger seat. The woman kept looking into the rearview mirror while her partner talked to Dale. Neither of them looked like cops, but she supposed that was the point. She waited until Dale finished her conversation and then followed Dale back toward the warehouse when she was done. She couldn't help but feel the entire exchange was very strange.

"You know them?"

"Not well. They were involved in the bust that brought Carmen Chavez in. We used Mesquite PD to make the traffic stop on the car carrying the drugs. Why?"

Peyton looked back at the detectives' car. "I don't know. They seem pretty disinterested."

"Not surprising. We take all the big cases away from them. The Mesquite mayor likes to make a big deal about cooperating with federal agencies, so they're stuck working with us, but the rank and file aren't always big on the idea. Those two seem okay to me."

"Where's the other car?"

"Parked around back, down the way. You want us to go size them up?" Dale's tone told her she thought it would be a waste of time.

"No." Peyton decided to trust Dale's instincts since she didn't have anything concrete to support her nagging feeling something was off. "What's the plan?"

"Nothing fancy. Let's go in and ask some questions. Follow my lead and keep your eyes open for anything out of the ordinary."

"Fair enough." Peyton followed Dale around to the back of the warehouse. One of the large loading dock doors was open and she spotted a tall, lanky man pushing a dolly loaded with boxes down the ramp of a trailer. Dale waved at him as they approached.

"Hey, you have a minute?"

The guy shot a glance up into the trailer before answering. "We're not open for business."

Dale smiled broadly. "It would suck if you were, right? I mean having to work this late and then deal with the public on top of it. That would be a gross injustice."

The guy looked confused, but before he could say another word, another man strode out of the back of the trailer. This one was tall too, but loaded with muscles that made him about twice the size of his buddy. Neither wore uniforms. They were dressed in jeans and T-shirts and they didn't look happy to have visitors. Dale waved at the second guy, but her friendly greeting was met with snarled words. "Private property."

Peyton watched Dale reach into her jacket and pull out her badge, taking care to let her holster show. She held up the badge and smiled. "We've gotten some reports about one of your neighbors and wondered if you've seen anything out of the ordinary."

The beefy guy pointed at Peyton. "This your partner?"

Dale looked over at her. Peyton may not know her well, but she knew her well enough to detect the fake smile. Dale's voice dripped false charm. "Yep. We feds like to travel in packs."

The guy ignored her attempt at humor. "We don't know any of our neighbors. We have enough of our own business to deal with." He looked over at his pal, who kept unloading the trailer as if no one else was in the room. "Right, Bob?"

"That's right."

The big guy crossed his arms over his chest. "See?"

Dale shook her head. "I get it. You've probably never crossed paths, but maybe you hear gossip? Word is the body shop down the way is a front for a chop shop. Most chop shops operate late at night, when they think no one else is around. Maybe you noticed something and didn't even realize what you were hearing or seeing?"

Peyton barely listened to the conversation. Instead she was mentally cataloging the contents of the warehouse. Wasn't hard.

She could tell by the size this was the only room and it consisted of nothing more than bare walls and a small desk in the corner that was empty except for a clipboard bulging with sheets of well worn paper. Bob's work buddy was stacking the boxes from the trailer along one wall. Based on the way he worked the dolly, the boxes appeared to be heavy, but nothing about the unmarked cardboard signaled their contents. What did an oil company need that would come in small, yet heavy cardboard boxes? Office supplies?

The words "chop shop" burst through her concentration. She caught Dale's eye, detected a slight wink, and was impressed Dale hadn't brought up the subject of drugs. If these guys, or anyone at Gantry was involved with the Vargases, better to let them think the feds were chasing their tail rather than hot on their trail. Dale kept them talking for a minute, and Peyton took advantage of the moment to edge over to the desk. She scanned the first page on the clipboard. The Gantry logo was at the top of the sheet, but everything below was a jumbled mass of dates and numbers. She slid a finger between the papers and looked at a couple more pages to find more of the same.

"All done."

Peyton looked up to see Bob, pushing the dolly back into the trailer and pulling the door shut. The big guy, on the other hand, was staring straight at her hand that was no longer touching, but still within inches of the clipboard. She attempted to deflect his attention by saying, "You guys looking for help? I have a brother who's about to be out of a job."

"Might look easy, but not everyone has the skills it takes," Bob said with a smug look. Big guy shot piercing dagger eyes his way and the smirk disappeared. "We're shutting down for the night," he said as he walked over, swept up the clipboard, and then strode back to the trailer.

Peyton looked at Dale who shrugged. They both walked outside and watched while Bob shut the warehouse door while big guy started the truck. Within seconds, they were driving down the back road toward the highway.

Dale turned to Peyton. "You see anything?"

"Plenty, but I'm not sure what to make of it. It's what I didn't see that bothered me the most."

"Tell me about it. Looked more like an abandoned storage shed than any business I've ever seen."

Peyton looked back at the building. "I'd love to get a look into one of those boxes."

"Money or drugs. Probably both. Good one about your brother looking for a job."

"Thanks." Peyton sighed at the foreshadowing. When Neil found out she planned to take over management of the ranch, he probably would be job-hunting. When had she decided to take that step? Didn't matter. Now that she'd made the decision, she just wanted to get home and talk to her mom about how they would make it work while she kept her current job. "Let's go. Do you need to let the cops know we're headed out?"

Dale looked down the way. "I don't see the second car. Let's go around front and those two can spread the word." She turned and took two steps before shots rang out. She hit the ground yelling, "Down! Down!"

It only took Peyton a second to wrap her mind around the fact they were being fired on. She pulled out her gun and fired toward the muzzle flash before grabbing Dale and shoving her around the corner of the warehouse. Dale leaned against the wall, a spray of red flowering along her shoulder. Peyton patted her down. "You hit anywhere else?"

"No. You?"

"No. We can't stay here. There's no cover."

"We can't go back through there. One of the jackasses firing at us has an automatic and it's coming from the roof, over there." Dale pointed at a building behind the warehouse. "Our best bet is to keep going this way and try and make it to my truck."

Peyton looked at Dale's pale face. She was losing blood fast. "Can you make it?"

"Do I have a choice?"

"Seems like our backup should be showing up about now." Peyton glanced around, but there was no sign of help.

"I think we're on our own." Dale winced as she reached into her jacket and pulled out an extra clip. She handed it to Peyton. "Here, you might need this."

Peyton shoved the clip in her pocket. Then she picked up a rock and held it over her shoulder. "Get ready. One, two, three." She hurled the rock toward the back of the warehouse, waiting until it hit pavement to shoulder into Dale and half carry her on a mad dash toward the front of the building. The rapid sound of automatic gunfire exploded in their wake.

Seconds later, Peyton shoved Dale into the passenger side of the truck and grabbed her keys. She spun out of the parking lot and sped toward the highway. As she pulled onto the entrance ramp, she pulled out her phone.

"What are you doing?" Dale asked, her voice thin and reedy.

"Calling in a shooting."

"You drive. I'll do it."

"Who're you going to call, 911? Mesquite PD? We were just set up. You know that right?"

"So who are you calling?"

"Don't worry about it." Peyton looked over at Dale. She was trying to look tough and ready despite her obvious pain. As fast as she was driving, they'd be at Baylor Hospital in just a few minutes, but in the meantime, she wanted to make sure they'd be safe when they got there. "We're going to need a bigger task force."

CHAPTER THIRTEEN

L ily waited later than usual to come down to breakfast. She didn't want to risk her father asking about the trust again, and she definitely didn't want her mother to know why she had declined to sign the papers. On top of that, she was still stewing about her encounter with Peyton last night. She'd seen her meet up with another woman at the valet stand, get into her truck, and ride away. What kind of work was she up to at that time of night? Was the other woman a colleague? Peyton sure was seeing a lot of women under the guise of business. And what was with the ominous warning to stay away from her father's business?

When Lily pushed through the double doors of the dining room, her mother looked up from the lifestyle section of the paper. Damn, her timing had been off. She started to say she was just going to grab a cup of coffee, but her mother insisted she join her. As Lily sat down, her mother scooted a bowl her way. "Joelle found this beautiful grapefruit at the farmer's market yesterday. She'd be sad if you didn't have some."

Lily obliged and filled a small dish with some of the ruby red fruit. She may have been able to say no to her mother, but Joelle, the long-standing family cook, never took no for an answer. Her mouth was full of citrus when her mother opened the conversation.

"There's a tea today at Martha Johnson's. We have a lot of planning to do for the holiday event. You'll accompany me, of course."

Lily swallowed the fruit and mustered a bright smile while her mind whirred through acceptable excuses for bowing out. She settled on vague. "I'd love to, but I have some things to take care of today."

"Work things?" Her mother didn't try to hide her distaste for the word. Her father must have mentioned the plans she'd shared with him.

"Yes. Does that bother you? Me working?"

"Don't be silly. I suppose what bothers me is that there's already plenty of work for you to do. A great deal of the Gantry money is spent on charitable causes, but you don't appear to be at all interested in that aspect of the family business. You'd rather be trudging around in a field somewhere with a bunch of windmills or trying to harness the sun than dressing up and helping me coax donations from Dallas's other wealthy families. One pursuit is not more worthy than the others."

"And I didn't mean to imply that it was."

"Then I don't understand. Your cousins are happy to accept their share of the family fortune and use their time to help those less fortunate. Darla will be at the tea today. When's the last time you two saw each other?"

Her cousins Darla and Lance probably thought keeping a fleet of servants employed was their contribution to helping the poor. The threat of Darla's presence at the tea sealed the deal. "It's been a while. I'm sure I'll run into her over the holidays."

Her mother opened her mouth to protest, but miraculously Lily's cell phone rang. A quick look at the screen told her it was Skye. "Sorry, Mom, I need to take this." She stood and gave her mother an airy kiss on the cheek before ducking out of the kitchen and answering the call. "Skye, do you have any news?"

"A little. One of the nuns who assisted with adoptions at Our Lady of Guadalupe around the time of your birth has agreed to talk to me. I would normally suggest that I go alone and see if she has any helpful information, but there are some special circumstances, and I think it might help if you join me."

Lily's heart pounded at the prospect of a solid lead. She hadn't expected to find out anything so soon, but now that she had a glimmer of hope, she didn't want to wait any longer to learn what she could. "Can we go now?"

"Actually, yes. I already made an appointment on the chance you were available. She's in Waxahachie. Let's meet near downtown and ride together."

"Okay. Are you still working on that job at the Adolphus?" Lily asked, telling herself the location was more about convenience than proximity to Peyton's office.

"Not today. The area around the courthouse is a security nightmare today after the shooting last night."

Lily gasped. "There was a shooting at the courthouse?"

"Not at the courthouse, somewhere in Mesquite. It was all over the papers this morning. A federal prosecutor was involved and the whole federal building is on high alert, which makes it hard to park anywhere near that block. I figured..."

Skye was still talking, but Lily was no longer listening, her ability to concentrate obliterated by the words "a federal prosecutor was involved." It could have been anyone. There were probably dozens of federal prosecutors in Dallas. But she only knew one, and the idea of Peyton being shot was unbearable. But Skye hadn't said anyone was actually injured. Her fear was probably unwarranted, irrational even. She took a deep breath and asked for confirmation that there were injuries.

"Yes, but the papers didn't give any names. I only know a prosecutor was involved because Morgan mentioned it. She had a hearing at the courthouse this morning that was canceled because of this. Word is the U.S. attorney's office is huddled up, preparing a response."

Lily pictured her mother at the dining room table, reading the paper. She wanted to hang up, run in, snatch the paper out of her hands, and scour it for every last detail on the shooting. Talk about irrational. She had her own chaos to deal with. She didn't need to borrow someone else's, someone who wasn't interested in her.

But Peyton was interested. If she wasn't, she wouldn't have joined her at the bar last night. She wouldn't have counted their dates. She wouldn't have been so adamant about warning her from doing business with her father, a warning that had left Lily unable to sleep the night before. *Damn you, Peyton. How did I let you get so close when you obviously don't want to be?*

She knew how to get answers, and she wasn't going to rest until she had them. "Skye, I need about forty-five minutes to get ready. In the meantime, I need a favor. Is there any way you could find out the name of the person who was shot last night?"

"Probably. Mind if I ask why you want to know?"

She didn't want to get into it on the phone and prayed Skye wouldn't push her to. "I'll tell you when I see you."

They settled on a time to meet at Morgan's office and Lily hung up, excited about meeting someone who might know something about her birth family, but anxious about whether Peyton was okay. Hopefully, Skye could find out something before their meeting. If she didn't, Lily was going to march down to the federal building and ask for some answers. Come hell or high water, by the time this day was over she'd know if Peyton was okay and what the hell the mysterious warnings Peyton had delivered the night before meant.

Peyton set the file on the nightstand and stood up, careful not to wake Dale. If the hospital bed was as uncomfortable as this chair, she expected Dale would want a discharge the minute she came to.

"You can quit tiptoeing around." Dale's voice was low and scratchy.

"Sorry. I was trying to be quiet."

"I'm not great with quiet. Makes me edgy."

"Noted. Next time I'll bring a drum set."

Dale struggled to sit up. "I'm good with there not being a next time, if it's just the same to you."

Peyton grinned. "I guess getting shot didn't make you any less of a grouch."

"Oh, you think just because we were in a shootout together, you can make jokes?"

"It was really more of a getting shot at than a shootout. We were mostly running away, if I recall."

"That's what smart people do when they're outgunned and outnumbered." Dale paused and looked at the ceiling. "If they get the chance."

She closed her eyes, and Peyton looked away, not wanting to intrude on the private moment of reflection. Maria Escobar had had no such chance. Witnesses said she'd taken a couple of steps out the front door of the house she shared with Dale when two cars rolled up and the occupants opened fire, riddling Maria's body with bullets. Dale was out of town or she might have met the same fate. There were probably days she wished she had.

"She was braver than me." Dale's voice shook as she spoke. "She got threats on a daily basis, but she wouldn't let it change how she operated. Said any deviation on her part from her normal routine was a win for the other side. It was the only thing she was ever wrong about."

"She died a hero."

"Doesn't change the fact she died." Dale fell silent, and for the next few minutes, Peyton stood in place, waiting until Dale was ready to say more.

"What are you doing here anyway?" Dale asked. "Shouldn't you be getting a warrant for that warehouse so we can hunt down whoever did this?"

Peyton didn't think Dale wanted to hear that she'd stuck around to make sure she didn't wake up alone, so she shifted to her second reason. "If you're up for it, I wanted to bring in a few folks so we can come up with a new game plan."

Dale looked around. "Here?"

"Yes, here. Doctor says you can't leave until tomorrow at the earliest and we don't have time to wait. You up for it?"

"Sure."

Peyton walked to the door and whispered instructions to the guard outside. She closed the door and said, "They'll be here in about thirty minutes."

She hoped they'd have enough room. She'd called Gellar the night before and insisted on a meeting, threatening to quit if her demands weren't met. He'd come down to the hospital since she refused to leave, and she'd outlined what she needed. He'd grumbled about the money, the resources. Said he didn't understand what was taking so long to bring down the Zetas and implicate Gantry. Peyton was prepared with a letter of resignation, handwritten on the back of a blank hospital insurance form. She waved it in his face and told him if he didn't double the size of the task force and let her and Dale handpick the members, she would get the next flight back to D.C.

He'd succumbed, and she was almost sorry he had. If she'd been forced to quit, she wasn't entirely certain she would've gone back to Washington, especially since she had a place here in Texas, at the ranch. But running the ranch wouldn't bring whoever was responsible for last night's events to justice, and she needed justice. She'd have to do this job and deal with the ranch too and find a way to make it work.

Within the hour, Dale's hospital room looked more like a war room than a place of healing. Peyton counted heads. Everyone on the current task force was there, and Bianca Cruz had brought the big white board she'd asked for. She looked over at Dale and waited for her to nod that she was ready before speaking. "You're probably all wondering why I've asked you here."

Their expressions were curious, but no one said a word. "Last night, Agent Nelson and I were cornered in a gunfight, and there was overwhelming force on the other side. We're lucky to be alive. It's time to meet overwhelming force with some overwhelming force of our own, so we're adding some folks to this team. We're going to meet daily to review strategy, and we'll work as a team."

She looked around the room and saw heads nodding and murmurs of "that's right." She held up a marker to the whiteboard. "Let's have some names. Who should we get to help us?"

❖

"I don't have any information yet," Skye said, "but I have someone working on it."

"Okay." Lily felt the tension that had been building in her shoulders all morning jump up a few notches. They'd just pulled onto the highway, headed toward Waxahachie, and instead of being able to concentrate on the meeting ahead, she was worried about Peyton.

"Is there something you want to tell me?"

Oh yeah, she'd promised to give Skye a reason for her request. She cast about for something reasonable, but finally decided the truth was easier than a hastily thought up falsehood. "You remember the woman who stopped by our table the other day?"

"Yes."

"She's an assistant U.S. attorney. When you said a federal prosecutor was involved, my mind went right to her. I'm worried."

"What was her name again?"

"Peyton Davis."

"You should call her."

"I was hoping you would have answers so I wouldn't have to resort to that."

"Uh huh."

"Look, we dated. It was only a couple of times, and I thought she was interested, but it appears that she's not. There's nothing more to it. I just want to make sure she's okay."

"So, call her now. What's the worst thing that can happen?"

Lily knew Skye was right. She pulled out her phone and dialed Peyton's number. The call went directly to voice mail, and she clicked off without leaving a message. "Either she's in the hospital or she just doesn't want to talk to me."

"If she's ducking your call, it's her loss."

"Thanks. You're sweet. I guess it wasn't meant to be."

"You know this after two dates? Wow."

Lily couldn't miss Skye's teasing tone. "What's that supposed to mean?"

"I think you know exactly what it means. When my wife and I met, I was in a very dark place. If she hadn't been so persistent, we would have never gotten together. She saved my life in more ways than one."

Skye's voice got very quiet, and Lily reached over and squeezed her shoulder. "Your wife is a very lucky woman." She sighed. "Maybe you're right. Maybe I gave up too easily."

"Don't be so hard on yourself. After all these years, you're not giving up on learning about your family."

"True." Relieved to switch topics, Lily asked, "What can you tell me about the woman we're going to see?"

"Her name is Sister Agatha. She was assigned to Our Lady of Guadalupe, and she helped handle your adoption. She moved to another church shortly after."

"How did you find her?"

"I come from a long line of Catholics, and one of my uncles is a priest. He helped me track her down. But I don't want you to get your hopes up about this meeting."

"Why not?"

"Sister Agatha is in a home for Alzheimer's patients. According to my uncle, she has good days and bad, but mostly bad. There's no way of knowing which until we get there."

Lily tried not to be disappointed that the first lead Skye had developed might be a black hole. She spent the rest of the drive thinking positive thoughts. She needed some good news.

Finally, they arrived at the nursing home. The plain brown brick complex looked dated, and the inside wasn't much better. Clean, but basic with very few amenities in sight. Certainly not how she would want to spend her twilight years, but she supposed if your mind was gone, what difference did your surroundings make?

Skye checked in with the receptionist and picked up their visitor badges. An aide led them to the great room where Sister Agatha was waiting. Intent on the playing cards in front of her, she didn't look up as they walked into the room. Lily stepped closer and saw that she was playing solitaire. "I don't remember the last time I saw someone playing this game with an actual deck of cards."

Sister Agatha looked up and smiled. "They don't let me have unfettered access to a computer. Guess they're scared I'm going to do something crazy like post what they're feeding us on Facebook."

Lily returned the sister's smile. The nun's face was wrought with wrinkles, and a milky film covered her eyes, but her positive thinking must have paid off because Sister Agatha seemed perfectly lucid. "May I sit down?"

She waved an arm. "Free country."

Lily introduced Skye and they both sat across from the nun. Dressed in charcoal gray sweats and pale pink tennis shoes, she didn't look much like a nun, but Lily didn't care about how she appeared now. All she cared about was what she remembered from the past. She looked at Skye and waited for her to announce the reason for their visit.

"Sister Agatha, we understand that you worked in the adoption program run by Our Lady of Guadalupe about thirty years ago."

Sister Agatha plucked an ace of spades from one of the piles of cards in front of her, set it off to the side, and then gazed up at the ceiling for several seconds before answering. "Indeed I did. I remember that. Lots of little babies needing good homes. Some cuter than others, but all deserving."

Lily said, "I know you probably worked with a bunch of children, but there's one in particular we were hoping you'd remember." She pulled out a copy of her birth certificate and set it on the table. "I was adopted as part of the program, and I'm trying to find out more about my birth family. Maybe this will refresh your memory."

Sister Agatha lifted the paper and held it close to her face, squinting as she skimmed the words. "Sophia Valencia. Sophia Valencia. Sophia Valencia."

Lily was startled to hear her birth mother's name spoken out loud. Maybe she hadn't been clear. She didn't expect anyone involved with the adoption to know her mother. As far as she knew, her mother had died in the hospital and she'd been placed in the care of the church until the Gantrys adopted her. She started to say as much to Sister Agatha, but before she could speak, she saw the sister's eyes slide shut and she started to hum.

Lily looked at Skye and mouthed "help," desperate to stop what appeared to be the decline of the sister's mental state. Skye leaned forward and gently said, "It would have been a long time ago. It's okay if you don't remember. Maybe you could keep the birth certificate and see if it comes back to you later."

Lily watched Sister's Agatha's face for any sign that she'd heard Skye's words, but her only response was continued humming as she began to rock back and forth in her chair. She shook her head in defeat and whispered to Skye, "We should go."

"We'll come back. We'll pick a different time of day, and I bet that will make a difference."

"Okay." Lily couldn't match Skye's optimism, but they really had no choice since it was clear Sister Agatha had checked out of the conversation. She stood and started to walk away when she felt a piercing grip on her wrist.

"Miss V.V. we called her. So sweet she was. Young." Her voice dropped to a whisper. "And scared. So scared." Sister Agatha delivered the words in a singsong voice. "She kept one V and changed the rest. I've got to hide. From all of them." She started humming again. "Sing songs to my little one. I'll never know her, but he will keep her safe. He's her daddy."

Lily looked down at the aged and wrinkled fingers still clutching her wrist and worked to sort through Sister Agatha's jumbled words. Who had to hide? Sister Agatha? Her mother? If it was her mother, her need to hide had disappeared when she died. What was she so scared of before that? Would knowing give Lily insight into her birth mother's family?

Sister Agatha released the grip on her wrist and dropped her hands onto the table. She stopped humming and started stacking cards again, apparently resuming her game. Lily took a chance on one last question. "Sister Agatha, how did you know my mother?"

Sister Agatha placed the king of hearts in a blank spot, drew a set of cards, and placed them back on the deck before meeting Lily's gaze. "Is it time for my lunch? Please make sure there's no mustard. I do not like mustard. Thank you and good-bye." She drew another set of cards and resumed focus on her game.

A few minutes later, Lily and Skye were back in the car. "I'm sorry," Skye said. "They told me that this is usually a good time of day for her."

Lily stared straight ahead, frustrated at the abrupt end to their visit, but desperate to process what she'd heard. "There's something there. I just can't put my finger on it."

"It's possible that she's confusing your adoption with someone else's. It was a long time ago."

Lily knew Skye's words made sense, but her gut told her Sister Agatha remembered her adoption very well, so well it had burned through her disintegrating memory to emerge in bits and pieces. It was up to her to put those bits and pieces together, but she needed Skye's help. "Skye, I need you to get a copy of Sophia Valencia's death certificate."

Before Skye could respond, her cell phone rang. She glanced at the display. "I should get this. It's that source about the shooting."

She answered the call, and Lily watched while she listened to the voice on the other end, offering a few yeses and uh-huhs in response. By the time she hung up, Lily was coming out of her skin. "What is it?"

"I still don't know much," Skye said with a frown.

"But you know something. Skye, tell me."

"Names. I only have the names of who was at the scene, but I don't know who was shot. A DEA agent, Dale Nelson, and your friend, Peyton Davis."

Lily felt the icy prick of fear travel down her spine. For a moment, it paralyzed her. But only for a moment. She picked up her phone and dialed, once again reaching Peyton's voice mail. She hung up and redialed again. Same thing. While she was dialing the third time, she mustered all the calm she could find and said, "Skye, I'm going to need you to drop me off at the federal building."

CHAPTER FOURTEEN

Peyton tapped her watch. "I need to get back for the afternoon docket." After she and the rest of the task force left the hospital, Gellar had insisted she join him for lunch for what he said would be a strategy session. Instead, she'd listened to his war stories with increasing impatience for the last hour and a half. What she'd rather be doing was working on the case. Short of that, she needed a nap.

Gellar paid the check and they walked back to the office. They were alone in the elevator when he took the opportunity to emphasize, again, how much he wanted Gantry to go down. "Cyrus Gantry acts like he owns this town, and I want him stopped. Do you understand?"

Funny how he was in a take-charge mood now despite the fact she'd had to beg him for the resources to see this case through. "Yes, sir." She injected what she hoped was the right amount of deference into her tone, but no matter what he ordered, she would only go where the evidence led. If something illegal was happening at that warehouse, everyone involved would go to prison, but in order to tie Cyrus Gantry to the crime, she'd have to have some pretty solid evidence.

The elevator stopped on the third floor, and when the doors opened, Bianca was waiting in the hall, looking anxious. Peyton, standing just behind Gellar, shook her head. Whatever Bianca had to say, she wanted to hear it first, not here in front of her boss. She hoped Bianca could read her signal.

"What is it, Cruz?" asked Gellar. "You have something to report?"

Bianca looked at Peyton and cleared her throat. "Uh, not yet, sir, but we have some leads. I'll make sure you get a briefing by the end of the day."

"See that you do." He turned to Peyton and shook his finger. "Remember what I said. I'm counting on you." He didn't wait for a reply before he strode down the hall.

Peyton waited until he was gone before turning to Bianca. "What is it?"

"Lily Gantry. Ida called me up to the front desk. She's here and she has a lot of questions. All I told her was that you weren't here, but she refuses to leave. Insists she has to talk to you. Now."

Peyton held up a hand to stop her while she endeavored to wade through the rushed words. "Wait a minute. Lily's here? Right now?"

"Yes. I wanted to get to you first, so you could go in the back. We can get someone from the marshals service to escort her out."

Peyton had stopped listening, but she was on the move. She didn't know if she was propelled by the thrill of seeing Lily or anxiety that she'd shown up here where some would view her as the enemy, but she didn't take the time to sort through the complexities. A few seconds later, she stepped in the lobby and spotted Lily pacing the carpet. She started to speak, but Lily beat her to it.

"Oh, my God, you're okay," Lily cried. "I was worried sick."

"Why?" Peyton asked, genuinely confused.

"The shooting. I heard you were involved. I've been calling and calling, but you never picked up, and I understand you don't want to talk to me, but I had to know you were okay. I even called the office, but no one would tell me anything."

Peyton pulled her phone out of her pocket. Damn. She'd turned it off when she was at the hospital and forgotten to turn it back on when she left. She switched it on and saw a long list of missed calls from Lily's number. She held up the phone. "It was off. I'm sorry."

Lily shook her head. "No, I'm sorry for acting like a fool. Nothing about this day has turned out the way I planned, and when I couldn't get hold of you, I had to make sure. Is Agent Nelson okay?" She stepped closer. "Are you?"

Lily's voice was silky soft, and Peyton wanted to pull her close, hold her tight, and tell her everything was okay. But then she remembered they weren't alone. She glanced back at Bianca who stood in the doorway, transfixed. Ida, the receptionist, had closed the glass partition, but not completely, and Peyton was certain she'd heard every word. The only way she could head off dangerous gossip was to immediately usher Lily out, and explain her appearance to the others as unexpected and unwarranted.

But she wanted to talk to Lily. How dangerous could it be to have just a couple of minutes alone? Would a few minutes really jeopardize her case? She was finding it hard to imagine Lily involved in her father's illegal dealings.

If you believed that, you wouldn't have warned her to stay far away from Gantry Oil.

So far, Peyton had sent mixed signals whenever it came to Lily. She'd broken off communications without explanation and then, when circumstances put them together again, she offered Lily vague warnings to steer clear of her family business. Yet, Lily had shown up here to make sure she was okay. She could have texted, or e-mailed, but she'd shown up in person, worried and anxious. Peyton owed her more than she'd given so far, no matter who was watching and listening.

She stepped over to Ida's window and tapped on the glass. "Ida, Ms. Gantry needs a visitor's badge." While Lily signed in, Peyton walked over to Bianca, who was still waiting near the doors and, in a low voice, said, "I'll explain later. I promise." She didn't wait for an answer before she led Lily back to her office. Once there, she shut the door and invited Lily to sit.

"I don't feel like sitting. I'm too keyed up."

"What's going on?"

"Well, this woman I'm fiercely attracted to blew me off, then showed up last night and bought me a drink. We had charming conversation and everything seemed to be going well until she got a call to go into work. As she was leaving, she gave me an ominous warning about my family.

"This morning I woke up to the news that the woman I had drinks with may have been shot, and the investigator I hired to find my birth mother's family has a lead. I paid the investigator to find out if the woman's okay and then I rode out to Waxahachie to meet with a senile nun who told me a bunch of stuff about my mother that doesn't make any sense. I only have a couple of weeks to find out what I can or risk losing my trust unless my attorney can work her magic, and what I thought was a simple task may be way more complicated than I thought."

Peyton grabbed Lily's hand and drew her over to the sofa and motioned for her to sit. As she sat beside her, she was careful to make sure she was close, but not too close. "I only caught some of that. How about we take it a piece at a time?"

Lily let out a breath. "I'm sorry. I didn't come here to dump on you, but what you said last night about my father has weighed heavy on my mind. You can't drop a bomb like that and walk away. I need to know what you meant."

"You're right. I was wrong and I'm sorry. I shouldn't have said anything at all, not unless I could tell you everything."

"So, you're not going to tell me now?"

Peyton started to waver, and she cast about for another topic, anything to delay her decision. "First tell me about this senile nun and your mother. And you hired an investigator to make sure I was okay?"

Lily punched her in the arm. "Don't act smug. I already had an investigator, but I did ask her to find out if you were the federal prosecutor involved in the shooting. When I heard there was a shooting it reminded me of one that happened last year. A prosecutor was gunned down in front of her own house."

"I know. That's a large part of the reason I have this job."

"You can't be serious." Lily reached for her hand and held it tightly. "Peyton, really? What happened?"

Peyton looked down at their clasped hands. Lily's concern was genuine, but her touch extended beyond comfort. It was like fire. She should draw back before she crossed a line. Instead, she changed the subject. "Tell me about the nun."

"I don't know what to tell you. Something's come up recently that spurred me to find out about my birth family. I hired Skye Keaton, the woman you met at lunch, to see what she could find out. The nun she located, Sister Agatha, helped with my adoption.

"I've always believed that my mother died during childbirth. That the church took me in afterward, but some of the things she said today...I don't know. I was supposed to get answers, but I wound up leaving with more questions."

"Maybe your mother knew she was going to die and contacted the church to make arrangements for you."

"Her death was sudden, unexpected. She didn't have a chance to make any arrangements."

"And this nun says something different?" Peyton kept her tone soft as she asked, "Who told you the original story?"

"It's not a story. You make it sound like I was lied to."

"Lied is a strong word, but maybe there was a reason for glossing over what really happened."

"What are you trying to say? That my mother had already made arrangements to abandon me, she just didn't live long enough to carry out her wishes? That my parents have lied to me my whole life about how I came into this world?"

This was the perfect opportunity to bring up her investigation into Lily's father and Gantry Oil, but Lily's desperate plea for reassurance dissuaded Peyton from tackling the subject. Instead, she searched for safer ground. "I'm not saying any of that. I was only thinking that sometimes it's hard to know what people's motives are until you have all the facts."

"Spoken like a true lawyer. Is that how you approach your job? By getting all the facts first?"

Now Peyton was the desperate one, seeking a way to steer the conversation away from anything that had to do with her job. She fished her memory and recalled Lily mentioning a trust, an attorney, and something spurring her to search for her birth family. She latched on to the latter. "What was the something that caused you to go looking for your birth mother?"

Lily looked into her eyes, her gaze long and deep, before she answered. "I love my parents, but knowing I might have other relatives out there, that I know so little about my birth mother...well, I suppose it's been building up for some time now. Sometimes I think my father is stringing me along with his promise of implementing my alternative energy plan just to keep me from digging into the past. I'm not a child, and I'm tired of being treated like one."

Her voice shook, and Peyton could tell she was holding something back, but she didn't want to push. Not now. Not when all she wanted was to act like neither of them had a care in the world, that they were on their third date, still getting to know each other, still under the spell of an undeniable attraction.

These moments might not constitute a third date, but the electricity between them was more powerful than ever. She wanted to run her hands through Lily's dark tresses, taste her lips, lose her way in the heady scent of her spicy perfume. The wall she'd erected between them was crumbling, and she was helpless to hold it in place.

As if she could sense her vulnerability, Lily leaned closer. "Peyton?"

"Yes?" The sound of her voice sounded distant, hazy.

"Kiss me. Please."

She did, and at the first touch of their lips, everything she'd guarded against fell away. Gentle at first, she kissed her way closer, driven by the burn of desire that flooded her entire body. Lily arched against her, and when their tongues met, she groaned with pleasure, losing her mind in the sweet taste of this woman who'd captivated her from the moment they met.

She had no idea how long they'd been kissing before she heard a sharp knock at the door. Lily smiled as she pulled away. "Better get that before someone walks in," she said.

Peyton kissed her on the cheek. "I suppose. Don't move. I'll be right back." She stood and smoothed out the wrinkles in her suit, looking back at Lily and savoring the memory of her touch. She cracked the door and was greeted by Ida's inquisitive eyes. "Hi, Ida."

"I rang your desk, but you didn't answer."

Peyton willed herself not to blush. "Sorry. What do you need?"

"Your mother needs to talk to you. Said it's an emergency. Do you want me to put her through?"

Peyton's thoughts flashed to her father. She glanced back at Lily whose eye's reflected concern. Lily mouthed "Do you want me to go?" and Peyton shook her head and then turned back to Ida. "Yes, put her through."

A minute later, with Lily at her side, she picked up the handset. "Mom?"

"Peyton, I know you're busy, but we've got trouble." Her mother's voice was calm, but laced with urgency. "Neil's got a drilling crew here ready to break ground, and Jim's not taking it well. I suggest you get here as fast as you can."

Peyton knew her normally stoic mother wouldn't ask her to come if it weren't important. Her mind raced as she processed the few words she'd spoken. Neil had apparently chosen to answer her ultimatum with a brazen act. She only hoped her father's reaction wasn't threatening his precarious health. "I'll be right there."

Lily was still watching her as she hung up the phone. "Are you okay?" she asked.

"I guess today's the day for family conflict." She offered a strained smile.

"I'm sorry. Is there anything I can do?"

Peyton looked at the closed door, and then crossed the room and took Lily in her arms. "I have to go."

"I know."

"Kissing you. It was—"

Lily placed a finger across her lips. "I imagine you're going to say it was amazing, but the tone of your voice sounds like a good-bye. You can say good-bye for now, but if you pull that stunt where you promise to call me later, but then you don't, you'll be missing many more amazing bouts of kissing. And you don't want to do that. Are we clear?"

Lily smiled, and Peyton couldn't help but smile back. "We're clear."

"Now go. Deal with whatever you need to. Take as long as you need. I'll be waiting and, if you need my help, just let me know. Okay?"

Peyton nodded. Seconds later, they walked out of the building together and parted ways, but she knew for sure this time it wasn't for good.

CHAPTER FIFTEEN

Peyton skidded her truck to a halt on the gravel drive and slammed it into park. Her mother was waiting on the front porch and Peyton took long strides toward her. "Where is he?"

"They're setting up below the back pasture. Zach left a little while ago to talk to Neil, but I haven't heard back from him. Signal's no good down there."

Peyton nodded and started to walk back to her truck, but her mother stopped her. "Andy has Ranger saddled and ready to ride. You'll get there faster if you cut through."

Peyton paused to consider. Even though the area she was headed to was relatively close to the house and accessible by car, to reach it, she'd have to go back out to the main road and take the long way around. "Good thinking." She jerked her chin toward the house. "What about Dad?"

"He's settled down. Neil asked him to sign some papers. I don't even know what. Your father got agitated and Neil took off." She clasped her hand on Peyton's arm. "He's out of hand."

"I know. I'll handle it. Call Roscoe. Ask if he's up for a house call this weekend. I think it's time for a family meeting." She didn't wait for a reply before heading toward the stables where Andy led Ranger out to meet her.

He handed her the reins, saying only, "He's been waiting for you."

Ranger pranced in place like he knew something was up, and after Peyton mounted and gave the signal, he took off like a shot. They breezed past the breeding stables, the grazing pastures, and the hayfields. The view from astride Ranger showcased the timeless wonder of the ranch, and Peyton's commitment to maintain its glory grew with every gallop.

Just as she'd settled into the ride, they burst into a clearing full of large trucks and workmen. Peyton slowed Ranger to a walk and led him to a man who was holding a tablet and barking out instructions to the other men. She stayed in the saddle as she asked, "You mind telling me what you're doing here?"

Before he could answer, Zach emerged from behind one of the trucks and walked in her direction. "Hey, Peyton."

She nodded. "Hey, Zach. You already talk to these gentlemen about how they need to leave?"

He motioned for her to join him over to the side and she dismounted and walked toward him. "What's up?"

"I'm not sure. I talked to Neil yesterday, and he didn't mention anything about this, but today after lunch, he blurts out that he's got to meet some workers down here and then he holed up with Dad for a while and got him all riled."

"I think he's still riled. You know what that was about?"

"Not entirely, but I think it has something to do with this." Zach waved an arm toward the three huge trucks on site. "I just spoke with the foreman, and he's got papers giving him permission to start setting up a well."

"We'll see about that. Where's Neil?"

"That's the thing. He's not here. Foreman said he let them in and then took off."

Peyton shook her head. "Okay, well, I need you to introduce me to this foreman." She led Ranger and followed Zach over to the man with the tablet she'd seen when she entered the clearing. He smiled broadly and stuck out his hand.

"Ralph Winters, nice to meet you."

Peyton shook his hand. "Peyton Davis. I wish I could say it's nice to meet you too, but truth is I'm here to throw you out."

Ralph's smile didn't falter. "Sorry, ma'am, but we have authority to be here." He reached into his jacket and pulled out a thin stack of papers. "Mr. Neil Davis signed this agreement, and we're in the process of setting up a rig. Now, we're about to be making a lot of noise and I'd rather not spook your horse."

Peyton took the papers and gave them a cursory glance. Sure enough, Neil had granted access to these contractors with Ray Explorations, but there was another signature on the document that took her by surprise. James Davis. She couldn't tell if it was really her father's signature or not—it'd been too long since she'd seen his handwriting. If it wasn't really his, then Neil had forged his name, and if that were the case, he was a lot further gone than she'd imagined.

She folded the papers and put them in her pocket. "We have a problem. I have reason to believe this agreement isn't valid, and until it's settled, I'm going to have to ask you to clear out."

Ralph's smile disappeared and his eyes took on a hard edge. "I'm afraid that's not possible."

Peyton glanced at Zach and he came over to stand behind her. "I apologize if I made it sound like I was giving you a choice." She reached into her back pocket and Ralph and his men stiffened. She pulled out her wallet and reached for her badge. She didn't want to use the trappings of her job for personal matters, but she wanted them gone and she wanted them gone now.

"Neil Davis doesn't have authority to grant you access. I'll be back with a court order to that effect, but in the meantime, I don't think you want to run afoul of law enforcement. They might come looking to make sure this property looks exactly how you found it." She held up her badge and waited for Ralph to back down.

Didn't take long. He waved his men back to their trucks. "Fine, but we'll be back. You can count on it."

Peyton waited with Zach while Ralph and his men cleared out and then she handed the papers to him. "You know anything about this?"

Zach leafed through the pages, stopping on the signature page. "That looks like Dad's handwriting, but I can't swear to it."

"Dad wouldn't sign this. Not on his own."

Zach shook his head. "Maybe Neil made a good case."

"Maybe Neil made such a good case, Dad didn't have a clue what he was signing." She looked at Zach, but he still appeared puzzled, as if he couldn't understand why she would think things weren't as they appeared to be. They weren't going to get to the bottom of this standing in a field. Time for that family meeting.

❖

"Why did you volunteer us for this again?"

Lily looked up from the table she'd just arranged and smiled at Courtney who'd just hung the final set of signs by the door to the convention center. They'd spent the last few hours with the rest of their Junior League chapter, helping decorate the venue for their annual holiday bazaar. "I'm trying to keep my mind off a few things, and you're being a good friend by helping me out."

"And you thought manual labor was the solution?"

"Oh, please. Don't act like you're such a princess," Lily said. "We both know better."

Courtney put her hands on her hips. "I'm not a princess, but if you'd asked me, I could've listed a million other things we could do to keep your mind off whatever's bothering you."

"Like shopping?"

"Maybe. Don't knock the restorative powers of a day at Neiman's."

"All a day of high-end shopping would do for me is to drain my already dangerously low savings."

"Something you're not telling me?" Courtney asked. "Do I need to sell my oil company shares?"

"The family business is fine."

"Whew. Now, if you would only dip into your trust, you wouldn't have to worry so much. I know you're feeling conflicted about it, but your grandfather wanted you to have that money."

Lily knew she meant well, but Courtney had never understood her reluctance to embrace the trappings of her family's wealth.

"I'm not giving up my trust, but I'm also not touching it. I have enough of my own hard-earned savings to keep me afloat for a while."

"Then why are you so hell-bent on keeping the trust if you're not going to use it?"

While they'd been setting up, she'd shared some of the details of the waiver her father and Nester had asked her to sign and her reasons for holding off. "Just because I don't want to use it now doesn't mean I won't want to pass it along someday."

Courtney punched her in the arm. "I get it. Future Gantry-Davis babies. You and Peyton will be the best looking parents at the PTA."

"Don't be silly."

"Tell me you haven't thought about a future with her."

"Oh, I've thought about it all right, but we're a long way from making babies. I don't even know if she wants children."

"Then you better start asking. Do you two have plans tonight?"

"No. There's something going on at the ranch and she needed to be there." Peyton had called on Saturday just to check in, but their conversation hadn't included any mention of whatever was going on. Lily was very curious, but she kept waiting for Peyton to bring up the subject. "Did Zach mention anything to you?"

"Nothing specific. He did cancel our date yesterday, but I'm supposed to see him later today. He said he'd call when he broke free." Courtney's eyes sparkled with mischief. "I have an idea. Why don't we both go out to the ranch and surprise them?"

"No." Lily had a feeling Peyton wasn't big on surprises. "I don't think that's a good idea."

"Sure it is. He's been promising me a tour of the place, which I hope is code for finding a secluded area to make out."

"What are you, sixteen? Besides, I got the impression things were a little heated out there. Probably not the best time for guests."

"Surely whatever was going on has blown over by now. Guests are good diversions. We'll pick up one of those chocolate seduction cakes from Breadwinners. Who's going to turn away guests bearing dessert?"

Courtney had a point. What was the worst thing that could happen? Peyton could turn her away, but after yesterday's kiss, that didn't seem likely. She spent the next few seconds reliving the feel of Peyton's lips on hers, strong and sure, tender and soft. She savored the memory of being wrapped in Peyton's warm embrace, and all she could think about was seeing her again. Soon.

She held up her hands in mock surrender. "It's a date."

Peyton promised Bianca she'd be back at the office on Tuesday, and then she hung up the phone. Bianca had assured her the task force had been working around the clock since Friday in an attempt to find concrete evidence to tie the Vargas brothers to Cyrus Gantry. She itched to be back at the office, but instead she'd spent the weekend with her mother, reviewing all of the business records for Circle Six and developing a plan of action to wrest control from Neil. Bianca's update made her feel even more guilty about staying here at the ranch, but family came first, and Bianca had assured her they had things under control.

What wasn't under control was the operation of the ranch. Understandably, her mother had let Neil take a bigger role in ranch operations when her father fell ill, but he'd run up the debt in a way that was unsustainable. Likely, he thought this oil deal would be the quick and easy solution to the problem he'd created.

In the midst of her musings, Peyton heard a car approaching and looked at her watch. Roscoe had said he'd be there at four, but it was only two o'clock. She strode to the window, held back the curtain, and looked outside, surprised to see Lily's car parked in the drive. As Lily stepped out of the driver's side, Peyton felt a swirl of emotions. She touched her lips and resurrected the burning passion of that first embrace. All she'd wanted to do since Friday was go to her, kiss her again, and forget everything having to do with the ranch, her feud with Neil, and the investigation into Lily's father. But, out of a sense of duty, she'd resisted. She had to get her own life in order before she could find room for Lily to be a part of it. More importantly, she'd have to tell Lily about her father, even if it meant risking fallout on the job.

But right now, all she wanted was to hold Lily in her arms and pretend everything around them was settled and sure. She dropped the curtain, walked to the front door, and swung it wide to find Lily standing on the front porch with Courtney Pearson beside her.

Lily could tell from Peyton's expression the impromptu visit was a bad idea. She tried to catch Courtney's eyes to signal they should leave, but after a quick hello, good to see you, Courtney plowed her way into the Davis house and Lily had no choice but to follow.

"Is Zach here?" Courtney asked.

"He's out back," Peyton said. "I can walk you out there."

Courtney smiled brightly. "I can find my way. Besides, I think Lily would like some time alone with you."

Lily watched, mortified, as Courtney flounced out of the room. She closed her eyes for a second, hoping she might melt into the floor, before facing Peyton. "I'm sorry about that. She can be a bit…"

"Forward?"

"That's a nice way of putting it."

Peyton stepped closer and her voice was barely a whisper. "Forward can be nice."

"I suppose. If you like that sort of thing."

"I'm glad you're here."

"You didn't look glad when you opened the door."

"I'm sorry. It's been a trying weekend and we have an appointment in just a bit. When I heard the car pull up, I thought you were the family attorney."

"An attorney needs an attorney? Sounds serious." A shadow crossed Peyton's face, and Lily regretted her teasing tone. "Now it's my turn to be sorry. We shouldn't have just dropped by. I promise you I was raised better than that. I'll go get Courtney and we'll get out of your hair." She took a step, but Peyton touched her on the arm.

"Wait."

She looked back and tried to read the expression in Peyton's eyes. Longing mixed with regret. Did she really want her to stay or was she just being polite?

As if she could read her mind, Peyton said, "I'm glad you're here. Seeing you…well, seeing you makes me happy." She pointed to the cake box Lily was still holding. "Besides, I'm very curious about what's in that box."

Lily could tell Peyton was torn about something, but she was equally certain Peyton really was glad to see her, and she resolved to enjoy the moment. She thrust the box at Peyton. "It's called chocolate seduction. We brought it for the whole family, but having just said the name out loud, I feel a little foolish."

Peyton grinned. "Maybe I'll hide this in my room and pretend you brought it just for me."

"Only if we can eat it together." Lily covered her mouth. "Sorry, again. I seem to have a knack for putting my foot in my mouth around you."

"I like that you're so unguarded. I spend a lot of time around people who filter their every word. Now, how about joining me for a piece of cake before I have to get back to business?"

Lily hesitated, but Courtney was nowhere to be seen and she couldn't exactly leave without her. Besides, she didn't want to leave. "Okay, but we better eat it in the dining room. I won't be responsible if we wind up alone, fueled by chocolate. Lead the way."

A few minutes later, they were seated around a large kitchen table, digging into the cake. Peyton hadn't mentioned the rest of her family, and Lily hadn't seen signs that anyone else was home. "How's your dad?"

"He's had a bit of a setback. His doctor was here earlier and gave him a sedative. He's upstairs, resting. "

"That's too bad." Lily wondered if the setback had to do with whatever was happening at the ranch. "Everyone else out?"

"Mom's keeping an eye on Dad, and I imagine Zach is showing off for Courtney out back. Neil hasn't been home all weekend."

Peyton's eyes stormed with anger when she mentioned Neil's name, and Lily was certain he was the source of trouble. She placed her hand gently on Peyton's arm. "Is there anything I can do?"

Peyton's shoulders relaxed. "You mean besides delivering the best cake I've ever had?" Her smile slipped into a grimace. "No, this is something I have to deal with on my own. Besides..."

Lily watched as Peyton's gaze grew cloudy again. "Besides, what?"

Peyton shook her head. "Nothing." She looked at her watch. "Can you stay for a bit? Maybe walk off this cake with me?"

"There's nothing I'd rather do."

"Great. I'll just leave a note in case Mom needs me or Courtney gets tired of Zach."

Peyton scrawled a note and left it on the kitchen table, and then took her hand and led her out of the house.

"Where are we going?"

"Well, I already showed you one of my favorite places on the ranch. Would you like to see another?" Peyton cast a pointed look at her shoes. "It's a short hike."

Lily laughed. "Just because I like pretty shoes doesn't mean I hate my feet. I promise these are comfortable. Lead the way."

Peyton never once let go of her hand as they walked along the old bridle trail, past the stables and the hayfields. Lily enjoyed the connection. It was simple, yet incredibly intimate. After about twenty minutes, they emerged from dense wood into a small clearing and Lily gasped. "What a beautiful house."

"You think so? She needs a lot of work."

Lily's eyes swept the two-story Craftsman home. It had once been painted the same sage green as the big house they'd just left, but nature and time had left it looking weathered and gray. The railing sagged, and Lily could see several rotted boards in the floor of the porch. The stone chimney was crumbling, and twigs poking from the top meant a family of birds had probably taken up residence. In spite of its lack of polish, Lily could see the potential. She turned to Peyton. "I love it."

Peyton tugged her hand. "Come on."

Lily followed Peyton into the house and found the real surprise. As crumbling and weathered as the outside looked, the inside was clean and well kept.

"My great-grandmother had this built for her daughter, my grandmother, and she lived here with her family, including my mother, for years. When my great-grandmother died, my grandmother moved into the big house. No one's lived in this house since, but Fernanda takes care of the inside. Unfortunately, no one has kept up with the outside of the house."

"Someone should restore it. It would be a shame to let all of this go to waste." Lily stood with Peyton in the living room and admired the hand-scraped wood floors and high-pitched ceiling.

"There was a time I thought I might live here. Raise a family in this house."

Peyton's voice had dropped low, and Lily stepped closer and looked into her eyes. She saw mostly wistfulness, but it was laced with a trace of hope. She wanted to spark that hope. "Is there any reason you can't?"

Peyton started to shake her head, but stopped and met Lily's gaze. "There are so many things pulling at me lately that I suppose I've shoved thoughts like that down deep." She took both of Lily's hands in her own and held them to her chest. "But right now, in this moment, I feel like I could do anything."

The spell of Peyton's confidence was strong, and Lily was completely entranced. She leaned in close so their lips were almost touching and whispered, "What would you do first?"

Peyton answered with a kiss, a slow, burning, glorious kiss that spread heat through Lily's body like wildfire through a drought-ravaged forest. She slipped her hands free and pulled Peyton closer. She ran her hands down Peyton's strong back and murmured against her lips, "You feel wonderful."

Peyton leaned back and smiled. "Yes, I do. How could I feel anything else? You, Ms. Gantry, are an amazing kisser."

Lily raised her fingers and brushed them against Peyton's lips. "So strong, yet so soft." She toyed with the buttons on Peyton's shirt. "Makes me wonder about the rest of you." She slipped loose one of the buttons and then looked up to meet Peyton's eyes, drawing permission to keep going from her gentle gaze. Another button and then another. She slipped her hand inside and cupped Peyton's firm breast, pulling her into another kiss as Peyton arched against her stroking fingers.

"Talk about amazing," Peyton gasped. "Makes me wish this place was furnished. I'm not sure how long I can stay on my feet."

Lily looked around, but other than the hard floor, there weren't any possibilities to get Peyton on her back. "I guess we'll just have to see how long you can hold out." She reached for Peyton again, but Peyton beat her to it, catching her lips with her own and running her hand up her sweater and along the edge of her bra. It was Lily's turn to succumb to arousal, and she pressed into Peyton's skillful touch, craving more.

"Peyton? Are you in there?"

Peyton gave her a quick kiss, pushed her sweater back into place, and stepped toward the sound of the voice. "Yes, Mom. I'll be right there."

She grinned at Lily and Lily couldn't help but grin back, feeling like a teenager caught in the act. Peyton started to walk toward the front door, but Lily pulled her back and fastened the buttons on her shirt. One more quick kiss and then they both walked out to greet her mother who was seated on a four-wheeler in front of the house.

"Hello, Lily," Helen said. "It's good to see you again."

"Good to see you too, Mrs. Davis."

"Please, call me Helen." Her eyes swept the both of them, and her lips turned into a slight grin. "Sorry to bother you two, but, Peyton, Roscoe called and he just passed the front gate."

"Okay, I'll be right there."

"Great, see you at the house."

Helen rode away with a wave and Peyton waited until she was out of sight before speaking. "Sorry about that?"

"The interruption or what came before?" Lily asked in a teasing tone.

"I'm not sorry about anything that came before." Peyton's expression turned serious. "I want to spend a lot more time with you. Uninterrupted time, but there is something I need to tell you. It's important."

Lily stared into Peyton's eyes. She carried so much weight, so many worries. She wanted to take all that away, be the one thing that wasn't a source of stress. "Not now. Go do whatever you have to do and we'll talk later. Just promise it will be soon."

"Tomorrow night. We'll have a real date. Away from any family, away from work. Just us."

"On one condition."

"What's that?"

"Will there be more kissing?"

"Like this?" Peyton bent down and captured her lips with her own. Lily groaned as the heat of her touch spread through her belly and between her legs. She ran her tongue along Peyton's lips and savored the taste of her. She could hardly wait until tomorrow for more.

❖

Within moments after Lily and Courtney left, Roscoe pulled up in his older model Cadillac Seville. Peyton, who'd stayed on the porch after bidding Lily good-bye, ushered Roscoe into the house, showed him to the kitchen and the chocolate cake, and then went looking for Zach and her mother. When she returned with her family in tow, she took a moment to observe the old family friend. His face was wrinkled and his eyes were baggy and he looked a good deal older than the last time she'd seen him, which had been a number of years ago. Roscoe had handled the family's legal business for as long as she could remember, and he'd stood as her sponsor when she took the state bar oath. Until now, everything he'd done for them had been about keeping their family close. What they were asking him to do today threatened to tear it apart.

"Peyton. It's been a long time. It's good to see you, but I'm sorry about the circumstances."

"It's good to see you too. Can't be helped I guess, but we appreciate you making time for us on a Sunday." Peyton nodded to her mother to start the conversation.

"Roscoe, as I explained on the phone, things with Neil have gotten out of hand. He signed a contract with one of Cyrus Gantry's companies to explore drilling at the ranch without getting permission from anyone else in the family. We gave him a week to get out of it, but he flat out refused. On Friday, he showed up with a team ready to break ground, but Peyton ran them off. On top of all that, it looks like he either forged Jim's signature or he pressed Jim to sign the drilling agreement.

"Peyton has Jim's power of attorney and she's ready to use it. What do we need to do next?"

Peyton admired her mother's get to the point approach. No attorney would ever make a ton of money billing hours on work for her because she wouldn't stand for waiting around for them to figure out what they planned to do. Roscoe was used to her style, and Peyton couldn't wait to hear what he had planned.

"Well, I drew up that power of attorney, so I know it's solid. It doesn't require a declaration that Jim's not able to fulfill his duties at the ranch for Peyton to exercise control, but it wouldn't hurt to have such a declaration if Neil decides to challenge it, especially if he's pressuring Jim into signing documents that he might not understand."

"I've always included Jim like a partner, but the ranch is in my name," her mother said. "Does it even matter that we have the power of attorney?"

Roscoe rested his chin in his hand and appeared to ponder the question. "It's a little more complicated than that. There's the ranch land itself and then there's the family business. Jim's a legal partner in the business and, the way we have it set up, the business leases the land from the ranch. Problem is Neil's a part owner of the business too."

"But he's not enough of an owner to make decisions on his own," Peyton said. "Not important ones anyway."

"Not on his own, but with his father's shares and Zach's, they can outvote you both, and the lease gives extensive rights as to the use of the land," Roscoe said. "Zach, you haven't said much. Where do you stand in all of this?"

All eyes turned to Zach and he squirmed a bit under the scrutiny. "I haven't thought much about it. I mean Neil's always been fair to me. I know he's spent quite a bit of time with Dad, and I do think that was Dad's signature on the papers those oil men had on Friday."

"Do you really think Dad would have given permission for drilling without getting Mom's okay?" Peyton asked. She and Zach had spoken several times about the issue since Friday, and she'd grown increasingly frustrated that his perception of Neil seemed so skewed.

"I guess not."

He looked like he'd rather be talking about anything else. Peyton understood. He'd always hated conflict, but it was time to step up and she said so.

"I guess if it comes to a vote," he said, "you can count on me."

Peyton nodded and turned back to Roscoe. "Okay, what's the next step? I told Neil if he didn't get us out of the contract, we'll get a court order."

"We can do that, but it'll be difficult to walk it back once we file a petition with the court. Are you all prepared for a permanent rift with Neil?"

How did anyone really prepare for such a thing? Peyton pondered the question while her mind traced back through the events since she'd returned home. Nothing about her relationship with Neil had changed since she'd left for D.C. She hated the idea of losing any chance of a renewed connection with him, but his choices were what had gotten them to this point. *You don't pick your family.*

The thought brought Lily to mind. Her family *had* picked her and now she was stuck with a father that might be indicted and sent to prison. If she was prepared to saddle Lily with that kind of fate, she better be able to accept that her own family had its bad apples and she would have to deal with the fallout.

She knew what she had to do about Neil and she also knew she couldn't wait any longer to be honest with Lily about her father. She would talk to Lily tomorrow.

"File whatever you need to, Roscoe. We'll be ready for whatever comes next."

CHAPTER SIXTEEN

Lily's nostrils flared at the scent of pancakes, but she struggled to stay in the dream. She was standing on the edge of a cliff, and Peyton, astride Ranger, was riding toward her. She waved her arms in warning, willing her to stop before they got too close to the edge, but Peyton only smiled and rode faster. Just as she thought they would plunge to their deaths, Ranger came to a stop at her side and Peyton bent down and pulled her up into the saddle. She nestled back against Peyton, enjoying the strong warmth of her embrace. And then the pancake assault happened.

She sat up in bed, stretching to meet the new day, and resolved she would have to find her own place soon. Someplace where people didn't make pancakes every day that they expected her to eat as if she were still a kid with a crazy good metabolism. She'd put off calling the realtor that Courtney had recommended, but only because she wanted to have her future a little more set up before she made a commitment to a monthly mortgage. And she wasn't sure where she wanted to live. In town or closer to the Circle Six? Was it silly to think about finding a place closer to Peyton? She slipped into the memory of their last kiss and decided no, it wasn't silly at all. Both of them had things they needed to sort through, but it was obvious they were very attracted to each other, and any distractions were only bumps in the road—nothing that would keep them apart.

Resolving to eat only grapefruit for breakfast, Lily climbed out of bed and headed to the shower. Before she could get undressed, her cell phone rang and the display showed the number for Morgan's law firm. She pressed the button to accept the call and barely got out a hello before the voice on the other end started talking.

"Lily, it's Erica Osten. I've completed my research and I'm confident they can't prevent you from accessing your trust fund if you don't sign the waiver."

She stared at the phone, willing her brain to engage. Erica. The attorney she'd hired to look into whether she would really lose access to her trust fund if she didn't sign the waiver that stated she wouldn't go looking for her mother's family. The news kicked up a storm in her head, and she tried to stymie the effect by slowing Erica down. "Good morning, Erica."

"Sorry," she said. "I didn't mean to launch right in. I just thought you'd be glad to hear the news. You don't sound glad."

"What you're hearing is the sound of someone who's not quite awake yet. You might want to start with a gentler lead in when you're calling to deliver big news."

"Good idea." Then without so much as a breath, she asked, "So, how do you want to handle this? I can send a letter to Mr. Rawlins this morning letting him know you have consulted with me and I have advised you not to sign the waiver. If they are going to fight you on it, my letter will be the opening bell."

The call to action made her head hurt. "How about we slow things down a little. Remember the I just woke up part? I need a little time to think things over." She was awake enough to deal with decision-making, but she wanted to talk to Skye and see if she'd made any more progress in her investigation before she made any decisions that would stir things up with her family. "I'll give you a call later today and let you know what I've decided."

She hung up the phone and considered her next move. No way did she want Erica to send a letter to her father's attorney before she had a chance to give her father a heads up. Best-case scenario, she would tell him why the trust waiver Nester wanted her to sign wouldn't hold up in court and therefore there was no reason for her to sign. She picked up her phone and dialed her father's office. He wasn't in, but she spoke with his secretary and scheduled some time on his calendar for later in the morning. That settled, she dialed Skye's number, but had to leave a message.

Frustrated at her attempts to reach anyone, she closed her eyes for a moment and attempted to reconnect with her dream.

❖

The next morning, Peyton paced the kitchen until her mother barked at her to sit down. She sat reluctantly and said, "Roscoe's going to call any minute, and I wanted to give Neil one last chance to back down."

"He's not going to back down. You haven't been around to see it, but his stubborn streak has gone up tenfold since you've been away. If you're trying to give him one last chance for Zach's sake, don't you worry. He'll be fine. Now, eat your breakfast and relax."

Peyton picked at her bacon and eggs, but she had no intention of relaxing until things were settled with Circle Six. Neil hadn't been home since Friday, and she'd even ridden out to the old bunkhouse at the rear of the property to see if he'd decided to stay out there. No one had a clue where he was, and for some reason that had her on edge.

At her mother's urging, she ate some of Fernanda's cooking and then resumed pacing, but this time on the back porch. She'd called the office to check in with Bianca, but had been told she was in court. She considered calling Dale, but doubted she'd have much to report. Bianca had assured her she'd keep Dale in the loop, but she was probably at home recovering.

Peyton wished she'd spent more time over the past few weeks getting to know the other agents better, but they'd all been scattered in the field, gathering clues. The only report she'd received over the weekend was that an extensive search of the warehouse had yielded only cartons of innocuous supplies and volumes of records that might or might not be in code. At her instruction, forensic analysts were rushing to make sense of the records. It might be days before they had any actionable information, but she'd have to tell Lily about her father tonight or run the risk of her finding out on her own. The fact the warehouse had been designated a crime scene made it only a matter of time before Lily knew Peyton had been keeping the investigation into her father from her.

The ringing phone jerked Peyton from her thoughts. She watched while her mother answered, said a few short words, and then hung up.

"Well?" Peyton asked.

"Roscoe has an affidavit ready for you. He plans to file the request for a court order as soon as you sign it."

Peyton was already out of her chair and across the room. "I'll call you when I know more. Send Andy and a couple of the other guys down to the site to keep an eye on things. If Neil or any of Gantry's guys show up, let me know."

Minutes later, she was in her truck and headed for downtown. She used the thirty-minute drive to sort through the facts of the case against Cyrus Gantry and the Vargas brothers. They had enough from Carmen Chavez and the others they'd arrested to prosecute the Vargases as part of a drug conspiracy, but to take down their entire operation they needed to cut off their supply lines and funding. If Cyrus Gantry was the Vargases' secret weapon, bringing him to justice was their only method of shutting the Vargases down for good.

She shuddered to think how Lily would feel when she found out her father was working with drug dealers. Would Lily turn to her for comfort or lash out in anger? Whatever the outcome, she had no choice but to do what was right.

Roscoe's office was a restored Victorian house in Uptown, and Peyton pulled her truck into the small parking lot and walked across the wide porch. The door swung open as she approached, and she found herself enveloped in a hug.

"Peyton Davis! You're a sight for sore eyes."

Peyton returned the hug and stepped back to appraise her old friend, Charlene Farley. Roscoe's daughter had graduated from law school with her and gone directly into the family business. They hadn't seen each other in years, but Charlene looked exactly the same—petite, pretty, and blond, three factors that often caused opponents to underestimate her tenacity and skill. "It's great to see you. You look good."

Charlene held the door open and waved Peyton inside. "Dad said you were coming by, so I've been watching out the window. I'm glad to see you, but sorry about the circumstances."

"Me too. I hate going this route, but I don't think we have any other choice."

"Sometimes that's just the way it is. I'm sure Neil means well, but he's gotten a bit shortsighted. He got pretty upset when I told him there wasn't any legal way to avoid tax consequences on the advance. Stormed out, saying he didn't know why you all bothered to keep us on retainer."

Peyton's ears buzzed. "Advance? I think I'm missing something."

"On the contract with the exploration company." Charlene paused as if waiting for Peyton to catch on. "He wouldn't show me the contract, but apparently there was a hundred grand advance. He said he'd heard something about making cash deposits under ten grand at a time in order to avoid taxes. I told him that was probably the easiest way to trigger an audit. Banks watch for that kind of thing. It's called—"

"Structuring," Peyton said. "Hold up a minute. I've seen the contract with Ray Explorations. Neil didn't get an advance. It's a simple flat fee, not even a big one, for use of the land to conduct testing. We only earn royalties when the well comes in."

"That's the first I've heard about this," Roscoe said as he entered the room.

Charlene shrugged. "He came by last week. Maybe he was talking new terms with the company and the advance wasn't finalized yet. I'm sorry I didn't mention it, but I had no idea the original contract didn't contain an advance. I assumed you already knew about it."

"Not your fault," Peyton said, her mind whirring. What was Neil up to? If he'd collected a hundred grand from Gantry's people, the family sure hadn't seen any of it. And why would the payment be in cash, and what the hell was he thinking, assuming he could structure the deposits to avoid detection by the IRS?

Or maybe he had some other reason for his questions to Charlene. Cash deposits of ten thousand dollars or more required the depositor to fill out IRS forms, but the real reason for the rule wasn't to thwart tax evasion. It was to prevent money laundering. Financial paper trails were the most efficient method of tracking criminals trying to funnel their dirty money through legitimate sources. Money laundering—the very crime they suspected Cyrus Gantry was engaged in. And now Neil was involved with Gantry. Could Neil be part of the conspiracy?

Peyton couldn't wrap her mind around the possibility. Not now. She needed a lot more information before she would accuse her brother of anything other than reckless management of the family business. She looked at Roscoe and Charlene who were waiting for her to call the shots. First things first. Protect the family legacy. "I'm ready to sign that affidavit."

Lily took a seat in the reception area of Gantry Oil and waited for her father to finish his conference call. She'd arrived early for the appointment, having spent the morning dreading the discussion she was about to have and wanting to get it over with as soon as possible.

"You can go back now," the receptionist said.

She walked through the frosted glass doors of the office suite and strode through the halls, taking in the massive grandeur of the empire her family had built. Certificates showcasing the company's accomplishments graced the walls sandwiched between expensive works of art by some of the country's leading Western artists. When she reached the large corner office, she knocked twice on the door and then pushed it open.

Her father was sitting alone behind his massive desk, and his face broke into a huge smile when she entered. She couldn't help but smile in return. So many people over the years had told her that they shared the same smile. Nurture over nature, she supposed.

He looked at his watch. "It's a little early for lunch, but I can always eat. You want to join me at the club?"

She shook her head. "I'm not hungry, Dad. I need to talk to you." She sat down. She'd had all morning to plan what she would say, but now that she was here, she was at a complete loss as to how to start.

"How's business?" Lame, but since he was always eager to talk about the company, it would prime the pump.

"Couldn't be better. And I haven't forgotten about my promise. Nester is working on the paperwork to secure investors for your project. Should be ready any day now."

Lily's stomach clenched as Peyton's warning about going into business with her father echoed in her head. She couldn't think about that now. Her own business ventures were the last thing on her mind. She plunged ahead. "Dad, I had an attorney look at the trust waiver that Nester asked me to sign. She says if I don't sign it, the trust will still hold up. Something about estoppel and other legalese, but the point is, I'm not going to sign it." Her words skidded to a stop and she took a breath while she gauged his reaction to the first part of what she had to say. If it went well, she planned to tell him she'd hired an investigator.

She scanned his face, but she couldn't get an accurate read. His eyes narrowed and his cheeks were red, but she didn't sense anger. After a few seconds of silence, she finally asked, "Are you going to say something?"

He reached in his back pocket for a handkerchief and mopped his brow. She watched the action, and it triggered dozens of memories. The times she'd played rough like a tomboy and gone to him to fix her cuts. The times she'd cried with disappointment when childhood bullies mocked her for looking different than the rest of the neighborhood kids. Each time she'd gone to him, he'd pull an expensive silk handkerchief monogrammed with his initials from his pocket, and he'd wipe her tears and clean her wounds. "Say something, please."

He carefully folded the handkerchief and placed it back in his pocket. "I don't know what to say. I don't know who this lawyer is that you went to see, but obviously you don't trust Nester, and if you don't trust Nester, you don't trust me. Have I ever given you a reason not to trust me?"

"I guess a part of me hoped you'd be relieved that my not signing wouldn't affect the terms of the trust. I love you and Mom, but like I tried to explain before—"

The phone on his desk rang and they both looked at it. "I'm sorry," he said. "I need to get this."

Lily watched while he answered the call, relieved at the interruption, but after his initial hello, the hanky came back out and he was wiping his brow in earnest. Worried at the increasing redness on his face and the sweat pouring from his brow, she honed in on his half of the conversation.

"What do you mean, they're here right now? I'm meeting with my daughter. Tell them to go away…That's ridiculous…Call Nester and tell him to get a team of his best over here right now. I'll be right there." He slammed the phone down and stood up.

"Dad, what's wrong?"

"Nothing, sweetie. Tell you what. Let me buy you lunch and we'll talk more. Take the back way and meet me at the club. I'll be there in a few minutes. I have a little something I need to take care of first." While he spoke, he pulled several stacks of paperwork from his desk drawer and hurriedly shoved them into a large envelope and sealed it. He pushed the envelope into her hand. "Take this with you and I'll get it back at lunch. I need to run it by one of the sites later." He leaned down, kissed her on the cheek, and was out the door before she could protest.

She rocked back in her chair and contemplated his abrupt departure, already deciding she was going to wait right there and find out what was going on. She glanced at the envelope. She didn't believe his story, but she didn't want to violate his trust by peeking inside.

Waiting got old after a couple of minutes, and she got up, ready to wander up front and figure out what was going on when her cell phone rang. The display showed it was Skye. "Hi, I've been hoping to hear from you."

"Sorry," Skye said. "It's taken me a while to confirm some facts. Do you have time to meet this afternoon?"

"I'm dying to know what you found out. Can you just tell me now?"

"Uh, well, I have some paperwork I'd like to show you. It'd be better if we met."

Lily glanced at the door. She didn't want to be on the phone with Skye when her father returned. "Quit with the cloak and dagger. Out with it."

"I didn't find a death certificate for your mother."

"Well, keep looking. If it's a matter of money—"

Skye cut her off. "It's not. It's a matter of there isn't one. There's no death certificate for a Sophia Valencia or anyone named Sophia or Valencia on the date of your birth or even in the days surrounding. In any county in Texas."

Lily sat back down as she struggled to digest Skye's pronouncement. "I don't understand."

"I'm not sure I do either, but I did find some records I think you need to see."

Lily started to reply, but the sound of heavy footfalls and shouting in the hall outside distracted her. She went to the door and pressed her ear against it, but she couldn't make out what was going on. "Hang on," she said into the phone as she cracked the door.

Within seconds, she was surrounded by armed men and women in black jackets. Letters swam before her eyes. ATF, DEA, ICE. One of them barked at her, "Hang up the phone and sit down. Keep this door open and don't touch anything. Do you understand?"

Lily could hear Skye on the other end of the line. "Lily, what's going on? Is everything okay?"

She nodded at the officers to let them know she understood and murmured into the phone. "I have to go."

As she sank into the chair and placed her phone on the table in front of her all she could think of was Peyton. Whatever was going on, Peyton was the only person she knew who could get them out of it.

Chapter Seventeen

Peyton saw the camera crews in the lobby of the federal building and wondered which of the other prosecutors in the office was starting a big trial today. Several dozen AUSAs worked under Gellar's direction, but she'd been so busy with the task force work she'd only met a handful.

She stepped around the crowd and rode the elevator up to the third floor. After entering the back door to the suite of offices, she headed to Bianca's office but found it empty. She stopped at the task force war room on the way to her own office and found it empty as well. Her desk was exactly as she'd left it, lined with stacks of files she still needed to review. Dale and Bianca had brought her all the files from the last few years that had any connection to the Zetas.

She sank into her desk chair and pulled the closest stack of files toward her. Roscoe had said he would go to the courthouse this morning and request an immediate hearing on the request for an injunction. She wanted to stay close by in case he needed her for any reason, and with the office so quiet, it was the perfect time for her to catch up on these files. A couple of the agents had reviewed them before, but in light of recent events, she wanted to see for herself if there were any clues.

Most of the cases involved street crimes, drugs, guns, and human trafficking, the Vargases usual fare. File after file documented these deeds, but up until the recent incident connecting the trailer full of dead bodies to Gantry Oil, they couldn't figure out how the Vargases laundered their enormous wealth. The potential to crack that part of the case had Gellar salivating, and Peyton really couldn't blame him.

Money laundering. Peyton mentally played back the conversation she'd had with Charlene. Were Neil's questions about avoiding tax consequences born of naiveté or something nefarious? No matter what, if he'd gotten an advance from Cyrus Gantry, she and the rest of the family had a right to know about it. She mentally added this topic to the long list of things she planned to address with him when he showed his face again.

A knock on the door interrupted her thoughts. She looked up to see Dale, her arm in a sling, standing in the doorway. She motioned for her to enter. "I didn't expect to see you for a while. Come in."

Dale took a seat in one of the chairs across from her desk. "I'm bored sitting at home. Besides, I don't need two arms to go through files." She nodded at the stack on Peyton's desk. "I see you've been doing your share of crap duty."

"That's right, but I haven't found anything enlightening yet. I figured I might as well wade through the rest of these while it's quiet."

"Where is everyone? I wanted to talk to Bianca about that search warrant affidavit I e-mailed earlier."

"I haven't seen anyone yet this morning." Peyton paused as Dale's statement sunk in. "Wait, what affidavit?"

"She asked me to go ahead and prepare an affidavit for a search warrant for Gantry's offices. Apparently, the FBI's forensic accountant, Samantha Reed, believes that the documents seized from the warehouse are a duplicate set of Gantry Oil records. They're coded somehow, and the theory is that the code is Cyrus Gantry's way of tracking the funds he's funneled for the Vargases. Bianca said they were going to use an affidavit from Agent Reed, along with an affidavit from me about the shooting, to support the warrant. I sent my affidavit to her late last night, but I figured she might want to go through it with me in person before y'all take it to Nivens."

Peyton felt a chill along her spine. She'd spoken with Bianca yesterday afternoon and she hadn't mentioned word one about a search warrant for Gantry Oil's corporate office. While it was inevitable that they would need Gantry Oil business records to make their case, she wanted to make absolutely sure any search warrant was ironclad before taking action. The shooting at the warehouse had given them clear probable cause they needed for that search, but a search of the head office would be met with strong resistance from the team of lawyers Cyrus kept employed. The fact that Bianca had left her out of the conversation entirely was disturbing.

And where was Bianca anyway? She glanced at the daily docket sheet on her desk and didn't see any court settings for the morning. She picked up her phone and dialed Ida's number. "Ida, I'm looking for Bianca. Did she check in with you this morning?"

"She left before I came in, but they left a copy of the warrant here. I made a copy for Mr. Gellar and I'm supposed to wait until they get back with the return before filing it. Did you need to see it?"

Peyton's insides froze. "Yes. I'm coming up there now." She motioned to Dale. "Come on."

"What's going on?"

"Nothing, I hope, but I have a feeling our missing task force is serving a search warrant on Cyrus Gantry's offices as we speak."

"Holy shit."

When they reached the front office, Peyton reached across Ida's desk and practically grabbed the papers from her hand. She skimmed the pages, chasing to the end. Judge Nivens had signed the search warrant early this morning, and it authorized the seizure of business records and computer servers. Bianca would have had to rush to get a team in place to execute the warrant today, and it would have had to be a big team, with enough agents to guard all the employees to make sure nothing was compromised or destroyed while they conducted the search.

She looked up from the document. "Ida, you said Mr. Gellar has a copy of this?"

"Yes, he wanted to review it before the press conference."

The camera crews downstairs. Suddenly it was clear. Gellar planned to make the afternoon news cycle with his raid on Gantry Oil. Holy shit was right. In a few hours, if not sooner, Lily would know the U.S. attorney had just devastated the family business. Once news of the raid hit the Internet and airwaves, Gantry's clients would scatter to the wind.

She forced herself to take several deep breaths. Maybe the raid hadn't happened yet. Maybe she could get in touch with Bianca and have her hold up until she could talk to Lily and...

And what? She couldn't say anything to Lily that might be perceived as interfering with her office's investigation. But she had to do something. She looked at Dale as she processed the possibilities, but before she could come up with a solution, her cell phone rang and she saw Lily's name on display. She jabbed the accept call button and feigned calm. "Lily, it's so good to hear your voice. We need to talk."

Lily was anything but calm. "Peyton, something terrible has happened. I need your help. I'm at my father's office. Police are everywhere. They just busted in and are totally taking over the place. They said I can't leave. They said I couldn't make any calls either, but I had to reach you. I need you."

Peyton's stomach sank. She didn't have time to come up with the perfect plan, but she knew what she needed to do. "Hang up and wait for me there. I'm on my way. Don't talk to anyone until I get there." Peyton clicked off the call and turned to face Dale who she was certain had heard every word of Lily's frantic pleas for help. "I guess you want to know what that was about."

"I figure you'll tell me when you're ready."

Relieved at Dale's matter-of-fact reaction, she folded the copy of the warrant, stuck it in her pocket, and started for the door. "Come with me and I'll explain on the way."

"We going to Gantry's office?"

"Damn right we are."

"You have a plan?" Dale asked.

"We have about three blocks to come up with one."

LAY DOWN THE LAW

❖

"This will be much easier if you just tell us everything you know about your father's connection to Arturo and Sergio Vargas."

Lily looked at the agent who'd asked the question and projected what she hoped was steely resolve instead of the gut-churning agony she felt.

Since the halls of her father's office had filled with men and women in black jackets, she'd been trying to figure out what the hell was going on. A man in a jacket labeled FBI stayed in the office with her, but he hadn't said a word. Within a few minutes, she'd heard voices barking commands and the sounds of things being moved around. The man went to the door and opened it, and she'd seen other officers carting boxes and computers, bound with tape labeled "evidence" down the hallway. While the man talked to someone outside the door, she took advantage of the opportunity to call Peyton. She felt better when Peyton said she was on her way, but as the moments passed, she couldn't stand not knowing what was going on.

A short while later, a woman walked in wearing an identical jacket to her guard. She nodded at the man and both of them took seats across from her. The man introduced himself as Agent Jeffries and the woman as Agent Cohen, and then he launched into the first question. When she didn't answer, the woman took a softer tact.

"Ms. Gantry, would you like me to get you a glass of water? You look awfully pale."

Lily decided to take advantage of their desire to make her comfortable. "I'd like to speak to my father."

"I'm afraid that's not possible," said Agent Jeffries.

"Oh, I'm sure it's possible. He's here isn't he?"

Agent Cohen started to answer, but Jeffries beat her to it. "He's here for now, but he'll be headed to prison soon. You don't want to join him there do you?"

"I have no idea what you're talking about." Lily bit her bottom lip to keep from saying more. Peyton had warned her not to talk, but it was impossible not to respond to these ridiculous allegations.

The only way she could keep her cool was to get out of here as quickly as possible. Was that even possible? Only one way to find out. "You can't keep me here."

Jeffries stood and stepped toward her, waving a leather-bound folder before her eyes. "You recognize this don't you?"

It only took a glance for Lily to see it was the prospectus she'd given to her father and Nester the day they'd asked her to sign the trust waiver. She had no idea why this agent had the prospectus, but she sensed trouble. She schooled her expression to hide any reaction and waited for the agent to speak.

Jeffries started flipping through the pages. "Looks like you're in business with your father. Guess that means whatever he's up to, you're right there with him." He pointed at the door. "So, sure, you're free to leave right now, but if you do, we might not be interested in hearing your side of things when we come to arrest you."

Peyton's calm voice echoed in her head, telling her not to talk to anyone. She should wait for Peyton to arrive and guide her through this mess. Peyton worked with these people all the time. She would know how to handle them. Lily fought the instinct to react, but it went against her nature to leave their assumptions unchecked. She stood up and spoke slowly, over enunciating each word. "Neither my father nor I have anything to hide. I'm leaving now and when I find my father, he'll be leaving too. Now, get out of my way."

Hoping they couldn't detect that she was shaking inside, Lily walked to the door and swung it open to find her father and Nester Rawlins standing on the other side. No longer caring what these agents thought, she hugged her father and asked if he was okay.

"Of course. This is all just a big misunderstanding." The shaky tone of his voice told her he was as nervous as she was. She looked at Nester for reassurance. Nester motioned for them to stop talking and then he turned to the agents. "I'm leaving with my clients. If you want to ask more questions, you'll do it the right way—through me."

Nester ushered them down the hall, but when they reached the lobby, Lily stopped them. "Wait. I need to stay."

"I've left a few of my associates here," Nester said. "They'll make sure that nothing is taken that wasn't included in the search warrant, but I want you two out of here now."

"But I..." Lily wasn't sure what to say. She wanted to leave, but she needed to stay. Peyton would worry if she was gone when she showed up. She had to at least call her and let her know she was leaving.

"Lily, we really need to go." He punched the button for the elevator as if the subject were closed.

"A friend is coming to meet me. She's with the U.S. attorney's office, and I called her when these people showed up. She said she would help and she's on her way."

Her father punched the elevator button again and Nester asked, "Who's your friend? Maybe we can contact her and see if she can convince her colleagues to call off their witch hunt."

"Peyton Davis." Just saying Peyton's name gave Lily comfort. She reached for her cell phone. She'd call her now, tell her they could meet somewhere else. Peyton would find a solution. As Lily was beginning to think everything would be okay, she noticed Nester's face had taken on a gray pallor. "What is it?"

He pulled a sheaf of stapled papers from his briefcase and thumbed through the pages. When he found what he was looking for, he shoved it toward her, his finger jabbing at a section in the middle of the page. She read the first line, then grabbed the papers and devoured the rest of the page.

This agent accompanied AUSA Peyton Davis to the warehouse at 1420 Rochester Road, Mesquite, Texas. The warehouse is owned by Gantry Oil. Following questioning of the employees at the warehouse, this agent and AUSA Davis were fired upon by persons unknown. Subsequent search of the premises revealed business and banking records for Gantry Oil. These records have been examined by a forensic accountant (see attached affidavit) and determined to represent coded entries consistent with the type used by individuals engaged in money laundering in violation of 18 U.S.C. Section 1957.

There was more, a lot more, but Lily stopped there and attempted to digest what she'd read. AUSA Peyton Davis. Gantry Oil. Money laundering. The words blurred on the page. What she needed to know was staring her in the face, but she couldn't make herself believe it.

Nester's voice burst into her silence. "Your *friend* Peyton Davis is investigating your father. How long have you known her?" He didn't wait for a response. "For all we know she's gotten close to you for no other reason than to find out about your father's business. I'm going to need to know every detail of every conversation you've had with her."

Lily looked at her father, the expression on his face one of stark betrayal. At that moment, the elevator dinged and the doors opened. He stood aside to let the occupants out, and Lily was suddenly face-to-face with Peyton and the woman she'd left the Adolphus with the night of the shooting.

Peyton's face was drawn and her eyes wide with concern. Lily watched as Peyton walked closer, seemingly oblivious to the presence of her father and Nester. When Peyton reached her side, she glanced back at the other woman before leaning in and asking, "Are you okay?"

Lily stared into Peyton's eyes. She looked sincere, concerned. She looked like the same Peyton she'd kissed less than twenty-four hours ago. But the events of the last hour told a very different story.

She stepped to the side and walked over to join her father and Nester who were already in the elevator. She met Peyton's eyes one last time and said, "If you want to talk to me again, contact my attorney." The doors closed, but not before she read the pain on Peyton's face.

She wasn't buying it. It was too soon for her to process everything that had just happened, but she knew one thing for certain. She'd completely misjudged the situation between herself and Peyton, and she'd put her family in jeopardy. She would not be fooled again.

❖

Peyton punched the button for the elevator, willing the car that carried Lily and her father to return. She punched it twice more before Dale touched her arm.

"She's gone," Dale said. "Let's deal with this." She pointed to the suite of offices. "And then you can figure out what to do about her."

She was right, but the knowledge that Lily thought she had betrayed her was devastating. *I should have told her about her father. I never should have let her find out this way.* The refrain of remorse chanted through her thoughts as she followed Dale back into the office suite. When they reached the reception desk, Dale took the lead.

"Who's the agent in charge?" she barked at the young FBI agent who'd been posted at the entrance to the offices.

The kid pulled himself to his full six feet and asked, "Who are you?"

"I'm the senior agent on this task force, DEA Special Agent Nelson." She pointed at Peyton. "This is AUSA Peyton Davis, the lead AUSA. Don't make either one of us show you our badges or you'll be tossed off this case faster than you can say J. Edgar Hoover. Now, are you going to tell me who's leading this mess of a search?"

"Yes, ma'am. AUSA Bianca Cruz and Special Agent Tanner Cohen, FBI."

"Get them out here now."

"I was told to stay right here. Not to let anyone in." The kid flicked his eyes at Peyton like he was looking for confirmation. She stared him down and said, "Go."

A few minutes later, Bianca walked through the interior office doors. "Hi, Peyton, Dale. Didn't expect to see either of you here."

"I bet you didn't," Peyton said. "Find an empty room. We need to talk. Dale, will you handle the other one?"

"No problem."

Bianca, to her credit, didn't ask any questions, but led Peyton to a small, unused office just inside the suite. Once they were both inside, Peyton shut the door and launched in. "What the hell's going on?"

"What are you talking about?"

"Why wasn't I told you were executing a search warrant this morning?"

Bianca shook her head. "I don't know what you're talking about. Mr. Gellar said he would fill you in. Have you talked to him?"

"When was he going to fill me in? After it aired on the six o'clock news?"

"Hey, I don't know why you're pissed off at me, but I'm only doing my job. Yesterday, we got the preliminary report from Samantha Reed in forensics about the records we pulled from the warehouse. Mr. Gellar was there when they came in, and he told me to go ahead and start work on the warrant. He said he would call you."

"We talked yesterday and you didn't mention anything about a search warrant."

"This all came together after we talked, and Mr. Gellar said he was going to run it by you. It didn't even occur to me to call you myself. Is there a problem?"

There was, but Peyton couldn't put her finger on it. Besides the obvious personal problem she'd caused by not telling Lily about her father before she found out in the worst way possible, there was something off about the rushed way this had been handled. She tapped her fingers on the desk as she thought it through. "I don't understand how anyone could have been able to tell that the records from the warehouse were duplicates of the ones Gantry has here at his offices. You're just now getting the ones from the office, right?"

Bianca looked like she wished she was anywhere else, but Peyton pressed the point. "What's going on?"

"Remember our first meeting? I mentioned the FBI has been conducting an investigation into possible fraud allegations against Gantry? They've been working with a confidential informant who's been sending them files to review."

Peyton felt her blood pressure rise. "Without a warrant? You realize any defense attorney worth their salt can get that evidence tossed? In fact, that could jeopardize anything you just turned up in this search if you used it as the basis for this warrant."

"I know. I just found out about it. I mean I knew about the informant, but I didn't know they were sending business records to the case agents. Those agents aren't on our task force and I wasn't in the loop."

"Well, we never should've asked Judge Nivens to sign a warrant unless we had all the facts. When he finds out about this, everything we send his way in the future is going to get extra scrutiny."

"I promise I didn't know."

Peyton could tell Bianca was telling the truth and decided to cut her some slack. "You weren't the one who asked the judge to sign the warrant, were you?"

"No, but—"

"Bianca, there'll be plenty of times to take the blame when the blame's yours. I'll deal with this. In the meantime, I need something from you."

"You bet."

"I want anyone who's not officially assigned to the task force out of here. As of right now, Dale is the agent in charge of this search. The agents who interviewed Lily Gantry need to report to her. Right now."

Bianca nodded and rushed out of the room. Peyton leaned against the wall and took a breath. The ranch, Neil, her father, the task force, Gellar—trouble was brewing on all fronts, but all she could think about was Lily and the pain in her eyes. It wouldn't be easy, but she could fix most of these things. As for the growing connection between her and Lily, she feared it might be permanently damaged. The idea was devastating.

CHAPTER EIGHTEEN

It was noon and Lily was in her room where she'd been since she'd left her father's office the day before. She dreaded going downstairs, especially since her mother had informed her that her aunt, uncle, and cousins had arrived to show their support for the family in this difficult time. More likely they were worried about their inheritance.

At some point she'd have to emerge and deal with the fallout of the day before. One of Nester's associates had already called to see when she could come in and debrief about everything that had happened during the search yesterday. She knew what they really wanted was to find out everything she knew about Peyton.

The prospect made her ill. How could she taint what she and Peyton had shared by holding up every detail for their prurient examination? Then again, hadn't Peyton already done sufficient damage with her lies? Peyton's promises, spoken and unspoken, had all been broken with this single betrayal.

She'd give anything to take back the things she'd confided in Peyton, about her mother, about her adoption. Her mind scanned her memories of every word she'd said to Peyton since they'd met, searching for anything that could be taken out of context, used against her or her family. Had Peyton ever really been interested in her or, as Nester had suggested, had she only gotten close as part of a ruse to learn more about the family business?

Lily had doubts. If Peyton had been faking her attraction, she was very good at it. Her soft smile, her gentle touch, the intense interest in everything Lily had to say—could all of it been a lie?

She didn't know who to trust anymore. Everything about Peyton had seemed so real, so genuine. And as for her father, what were the chances that a team of federal agents would descend on his offices for absolutely no reason? Peyton's vague warning for her not to go into business with her father echoed in her memory.

She'd longed to talk to her father about the allegations, but he'd been absent since Nester had hustled them out of the Gantry Oil offices the day before. The only conversation they'd had in the elevator had been about the envelope he'd handed to her. She'd completely forgotten about it in the chaos that ensued after he left her alone in his office. When she told him she'd left it behind, he had merely shaken his head.

He'd spent the rest of the day and this morning in meetings with attorneys, according to her mother. She knew he was doing what was necessary, but she needed to hear from him that everything would be okay. That everything the FBI agent had said the day before was a lie.

The words she'd read from the search warrant had haunted her every thought, the mention of the shooting especially. She'd scoured the online reports of the incident, but details were few and far between. When she searched the address she'd read in the report, it was indeed the address of a warehouse owned by Gantry Oil. If nothing illegal was going on, then why had someone shot at Peyton and Agent Nelson when they were there asking questions?

Frustrated, tired, and heartsick, she left the safe cocoon of her room, descended the stairs, and made her way to the dining room where the family was gathered for lunch. Her uncle Brock, aunt Clara, and her cousins, Lance and Darla, were already seated with her parents at the table. When she walked in, her father merely nodded, but Brock stood and gave her a big hug.

"Lily, it's been a long time. I'm sure your family is very happy to have you home, and we're very happy to see you." He shot a look at his wife and children who murmured hellos before returning to the food on the table.

Brock had always been kind to her, but he seemed oblivious to the rest of his family's icy reception of her. She'd learned early on that Clara and her offspring resented the fact her father, not Brock, had been chosen by Rufus to run the family business, and Clara hadn't bothered to hide her anger that a non-blood relative was first in line to inherit it all. Lily had never let Clara, Lance, and Darla get under her skin, but today her skin was thinner than usual and she braced for what was sure to be an uncomfortable meal.

She sat in the chair nearest her mother, and Joelle appeared at her shoulder with a warm plate of food. At the scent of pot roast and gravy, she realized she hadn't eaten since the grapefruit she'd had the morning before, and she dug in as the conversation continued around the table.

"Cyrus," Brock said. "I can meet with our investors, help put their minds at ease while you work with Nester on a plan to defend whatever's coming next."

He slapped the table with his palm. "There's nothing to defend. Besides, Gantrys don't work from a position of defense. I've already made arrangements to go on the offense. Nester has hired a PR firm, and they'll start providing statements to the press about how Hershel Gellar is a long time enemy of big business and he's had his sights set on me for years. Took this long for him to find a way into my inner circle." He stopped talking and shot a pointed look in Lily's direction. "But that doesn't mean that he's got hard evidence that I or anyone else at Gantry Oil has committed any crimes."

Lily put her fork down, her appetite gone. She knew that she was the path the U.S. attorney had taken into her father's inner circle, and the accusing eyes of everyone at the table made it clear they blamed her for the mess that threatened to take down the family business. She stood and placed her napkin next to her plate. "I apologize, but I'm afraid I'm not feeling well. Please excuse me."

She didn't wait for a response before striding briskly from the room. When she reached the stairs, Joelle called out to her. "Miss Lily, you have a phone call. I didn't want to bother you while you were eating, but…" She paused and her eyes were full of concern. "Are you okay?"

"Yes, I'm fine. Or I will be. You said I had a phone call?" Lily rarely got calls on the residence phone since most of her friends chose to use her cell number. Of course, she'd turned off her cell phone yesterday afternoon after Peyton's number showed up for the fifth time. She followed Joelle to the phone in the downstairs study and picked up the line. "Lily Davis."

"Lily, it's Skye. I've been trying to reach you since yesterday. Is everything all right?"

In the chaos of the day, Lily had completely forgotten she had been on the phone with Skye when the federal agents burst into her father's offices. Skye had said something about not being able to locate her mother's death certificate. "Have you found it? My mother's death certificate?"

"Look, I'd really like to talk about this in person. What are you doing right now?"

Lily glanced at the door to the study. What she should be doing is sucking it up and having lunch with her family. Acting like she was one of them even though they'd just made it clear that her actions had placed them all in danger. But what she wanted to do was get as far away as possible, from their accusing eyes and her regrets about Peyton. She made arrangements to meet Skye at Morgan's office in an hour and prayed that whatever Skye had to tell her would make her feel better.

Peyton kept her voice low, but she leaned across Gellar's desk and scowled to emphasize her anger. "Either I'm in charge of this task force, or I'm not. If you plan to cut me out of major decisions, then maybe I made the wrong decision taking this job."

Gellar looked unfazed at her anger. "Come on now, Peyton, you should know sometimes we have to make decisions based on the climate, not just the facts."

"I don't even know what that means."

"Don't tell me you worked in Washington all that time and didn't see any politics at play. I have a duty to protect the citizens of this district, but how I do it is up to me. Word is Cyrus Gantry has been talking to investors about diversifying into alternative energy sources—warm and fuzzy stuff. Better if we get this to a jury while he's still just a big bad oil tycoon."

Peyton shook her head in disgust. She'd watched Gellar's press conference on the evening news last night, and she couldn't believe the sweeping allegations he leveled at Cyrus Gantry, especially since they'd only just begun to review the evidence seized from his offices. She'd tried to get in to see Gellar several times yesterday afternoon, but he'd been too busy giving interviews to talk to anyone at the office. Unfortunately, she didn't have any recourse to deal with Gellar's methods. As a U.S. attorney, he was appointed by the president, and while main Justice in D.C. could make recommendations based on his performance, ultimately only the president could fire him.

Damn it. She was on the verge of telling him to shove his politics and quitting, but if she walked, Lily would be left without a safety net. In his zeal, Gellar was convinced everyone close to Cyrus Gantry must be guilty of something, and he wouldn't rest until they were all convicted. As much as she loathed his showboating, she had to stick around, at least until Lily was in the clear. She owed her that much.

An hour later, Dale walked into her office and shut the door. Peyton could tell she was trying to mask concern, but she was doing a lousy job of it. "What's going on?"

"You're not going to like this."

"I don't like much today. Go ahead, spill."

"I talked to Cohen and Jeffries, the agents who talked to Lily yesterday."

"And?"

"Cohen says Lily didn't talk much, that she seemed nervous. Based on what she did say, Cohen couldn't really get a read on whether she knew anything."

"So why do you look like whatever you're about to tell me is going to set me off?"

Dale set an envelope marked evidence on Peyton's desk. "Because they found this sitting on the floor right by her chair when she left. Their theory is that she left it behind by accident."

Peyton reached over and picked up the envelope. Dread gnawed at her insides as she broke the seal and pulled out a stack of paper. She thumbed through the pages, but nothing she saw made sense. She held up the stack. "Help me out here. What am I looking at?"

"According to Agent Reed, what you have in your hand are records a lot like those they found at Gantry's warehouse. Except these document recent transactions. As recent as last week."

"And they were in Gantry's office?"

"Yes. Jeffries is convinced Lily had them in her possession."

"Based on what? The fact she was there?"

"They weren't on Cyrus's desk or in his drawers. They were on the floor, right next to where Lily was sitting."

Peyton stood and started pacing. The idea that Lily would be complicit in her father's schemes was inconceivable. Or was she so blinded by attraction that she couldn't see the truth?

No, she was right not to jump to conclusions. So far everything about this investigation had gone against her instincts. Gellar may be in charge when it came to the showing off for the cameras, but at least for now, she was taking back command of what happened behind the scenes. She'd start by finding out who she could trust.

"What do you think?" she asked Dale.

Dale glanced at the envelope and then back up at Peyton. "I think we need a little bit more information before we start arresting folks."

Satisfied with Dale's answer, Peyton made a decision to confide in her. "You've probably already figured this out, but I have feelings for Lily. Up until yesterday, I think she had feelings for me too. Now what do you have to say?"

"Feelings are hard. They can cloud your judgment, but they can also sharpen your focus. Just depends." She reached over and picked up the envelope and tucked it under her arm. "What do you say we play it by ear? I'll go see Lily. If she'll consent to talk to me, I'll let you know what I think. Fair enough?"

"More than fair." Peyton walked out from behind her desk and stuck out her hand. "Thanks, Dale."

"Wait and see what I have to say after I talk to her before you go thanking me. And, Peyton?"

"Yes?"

"Watch your back. Not everyone around here has yours."

Peyton watched Dale leave, certain she was right.

❖

Skye was waiting in the lobby of the Bradley & Casey's offices when Lily arrived. "I'm sorry I'm late," Lily said. "There was a bad wreck on Central."

There had been a bad accident, but she would've missed it entirely if she'd taken the right exit. She'd been so distracted by the events of the past twenty-four hours, it was amazing she'd made it here in one piece.

"Are you okay?" Skye asked. "I heard about your father."

"Who hasn't heard? I had to shut the radio off on the way over. Whatever happened to innocent until proven guilty?"

"Good question. I can personally attest that principle is more theory than fact."

"Oh really?"

"A story for another time. Morgan said we can use the conference room. Come on."

Skye led the way, and a few moments later, they were seated at the spacious table. Lily remembered the first time she'd come here, a few weeks ago. If she'd known then what fate would soon befall her family, she never would have started this journey. Even now, she felt uncomfortable pursuing this track, but she needed some kind of distraction to keep her from thinking about Peyton and her father.

She'd ignored all of Peyton's calls, and finally, she'd stopped calling. The messages had all been the same. Simple requests for a callback and nothing more. No clues to signal whether she'd phoned for personal or professional reasons, although it didn't matter either way. Anything personal between them was over, and she had nothing to say to her about her father. Anxious to be immersed in something other than thoughts of her current troubles, she turned her attention to Skye who had set a small stack of papers on the table. "What are these?"

"First things, first. As I said on the phone, I've checked with every county in the state, and there is no death certificate for a Sophia Valencia around the time of your birth. I even checked for other first or last names. Nothing turns up."

"What does that mean?"

"Well, the obvious answer would be that she's not dead."

Lily felt a glimmer of hope before reality rushed in. "But that doesn't make any sense. Are you saying that the nuns lied to my parents? If she's alive and she gave me up, wouldn't she have had to sign papers so my parents could adopt me? Wouldn't those be on file somewhere?"

"Yes. If she gave you up for adoption, then there would be a record with the county where you were adopted."

Skye's tone was measured, and it only took a moment for Lily to pick up on the clue. "*If* she gave me up for adoption. Are you saying she didn't voluntarily give me up? What do you mean by that?" She stood up for emphasis. "Skye, I've had a really bad couple of days, and I don't have the patience for riddles. Whatever you're trying to say, just say it."

"I'm sorry. This isn't easy, and I don't know the why of it all, but here's what I do know." She reached over and picked up a couple of pieces of paper from the stack and lined them up on the table. She pointed to the first one. "Here's your birth certificate."

Lily looked down at a copy of the same document she'd shared with Skye when they first met. More confused than ever, she pulled the other document closer. "What's this?"

"Most hospitals ask mothers to fill these forms out for newborns. It helps them with record keeping, so they don't have a bunch of files labeled newborn baby XYZ. It's also for security purposes—to make sure babies aren't released to the wrong parents."

Lily picked up the paper and scanned it. It was a fairly simple form with a few lines to be filled in and boxes to be checked off. Her mother's name and date of birth were listed along with the address of Our Lady of Guadalupe.

Her eyes moved to the other side of the page where she expected to see blank lines and empty boxes where the information about her father should be. But the entire form was filled in. She devoured the information. It wasn't an official document, so there was no prohibition about including her birth father's name without his permission. But it wasn't the fact that the entire form was filled in that shocked her the most. What shocked her the most was that she knew the name listed on the line beside Father, and up until this moment, she'd thought she'd known everything about him.

She shook the paper at Skye. "Where did you get this?"

"From the hospital's archives. Maybe your mother filled out the form without him knowing."

Lily put her head in her hands and squeezed tight. It was too much. First Peyton's betrayal and now this.

"Lily, are you okay?"

She looked up into Skye's kind eyes and mustered a smile. "Why wouldn't I be? I just learned what every adopted kid probably wants to believe. I'm not adopted after all." She picked up the form and read it again. Sure enough, Cyrus Gantry was listed as her father. It was his date of birth, and she had no doubt it was true. All the qualities they shared weren't nurture after all. No wonder she'd always felt more of an affinity with him than with her mother.

Her mother, Rose. Did she know? Lily's stomach clenched and she put the thought aside. There was only so much she could process in one sitting.

"There's more, if you're up for it," Skye said.

"I'm not sure I'll ever be up for it, so you may as well go ahead and tell me."

"I think I've located your mother. Sophia."

CHAPTER NINETEEN

L ily wandered through Klyde Warren Park. The food
trucks had just set up, arriving early to beat the lunchtime
rush. Young mothers pushed strollers along the winding paths and
chased toddlers through the playground. A yoga instructor led a
class on the lawn. Everyone she saw was acting like this was just
a normal day. A bright, sunny day full of possibilities and promise.

She sank onto a bench and wished she felt the same, but for
her this day was full of broken promises and betrayal. Cyrus was
her father—that much hadn't changed, but all her life he'd lied
about their true connection. And what had her mother been to him
that he'd let her think Sophia was dead all this time?

Lily knew her father and mother had been married before
she'd been born. Had Sophia been a one-night stand? Her mother
couldn't have children of her own, so had he conveniently accepted
what Sophia could give and then...

And then what? Whose decision had it been to let her father
raise her? What kind of woman was Sophia that she could give
birth to her child and then walk away, letting her daughter believe
she was dead?

There was only one way to get answers. Right now she
wouldn't trust her father to tell the truth, and Skye said she'd
found Sophia. She could go see her, demand the truth. Hi, I'm the
daughter you didn't want, that you gave away. I thought you were
dead and I loved these nice people who took me in, but now it
turns out everyone is a liar and I'd like to know why.

She didn't know what to do. So she sat on the bench and watched the world go by, drinking in the normal as if she could become it by osmosis. She had no idea how long she'd been sitting there before she felt the weight of another person settling in next to her.

"Lily Gantry?"

She turned toward the voice and looked into kind eyes that belonged to the woman who'd accompanied Peyton to her father's office the day before. The same woman who'd picked Peyton up at the Adolphus the night of the shooting. She fished her memory and came up with a name. "Agent Nelson."

"You can call me Dale."

"Is that part of your shtick?"

"Pardon?"

"You know, good cop, bad cop? I already met the bad cops, so I guess that means you're here to try and smooth things over and get me to talk."

Dale laughed. It was full of genuine humor, and Lily almost caught herself smiling in return. "I won't lie. We do use that routine on occasion, but I don't work with those folks who talked to you yesterday."

"Is that so?"

"Yes, ma'am."

"Who do you work for?"

"I work with Peyton Davis and a team of other agents, and we're investigating your father because we suspect he's laundering money for a faction of the Mexican Cartel."

"So I gathered." Lily was torn. Common sense said she should get up and walk away, but instinct told her to hear Dale out. What harm could come from listening? It wasn't like her father had been truthful with her before. "I suppose you think I can shed some light on that?"

"Actually, I don't have any idea if you know anything about it. How about this? I tell you what I know and then you can decide if you want to talk to me?"

"Should I have a lawyer?"

"If you want to get a lawyer before you talk to me, that's fine, but can I make one suggestion?"

"Go for it."

"Get your own lawyer. A lawyer should only represent one client at a time, and Nester Rawlins represents your father. Do you get my meaning?"

She did and she didn't. Yesterday, federal agents threatened her with prosecution. Today, one was handing out advice. Everything about this day was so surreal, but she could see no harm in hearing Dale out. Plus she needed to hear the whole story if she was going to figure out what to do.

For the next half hour, she listened as Dale gave her a play-by-play of the investigation into her father's business dealings, starting from an FBI investigation into fraud allegations to the discovery that his business records reflected unusual activity. When she got to the shooting, Lily couldn't help but gasp at the description of Dale and Peyton, pinned down under automatic gunfire.

"How badly were you hurt?"

"It'll heal. Peyton saved my life that night."

Lily nodded, afraid if she spoke Dale would hear the shake of fear in her voice. If someone would try to kill a federal agent and a prosecutor to protect their crimes, what else would they do?

Dale finished her story with the execution of the search warrant. "I'm going to tell you something I shouldn't. Peyton didn't know they planned to search your father's offices and go public about the investigation. She wasn't even at work when it all went down."

Of course not. She'd been home dealing with her own family troubles. Lily knew that, but she'd suppressed the information and assumed the worst. Peyton had warned her about her father, maybe not as strongly as she could have, but Lily hadn't listened, choosing to brush off the warning. Still, the sense of betrayal was still there. Peyton must have known something was on the brink of happening, but Sunday afternoon she'd acted like everything was perfect.

Except Peyton had said she had something important to tell her. That she would tell her when they met again, Monday night.

Damn. Caught up in the passion of arousal, Lily had completely forgotten Peyton's words.

"Why are you telling me all this?"

"I have my reasons. Now, I'm going to show you something, and it's totally up to you to tell me what you know about it or not. Your call, okay?"

Lily nodded and Dale handed her an envelope. In the upper left hand corner was the return address for Gantry Oil. She hefted it in her hand and asked, "What is this?"

"You don't know? The FBI agents you spoke with yesterday found it next to the chair you were sitting in at your father's office. They seem to think it was yours."

Lily flashed to the memory of her father, pulling papers from his desk drawer, shoving them into an envelope, and handing it to her. *Take this with you, and I'll get it back at lunch. I need to run it by one of the sites later.* He'd lied to her. He'd wanted those papers far away from the prying eyes of the federal agents. She was certain, but she didn't know why.

She debated how to reply to Dale. She had no idea what was in the envelope. Would telling the truth get her father in trouble? Did she care? She looked at it again. It was stamped with the Gantry Oil address, and they'd found it in his office. There was no sense denying the truth, and she'd had enough of falsehood lately. "It's not mine. My father gave it to me and asked me to meet him with it later. I have no idea what's inside, and I must have forgotten it when I left the office."

"So you'd be surprised to learn this envelope contains coded records, just like the ones we found in your father's warehouse. If there was ever any doubt that he knew about the records at the warehouse, these prove otherwise."

"And your buddies think I knew as well? Well, I didn't. Up until a few months ago, I wasn't even in the country, and I haven't been working for my father. I know plenty about the science of energy and business in general, but I don't know anything about his private business dealings." She braced for the answer to her next question. "Are you going to arrest me?"

Dale drummed her fingers on the envelope. "Fact is, I've done a bit of checking around, and what you've just said is true. I know you've pitched some ideas to the company, but that's about the extent of your involvement. I believe you didn't have a clue what was in this envelope. So, no, I'm not going to arrest you. I suppose it's up to you as to whether you'd like to work with us or against us."

Lily supposed she should feel indignation at being tricked into ratting out her father, but all she felt was relieved not to be a target of Peyton's investigation. "Does Peyton know you're here?"

"Yes."

"I guess you're going to report to her now."

"We'll talk soon. I'd like to be able to tell her whether we can count on you."

"You're good at this."

"Pardon?"

"Pressuring people without seeming to. You should give lessons to those other agents." Lily leaned back against the bench and closed her eyes. Her head swam. Her mother was alive, her father had lied to her, and he might be a criminal. Everything she had believed to be true was crumbling down around her. It was just too much.

"Tell Peyton, I'm sorry, but I have nothing left to give."

Peyton spent the afternoon on edge. Waiting for news from Roscoe. Waiting for news from Dale. She could barely concentrate on the evidence logs detailing the items that had been seized from Gantry Oil. Every entry triggered thoughts of Lily and the expression of betrayal she'd witnessed the day before. When the phone on her desk finally rang, she grabbed the handset and answered on the first ring. "Davis."

"Peyton, it's Roscoe. I don't suppose you've heard from Neil yet?"

"No, have you?"

"I have my top investigator looking for him to serve these papers, but he's nowhere to be found. The judge has scheduled a hearing on a temporary injunction first thing tomorrow. If we can't find Neil to serve him, I'll put my investigator on the stand to tell the judge what he's done to try and find him, but I'd like to have you there on standby in case the judge wants to hear from you."

Peyton glanced at her calendar. "I'll be there." They discussed the time and where to meet, and she hung up the phone to contemplate what she would do between now and then.

She'd barely seen Gellar since her confrontation with him that morning. No doubt he was on another circuit of press appearances to discuss his latest coup. The problem was the more she reviewed the evidence the more convinced she was they'd chosen the wrong method to flush the Vargases out of hiding. Gantry had too much to lose in terms of reputation and investor money to come clean on his involvement with the Zetas. And he had enough money to keep Nester Rawlins and his fleet of lawyers working twenty-four seven on his defense. She knew from Bianca that Gellar had already raised the possibility of investigating Rawlins's firm to see if their fees were paid with funds from legal sources, but Peyton knew that path would result in a logjam. Indictments of lawyers had to be approved by the Justice Department and, after working there for a few years, she knew such requests were rarely granted. Lawyers took care of their own. Gellar's tactics would only delay a resolution of the case.

What she needed to do was assemble the task force and brainstorm another solution, and the best time to do that was when Gellar was out of the office so he couldn't interfere. She started to pick up the phone to call Ida and check Gellar's schedule, but stopped when she saw Dale standing in her doorway. "What did you find out?"

Dale shut the door and sat down. "I don't think she knew a damn thing about what her daddy was up to. Not many people can fake shock that well."

Peyton sighed with relief, but she needed to know more. "What did she say? Is she okay?"

"She's as okay as someone can be who's watching their world fall apart around them. She was leaving a lawyer's office with an ex-Dallas cop right before I talked to her. I think she realizes she needs to put some distance between her and the family business."

"Was the ex-cop a blonde with short, spiky hair?"

"That's the one."

"I think that's about something else entirely." Peyton was certain the blonde was Skye Keaton, the investigator Lily hired to help her find her birth mother's family. At least Lily had that venture to distract her from everything else that was going on. Peyton desperately wanted to call her, ask her how she was doing, talk to her about something, anything other than this case. Maybe this was an opening. She could ask about her quest to find her mother's family, assure her she would shield her from prosecution. "How did you leave things with her?"

"She gave us what we need to confirm that her father knew about the records in the envelope, but that's it. She's not going to have anything more to do with us."

"Us? What does that mean?"

"She's hurt, Peyton. Her world just fell apart and she thought you were to blame. I made it clear you weren't, but she's not going to just bounce back."

Dale was right and she knew it. The best thing she could do right now was leave Lily alone and focus on the job. There was no way they could mend the break between them while she was still working on evidence to put Lily's father behind bars.

Lily's father behind bars. That wasn't going to happen anytime soon. The nagging thoughts from earlier came roaring back. She knew they were going about this the wrong way, and she told Dale her concern that the only thing that was going to come out of yesterday's raid was a protracted battle in the media.

"So, what do you want to do about it?" Dale asked.

"I've been thinking we need a different approach. Maybe we should get the team together and brainstorm while Gellar's out."

"Remember what I said before about having your back?"

"You think we can't trust everyone?"

"I won't go that far, but I will say maybe it would be a good idea to start with a small circle and branch out when we have a plan."

"Good thinking," Peyton said. "Who do you trust?"

"Bianca." She held up her hand. "Before you say anything about yesterday, that was all Gellar's doing. She's young and inexperienced, but she was just following orders. She's got good instincts and I trust her."

"Who else?"

"Mary Lovelace, ATF. You met her your first day, but she's been working an angle in the field the rest of the time. I've known her for a while. We served together in Afghanistan."

"Perfect. You think they would be up for coming out to the ranch tonight? Give us a little privacy."

"Now you're talking. We'll be there."

After Dale left, Peyton started jotting down an agenda for the meeting as the beginnings of a risky plan already began to form. She should call and warn her mother and Fernanda to expect guests. Peyton hated that she didn't trust the rest of the group enough to have the meeting at the office, but better safe than sorry. Was this how Lily felt right now? That she couldn't trust the people who were supposed to be in her inner circle?

CHAPTER TWENTY

Lily stood in front of the open closet doors, scouring the racks for her garment bag.

"I moved your clothes to the guesthouse."

She turned and faced Courtney who'd just walked into the room. "What did you do that for?"

"Because it's obvious you're not going home anytime soon, and as much as I like you, I think you need your own space. You've been living out of your suitcase for a week."

Lily sank onto the bed. She'd spent the last seven days hunkered down at Courtney's house in East Dallas, ducking reporters, her parents, and anyone else who wanted to pry into her private life. She'd hadn't planned to stay in the small Tudor for more than a couple of nights, but since she'd arrived, she'd been paralyzed by indecision about what to do next. It was clear she was cramping Courtney's style.

"I'm sorry. I'll check into a hotel tonight."

"Don't be ridiculous. You'll do no such thing. You're welcome to stay. I like having you here, but the guesthouse will give you more privacy and space."

"You're sweet, but I can't hide out here forever. At some point, I need to make some decisions."

"Can I help?"

Lily wished she could, but the list was long, starting with what to do about her father. Nester had called her every day, the level of pressure in his tone increasing each time. His requests sounded simple enough. Come to the law firm to talk, but talking to him would not be simple. He would want to know everything she knew about Peyton Davis. She wasn't prepared to tell him the things she knew, things he wouldn't believe. Peyton was kind and funny, handsome, and smart. According to Agent Nelson, Peyton was a hero and a pursuer of justice. Nester wouldn't want to know any of those things. He was only interested in dirt, something he could use to discredit Peyton and her office's investigation of her father. Even if she had any mud to smear, Lily wouldn't use it, not when she was so conflicted.

Ignoring Nester had only given her more time to fret over whether she should attempt to contact Sophia. She'd had a lifetime to contemplate their first meeting, but now that she knew more about the lies surrounding her supposed adoption, the dream of a beautiful reunion threatened to become a nightmare. Skye had sent her a couple of texts during the week, just to check in and see where things stood, but the fear of the unknown left her undecided.

"You could get in touch with her. I bet she'd be glad to hear from you," Courtney said.

"Who? My mother?"

"Well, her too, but I was talking about Peyton. She's been working from the ranch quite a bit over the last week, and Zach said she seems to have a lot weighing on her mind, more than just Neil. I bet she's missing you."

Lily sighed. "It's not that simple. I wouldn't know what to say. Besides, I think the only reason she'd want to talk to me is if I can help prosecute my father. Don't get me wrong, if he broke the law, he deserves whatever's coming his way, but I don't want to be in the middle of it."

"But, honey, you kinda already are. I saw the way you and Peyton were acting at the ranch, and I've never seen you look so head over heels before. You like her. She likes you. The rest is just background noise."

Could Courtney be right? Maybe she should pick up the phone and call, gauge Peyton's reaction, see if there was any chance they could mend the broken trust between them.

The idea was a good one in the abstract, but the reality of their situation was that Peyton was out to get her family, and Lily could never be sure Peyton wanted to be with her for her and not for the access she provided. "If only. It's not going to happen."

Courtney's narrowed eyes signaled she wasn't happy with her answer, but she pressed on. "Well, then what about your mother? Sophia. Why not get in touch with her? You have all these unanswered questions. You deserve to know the truth. Maybe you need to know before you can move forward. Face it. You've had a week full of open wounds. Why not get some closure? What's the worst thing that can happen? She's already abandoned you."

Good question, and Courtney's blunt assessment was a wake-up call. She already thought the worst about Sophia and her father. If she met Sophia and the truth of why she'd given her away was ugly, it wouldn't be a big surprise and she had time to brace for it. But if there was some good reason, some vital reason, why her mother had chosen not to raise her daughter, or to know her at all, she wanted to know what it was. Maybe then she could pick up the pieces of her shattered trust and move on.

❖

Judge Nivens's secretary looked up from her desk. "He's ready to see you now."

Peyton followed Bianca and Dominic Fowler into the judge's chambers. He waited until they were all seated to start talking. "Ms. Cruz, I've read your motion, but it was a bit sparse on detail. I get the impression there were a few things left unsaid. Would you like to fill me in?"

Peyton met Bianca's eyes and nodded, confident they'd gone over what she needed to say enough times for her to handle this on her own.

"Yes, sir," Bianca said. "Although charged as an equal party in this conspiracy, we have met at length with Ms. Chavez and her defense counsel, Mr. Fowler. Based on these interviews and other evidence we have developed, it is the government's intention to reduce the charges against Ms. Chavez such that she would be probation eligible. Because of this, we would like to rescind our earlier request that she be held without bond."

"Interesting, Ms. Cruz." The judge turned to Dominic. "Mr. Fowler, I assume you have no objection to the Court considering bond conditions for your client?"

"No, your honor. None at all."

"And, Ms. Cruz, I assume you would like this motion to be sealed?" Nivens asked.

Bianca shifted in her seat and looked back at Peyton who simply nodded. "Yes, sir," Bianca said. "We would like that."

Peyton was staring at the judge, watching him talk to the others, when he looked up and met her eyes. His wink was almost imperceptible, but she was certain she'd seen it.

"Ms. Davis, do you have anything to say or are you just here to observe?"

"I have nothing to add, Judge," Peyton said with a smile. The wink had told her the judge probably knew what they were up to and he was going to do as they asked. There was no point in piling on.

"Fine then. I'll implement the usual bond conditions," Nivens said.

A short while later, the three attorneys stood in Peyton's office with the door shut. "That went as well as could be expected," Peyton said. "Dominic, you sure Carmen's up for this?"

"You picked her. She's not a criminal, so it's not easy for her to think like one, but she'll do what you ask and that's all you can expect."

"Fair enough." Peyton knew the plan was a long shot, but when she'd pitched the idea of releasing Carmen Chavez and using her to lure the Vargases out of hiding, Bianca, Dale, and Mary Lovelace had all signed on. The past week had been spent working out the details, including meeting with Carmen several times to get her ready to be the bait in their trap. Peyton knew they were asking a lot from her, but the promise of her freedom and protection for her family had convinced her to cooperate.

After Dominic left, Peyton told Bianca to close the door and take a seat. She called Dale and put her on speakerphone. "Dale, she'll be out this afternoon. I need you to make sure Mary has everything in place."

"Not a problem," Dale said. "Mary's already set up in an apartment next door to Carmen's and Carmen's place is all wired up. I vetted the cops who are working with Mary, and we've got a whole network of CIs who're putting out the word that Carmen's being released because we messed up the evidence, and she has important information for the Vargas brothers."

"How long will it take for them to get in touch with her?" Bianca asked.

"No telling," said Dale. "She lost her job when she got arrested, so she'll be staying put most of the time. If they're going to approach her, it'll be through a third party. Probably someone we haven't seen before who can risk showing his face around Carmen without raising suspicion. Mary and her team will be right there, ready to listen in."

"Okay, we've done all we can do for now," Peyton said. "I want reports at least twice a day, and if there's any movement, find me, no matter where I am."

A few minutes later, alone in her office, Peyton called her mother to check in. The week since the temporary injunction hearing had passed with no word from Neil. Based on Roscoe's arguments and Neil's seeming indifference to the whole procedure, the judge had granted a thirty-day injunction, preventing any drilling during that time. If no agreement could be reached, then he would schedule a full-blown hearing and, if Gantry Oil wanted to enforce the contract, they'd be pitted against each other in a court of law. Not only would that impact the future of the ranch, but if Gantry's attorneys alleged a conflict of interest, it could derail the criminal prosecution. Cyrus Gantry had millions at his disposal, and her only real weapon was the desire to do the right thing. Frustration clouded Peyton's outlook. Why was she doomed to fight against the Gantry family at every turn?

After confirming with her mother that there was still no word from Neil, she closed her eyes and relived the memory of the first time she'd seen Lily at Cattle Baron's. The surge of attraction she'd felt when Lily's spellbinding gaze swept her way was fixed in her memory. From that moment, she'd been captivated. She still was, but she had a job to do, and if she did it right, she could minimize the pain she'd caused. Since Lily didn't want anything more to do with her, that would have to be enough.

CHAPTER TWENTY-ONE

L ily paced Courtney's front porch while she waited for Skye to arrive. Day before yesterday, when she'd called Skye to tell her she was ready to try to contact Sophia, she'd never expected the meeting would happen so quickly. Apparently, Sophia lived less than sixty miles away, and Skye was on her way to pick Lily up and drive her there. She was a nervous wreck.

When Skye pulled into the driveway, Lily contemplated telling her she'd changed her mind. She walked to the driver's side window and Skye lowered the glass. "You ready?" she asked.

Lily shook her head and looked back toward the porch. Skye touched her arm and said, "You don't have to do this, but if it makes any difference, she's very excited to meet you."

"Meet me?" Lily felt her voice rise with frustration. "I'm thirty years old, and this whole time she's had the advantage. If she wanted to meet me, she could have."

"I don't think it was that easy."

"What did she tell you?"

"Not much, but I have a sense about these things. She has a comfortable life, but I get the impression it hasn't been easy. Wouldn't you rather ask her these questions yourself?"

Lily wasn't entirely convinced she was doing the right thing, but she walked around to the passenger side and climbed into the large SUV. They rode the first half of the trip in silence while her thoughts skipped all over the place. Finally, tired of being in her head, Lily fished around for some banal conversation topic that would keep her mind off meeting Sophia. She noticed a child's car seat in the back. "You have kids?"

"One. Her name is Olivia. She's two years old."

"What a beautiful name. Is she…"

"Adopted? Kind of. My wife, Aimee, is her biological mother, but I adopted her so we could both be her legal parents."

"I'm sorry. That was none of my business."

Skye shrugged. "Doesn't bother me. Aside from the day I married Aimee and the day Olivia was born, the day I adopted my daughter was one of the most special days of my life."

"Do you plan to have more?"

"Sure. We'd like for Olivia to have a sister or a brother."

"That's good." Lily was sorry she'd broached this line of conversation. She wasn't in the mood to talk about other people's happy adoption experiences. She knew she wasn't being quite fair. Until the last few weeks, her own adoption experience had been idyllic. Raised by a rich family, living a life of privilege, she'd wanted for nothing. Her ability to reject the money from her trust was partly due to the fact she'd been educated at the finest universities and was able to earn good money on her own. That might not have been possible if her life had taken a different path. If Sophia had kept her, how would her life have been changed?

"We're almost there."

Lily shook off her musings and braced for what lay ahead. "You came out here to see her?"

"I did," Skye said. "I decided the news that her daughter was interested in a meeting would be best delivered in person."

"Tell me about her."

"She's beautiful. You look just like her."

Lily glanced out the window to hide the tears she felt gathering in the corners of her eyes. All her life, she'd watched as her friends grew up into versions of their parents. Such a simple thing, but one she'd thought she would never experience. She wiped the tears away. "Tell me something else."

"She raises horses. She gave me a tour of the stables. Even tried to get me to take a ride, but I'm more of a Harley girl myself."

Lily spoke fast to keep the tears from coming back. "I rode competitively for many years. My parents came to all my events, but it drove my mother crazy. She wanted me to have a more ladylike hobby."

Skye shot her a sympathetic look as she pulled off the main road onto a gravel drive with a sign marked Valencia Acres. Dense woods lined the road for about a hundred yards, but then gave way to a modest two-story, pale yellow house with red trim.

As Skye parked the car, Lily glanced around. A few hundred feet from the house was a barn, painted the same yellow as the house. Another large building was set farther back on the property, and she assumed it housed the stables. The setup reminded her of the first time she'd pulled up at the Circle Six, and she wished Peyton was at her side to support her through whatever happened next.

"Are you ready?"

She looked at Skye. Peyton wasn't in her life and that was her decision, just like coming here today was her choice. It was time to see if she'd chosen wisely. She squared her shoulders and took a deep breath. "As ready as I'll ever be."

They'd barely stepped onto the porch when a woman appeared in the doorway. Lily knew instantly that she was Sophia. They didn't merely share a family resemblance—Lily could swear she was looking into a mirror, and she was transfixed. Unable to speak, she stood rooted in place.

"Sophia Valencia," Skye said, "this is Lily Gantry."

"Hello." Lily followed the one word by offering her hand in a tentative greeting.

Sophia grasped Lily's hand in both of her own and offered a nervous smile. "Please, come in."

The next few minutes were surreal as Sophia pulled a cold pitcher of lemonade from the fridge and offered them a tray of homemade biscochitos. They discussed the unseasonably warm temperatures, the lack of rain, and the price of hay. All the while, Lily grew more and more uncomfortable. The curious gaze of the stranger who sat across from her didn't help. Sophia wasn't her mother. Biology didn't make a mother. Neither did cookies and lemonade or small talk about mundane subjects. Anger itched inside her. She wanted to throw the plate of cookies against the wall. Splash the cold lemonade in Sophia's face. Anything to distract her from thinking this was an afternoon tea party and not the biggest confrontation of her life.

But she'd been raised to be a lady, not to kick up a fuss. She wouldn't cause a scene, but she couldn't stay here and pretend things were normal. She stood abruptly, almost knocking over her chair. Sophia's eyes widened and Skye reached out to grab her hand, but she shook it away. "I'm fine. I just need some air." She backed toward the door. "I'll be outside."

Lily stumbled out the door to the porch and down the steps. If she'd had the key to Skye's SUV, she would have jumped in and driven away. She walked toward the stables, imagining herself on a horse, riding into the distance, leaving all her cares behind.

"Would you like to see the horses?"

She whirled at the sound of the voice that sounded so much like her own. Sophia stood several feet behind her, her expression expectant. Lily couldn't deny that as much as she wanted to escape, her need to know why Sophia had given her up and why she hadn't tried to make contact since outweighed her want. The sheer force of her need sent the words spilling out. "Why did you abandon me?"

"Oh, *mija*." Sophia took a step toward her and then stopped. "Please, can we talk? I mean really talk. There is so much I need to tell you." She pointed at the stables. "I have an office in here."

Lily looked back at the porch, but there was no sign of Skye.

"She's in the house," Sophia said. "I told her I wanted to talk to you alone."

Lily wavered. If she left now, she'd spend her whole life wondering why. She'd opened this Pandora's box and it was time to deal with whatever came out. She stood back to let Sophia lead the way. "Okay, let's talk."

❖

Peyton walked through the doors of the federal building and checked the time. She had a meeting scheduled this afternoon with Agent Reed to go over Reed's preliminary analysis of the records seized from the Gantry Oil offices. Peyton had a knack for numbers, but after spending the last few years in D.C. focused on white-collar crime, the sameness of it bored her. She'd much rather be interviewing witnesses and sifting through crime scene photos than poring over credits and debits on a financial statement. The only reason she'd agreed to meet with Reed was to keep Gellar in the dark as to what she was really up to.

She wouldn't be able to keep up the charade for long. Eventually, he would notice that key members of the task force were spending a lot of time and resources without garnering much in the way of evidence to bolster the case against Gantry. She only hoped she would be able to bring him the Vargas brothers before he caught on.

Just as she was about to walk through security, she heard a voice call her name, and she looked up to see Dale walking toward her. "What's up?"

Dale waited until she was right next to her to talk. "Mary called. Carmen got the call and she's on the move. I'm parked down the street. Let's go."

Peyton phoned the office on her way to Dale's truck. She told Ida she had a personal matter to deal with and asked her to reschedule the appointment with Reed. After they climbed into the truck and were driving out of downtown, Peyton asked, "Where are we headed?"

"A ranch in Wise County. Don't know much about it. Carmen went out for breakfast this morning and some guy slipped her a disposable cell. She got a call not long ago, and Mary's convinced it was Arturo. Carmen told him her attorney got copies of all the evidence and she needs to talk to him about it. He gave her an address and detailed instructions about parking by the highway and taking a trail directly to the stables. Mary already had a tracker put on Carmen's car, so she sent her on her way. They're taking another route to try to beat her there. We could all be walking into a cluster."

"What do we know about this ranch?"

"Not a lot. It's owned by a company called VA Enterprises, purchased a year ago. They raise quarter horses. I called Bianca and she's seeing what else she can find out, but that's it for now."

Peyton looked out the window as the city scenery flew by. "Any chance we could get some of the local agencies involved?"

Dale shook her head. "Not a good idea. I don't have a good contact in the area, and we don't have enough time to bring someone up to speed. Besides, I don't have a clue what we're walking into and I don't want to risk it. By the way, your gun is back in the glovebox."

Peyton had turned in the gun she'd borrowed the night of the warehouse shooting. She opened the glovebox, pulled it out, and checked the slide. "Okay, what's the plan?"

"Mary got an aerial map and marked what looks like bridle trails." Dale handed over her phone. "You can pull up the map from her text. She and her guys are going to go in a back way and set up behind the stables. I'll park us off the highway and we can take another way in to cover the front. We put a listening device and GPS on Carmen's disposable cell phone that will record her conversations with Arturo. If we're lucky and he takes it from her, then we'll be able to track him if conditions aren't right to nab him there. I'd prefer to get Carmen to safety before we take him down. That's as far ahead as we can plan at this point."

"I guess that'll have to do." Peyton studied the map and then set Dale's phone on the console and pulled out her own. No new e-mails, texts, or messages. If they managed to arrest Vargas, they'd be up all night with the aftermath. She opened her messages and started composing a text to her mother to let her know she'd be working late, but stopped before she finished typing. She'd talked to her mother just before lunch and, if she texted her now, she'd think something was up.

Something was up. This was worse than the shooting at the warehouse where they hadn't expected to be walking into danger. If she didn't make it out of this alive, would she be content to let her earlier conversation with her mother be her last? They'd talked about the ranch and her mother's plans for the horses. Maybe it's time I looked into more modern breeding methods, she'd said. Try and turn things around. Before they'd hung up, her mother said her father was feeling much better today. He'd come down to lunch and was out on the porch enjoying the warm weather. If that was the last talk they had, it had been a good one.

Peyton backspaced over the letters and clicked the back arrow to return to the messages screen. Her last text from Lily was midway down the screen. She'd received it a week ago Sunday, the day she'd shown Lily the house at the Circle Six. Lily had sent it that night before she went to bed: *Thanks for showing me your special place. You have a special place in my heart. Can't wait to see you tomorrow.*

The tomorrow Lily referred to in her text had only brought heartache, but she hadn't been able to bring herself to delete the text. Now she'd give anything if this text had been their last conversation rather than the painful scene outside Cyrus's office.

"We're almost there," Dalc said. "Start looking for a place we can park the truck out of sight."

"Will do." Peyton tucked her phone in her pocket. She needed to focus on the future, not the past, but she made a silent vow that if everything went according to plan and they were able to arrest the Vargases, she would do whatever it took to win back that special place in Lily's heart.

CHAPTER TWENTY-TWO

How many horses do you have?" Lily asked. She may have shunned the small talk in the kitchen, but now that she was alone with Sophia, meaningless conversation was her shield.

"We had a big sale a few weeks ago, so we're down to fifteen. We stand five stallions including this one, Queen's Ransom. He won the All American Futurity this year."

Lily followed Sophia to the stall and was greeted by a beautiful Blue Roan who stood at least fifteen hands. All her anger dissolved in the face of his cheerful grin. "He's gorgeous."

"He's my pride and joy. I trained him myself. If only I'd been blessed to be petite, I would have raced him too."

"We're both tall." Lily felt silly stating the obvious, but she couldn't help it. "It's been both a blessing and a curse."

"You carry your height well. You've grown into a beautiful woman."

Too much, too fast. Lily wanted answers before they started getting melancholy for a past they hadn't shared. "We need to talk and I need some answers."

"You're right. My office is right down here."

Lily followed Sophia through the stables to an office in the corner of the building. Sparse, but neat, the small room contained a couple of file cabinets and a desk with a computer. The windows on each side provided plenty of light, and a door on the other side of the room likely housed a closet. Sophia invited her to sit, and she took the chair near the door while Sophia sat at the desk. After a few beats of uncomfortable silence, Sophia started talking.

"Your friend Skye, she explained how you found me. She said that you know Cyrus is your father."

"She's not my friend." The anger was back, and Lily didn't try to hold it in.

"I don't understand."

"Skye is a very nice person, but she's not my friend. She's someone I hired to find out whether I have any living blood family. I paid her because I had no idea my birth mother was alive and well and living an hour away. Imagine my surprise when I learned the truth."

"I can't imagine." Sophia looked at the floor. "You're hurt and I'm sorry for my part in it."

"Is that all you have to say?"

Sophia shook her head. "I've kept these secrets for so long, it's difficult to let go. You have to believe me. Everything I've done was for your protection."

"So you left me to be raised by a rich family, thinking I'd be better off? Like money would solve everything. What were you to Cyrus? What was he to you? Did you even care about each other or was I just a mistake you needed to cover up?"

"I loved your father, but I shouldn't have. He was married and I was young and impetuous. My brothers tried to control my every move, and I rebelled by having an affair with a man they couldn't stand."

Lily saw the fiery light of passion in Sophia's eyes when she spoke of her father. She couldn't recall a time when she'd observed her mother express that same intensity about anything. Maybe it was Sophia's passion that drove her father to have an affair. She had to know. "Did he love you too?"

"He did. Everything he did proved it to me."

"But he wouldn't leave my mother to be with you?"

Sophia shook her head. "It wasn't that easy."

"Love isn't always easy." Lily's mind flashed on an image of Peyton, standing in the old, run-down Craftsman, talking about her dreams of a future family. In that moment she'd felt the first tugs of new love, only to have them ripped away the very next day. No, love wasn't easy. What right did she have to chastise Sophia for not fighting for it when she'd turned and walked away from love at the first sign of adversity?

"My brothers, they are bad men. Dangerous men. I agreed to walk away from any chance with your father to save his life and yours. I didn't want you to grow up in their world."

Questions swirled in Lily's brain, but she didn't know where to start. What Sophia was describing sounded like a bad telenovela. She tried to piece together a coherent question, but her thoughts were interrupted when the door across the room swung open. Before Lily could process what was happening, a man stepped out and pointed a large handgun at them.

"Sophia, always the rebel," he said. "Both of you, over here." He barked the words and gestured with the gun, motioning them to the far wall, between the filing cabinets.

"What are you doing here?" Sophia shouted at the man. "I've kept my end of the bargain. You need to leave now!"

Lily looked between them. On some level, Sophia's bravado was impressive, but shouting at a man with a gun didn't make much sense. Her own hands were shaking, and terror spiraled down her spine with an icy chill. The man was tall and dark with jet-black hair and deep brown eyes. She glanced at Sophia to confirm her suspicions, but the man did it for her.

"Sophia, aren't you going to introduce the girl to her uncle Arturo?"

My brothers...Dangerous men. Lily closed her eyes. Her father had been right all along. There was nothing about her past worth finding.

Sophia wasn't backing down. "Leave, Arturo."

"No." He waved the gun in Lily's direction. "Her gringo father is breaking his end of the deal, so all bets are off. My regular business is having some difficulties, and I came here for your wonder horse, but I think I'll take my pretty niece instead."

"Where's Sergio? Did he betray you too or was he too decent to rob his only sister?" Sophia stepped closer to her brother, effectively shielding Lily. "I've worked hard for my life. Honest work. Your kind has no place here. Get out." She pointed to the door.

Lily watched them with a mixture of fear and confusion. She sensed that deep wounds were at play, but her fear won out over any desire to sort through the family history. She started looking around for a route of escape. The open door across the room was the path to freedom, but to get there, she'd have to be faster than Arturo's gun, and, as conflicted as she felt about Sophia, she couldn't leave without her.

Rather than contemplating escape, Sophia seemed intent on getting in Arturo's face. She was standing less than a foot from him now, his gun mere inches from her shoulder. Instead of being deterred by the weapon, she appeared to be galvanized by it. She jabbed at Arturo's chest and shouted, "I gave up everything because of you and Sergio, and I won't do it again. No amount of safety is worth the price of freedom."

Arturo looked flustered, confused at her unwillingness to yield to his authority. His gun was no longer pointed directly at Sophia, but his arm hung by his side as he argued with her. As Lily watched them, Sophia's daring doused her fear. Maybe between the two of them, they could overpower him. She inched closer, trying to catch Sophia's eye to signal her intent, but a timid voice from the hall outside the door froze her in place.

"Arturo, it's Carmen."

Arturo called out to the voice, telling her to come in. Lily had hoped he would turn to look, but he kept his eyes fixed on Sophia. A young woman appeared in the doorway. She looked terrified. Lily knew exactly how she felt, and she also knew this might be their only opportunity to get away from Arturo and his gun. She pointed toward the door and cried out, hoping against hope that her action would cause Arturo to turn away from Sophia for just a second, long enough for them to catch him off guard.

At the sound of her cry, Arturo did glance at the door, but before Lily could act, the young woman was yanked from the doorway and in her place were strangers wearing black jackets and carrying guns and shouting commands. She whipped her head around and saw Sophia lunge at Arturo's chest as he lifted his gun into the air. She heard several loud bangs and watched helplessly as Sophia collapsed and Arturo fell forward. Her feet were lead blocks as she pushed her way toward them. She barely made it two steps before she was wrapped in darkness and she sagged to the ground.

❖

When they were within sight of the property, Dale pulled out her phone and sent a text to Mary, requesting a status. While Dale typed the text, Peyton looked around. There was a house and two buildings, one of which looked like it could be the stables where Arturo had instructed Carmen to go. There was a truck parked in front of the house. She made a note of the license plate and pointed it out to Dale. "Get someone to run that. Maybe it will tell us more about who owns the property."

Dale typed another text. "Done, but time's running out. Mary says Carmen's on the trail to the stables and she'll need to get in there on time or risk blowing the whole thing."

"What's the plan?"

"Carmen goes in, talks to Arturo. Mary fed her some stuff to say about the investigation that's not public. We wait until she walks out and is clear of the building and then we either grab Arturo here or follow him and pick him up later. Mary's got a guy in place on the other side of the building and we're hoping he can find a way to see inside and let us know if Arturo's alone in there."

Peyton sorted through the possibilities. They'd had an arrest warrant for both of the Vargas brothers for a while, but catching them was another matter. To be within striking distance was exhilarating, but a lot could go wrong. She hoped the reward was worth the risk.

Dale seemed to hear her silent question. "It's not too late to call this off. This was your plan. It's your decision."

"What would you do?"

"Carmen may be a civilian, but she got herself into this mess. Arturo has no reason to hurt her, especially since she might be a valuable source of information for him. If anything, he plans to use her to protect his interests. I say this is the closest we've come to flushing him out of hiding and we go with it."

Peyton knew Dale was right. These decisions were hard for a reason, but they still had to be made. "Okay then. It's a go." She pointed toward the house. "We need to make sure that if there is someone in there, they aren't cover for Arturo, or even worse, some innocent person who might walk into the middle of this. Looks like the front door isn't visible from the stables. How about you and I check it out?"

"Good idea."

Dale sent another text to Mary and then led the way to the front of the house. The big wood door behind the screen door stood wide open, allowing them a full view of the front room of the house. Dale signaled to Peyton to stay on the far side of the door while she looked around. A second later, a tall blond woman appeared on the other side of the door.

"Can I help you?" she asked.

Dale started to speak, but Peyton interrupted. "I know you," she said in a low voice. "You're the investigator working for Lily Gantry. What are you doing here?"

"Excuse me?" The woman's tone was indignant, but quickly changed to curious. "Wait, haven't we met?"

Peyton's gut clenched as her instincts told her something was seriously wrong. What was this woman who'd been working for Lily doing at the home of someone who was probably harboring a dangerous fugitive? Could she have been wrong about Lily being innocent of any knowledge about the Vargases' connection to Cyrus?

She had to know. Right now. She fished her memory for the woman's name. "Skye, who's in there with you?"

"Not that it's any of your business, but no one."

Peyton looked at Dale who flashed her badge and said, "We're coming in. You okay with that?"

Skye looked at the badge, seemed to consider her options, and then opened the door and waved them in. Once inside, Peyton didn't waste any time. "I need to know exactly what you're doing here and I need to know right now."

"I can't tell you that," Skye said.

Peyton stepped closer, her hands close enough to throttle Skye if she refused to answer her questions. She heard Dale clear her throat, but she ignored her attempt to get her attention and pressed on. "If Lily's involved in this, we might be able to help her, but we need to know everything about her connection to the Vargases or I can't make any promises."

She'd said too much, but if Lily was here on some misguided mission for her father, Peyton was desperate to get to her before she traveled too far down that path.

Skye raised her hands. "I have no idea what you're talking about. Lily is here to meet her mother, Sophia Valencia. That's all I can tell you and I shouldn't have told you that much."

Of course. Lily had hired Skye to help her track down her birth mother's family. Peyton felt foolish for thinking Lily might be here for anything other than an innocent purpose, but she still had questions about why Lily's mother would be connected to the Vargases. She glanced at Dale and could tell she had the same questions. "Where are they?" Peyton asked Skye.

"They went out to the stables a little while ago." Skye looked at her watch. "I guess they have a lot to talk about."

The words after "they went out to the stables" were a blur. Peyton started to the door, but Dale grabbed her arm and held her back.

"Wait, we need to check in with Mary first."

The next few minutes lurched by as Dale sent a text to Mary and they waited for her to check with the rest of her team to find out what they could about Arturo's position. When Dale's phone rang, Peyton jerked with surprise. Dale put Mary on speaker and they listened to her report.

"Carmen's ready to go in. It appears Arturo didn't bring any of his men—he may not know who he can trust at this point. He's in there in what looks like an office. Problem is, he's not alone. There are two women with him and he has a gun on one of them."

Peyton knew before Mary spoke the words who was with Arturo. She glanced at Dale, whose eyes reflected the same fierce sense of resolve she felt. Mary's voice burst through the phone. "It's time, guys. Carmen is ready and so are we. Do we go in?"

"Take everyone you have and go in now," Peyton yelled as she took off running.

❖

Lily clawed at the cloth covering her head and gulped for air. Seconds later, light broke through and she realized she was on the floor of the stable office and she couldn't move her arms. Frantic to discover the source of her paralysis, she moved her head back and forth until a whispered voice calmed her fear.

"Shhh, it's okay. I've got you. You're safe."

The voice repeated the refrain, softer with each pass, and Lily closed her eyes and relaxed into what she now recognized was an embrace. She had no idea how much time had passed before the voice asked, "Lily, baby, do you think you can stand?"

Peyton. Peyton was here, holding her, and she'd never felt more safe in spite of her cloudy memories of what had happened mere moments ago. A man, who'd called himself her uncle, had threatened her. With a gun and…her memories came flooding back, and she jerked out of Peyton's arms. "Sophia!"

Peyton pulled her back. "She's going to be okay." She pointed across the room where paramedics were loading her onto a stretcher. "The bullet grazed her arm. They're taking her in, but she should be released tonight."

Lily glanced around the room and relived the events of the last half hour. She saw Agent Nelson and a small crowd of other federal agents near Arturo, who was also being loaded onto a stretcher. She gestured in his direction. "Is he…?"

"He's alive, but he can't hurt you," Peyton said. "As soon as they stitch him up, he'll be going straight to prison."

Lily sighed with relief. She'd thought her life was over, and she still had no idea exactly what had happened to alter that destiny. But Peyton was here now, and she'd never felt safer than she felt in her arms. But as safe as she felt, she remembered how Sophia had stood up to Arturo. "I have to go with her." Lily tried to stand, but dizziness stopped her halfway there.

Peyton stood and helped her get her footing. "We're both going. You've had quite a shock and I want to make sure you're okay."

"I'll take you."

Lily looked up to see Skye standing behind Peyton. A flash of memory flooded back, and she realized Skye had been part of the group at the door who'd rushed into the room to save them. "Skye, are you okay?"

"Not a scratch." She jerked her head at Agent Nelson and directed her words to Peyton. "I imagine your running buddy is going to be here for a while, but I can take you both to the nearest hospital. You ready to go?"

Lily watched while Peyton walked over to Agent Nelson and exchanged a few words. Nelson looked up and waved at her and then clapped Peyton on the shoulder. When Peyton came back, she asked, "Everything okay?"

Peyton answered by pulling her close. "It will be."

On the ride to the hospital, Peyton sat next to her in the backseat, and she and Skye filled her in about how they'd wound up at the stables and managed to use Arturo's own plan to meet with their cooperating witness to distract him from her and Sophia.

Lily shivered as Peyton told her more about why Arturo Vargas was a wanted man. "I had no idea what was happening. I really thought he was going to kill us both."

Peyton grabbed both her hands. "I promise you we had overwhelming force coming through that door. It was dangerous, but when we saw him in there with you both, we had to risk it." She pulled back a strand of Lily's hair and stroked her cheek. "I'm so relieved you are okay."

Lily raised her hand and placed it on Peyton's, grasping tightly. "I'm so glad you're here."

Skye cleared her throat and the two of them smiled, but didn't break contact. Lily finally felt safe enough to ask a nagging question. "Peyton, what you said about Arturo, the things he's done, that he's going to prison. How will that affect me?"

"I don't understand." Peyton looked puzzled.

"First my father, now my uncle. I swear to you, if my father is guilty of working with Arturo, I had no idea. You have to believe me."

"Wait, Arturo is Sophia's brother? He's your uncle?"

Peyton's tone was shocked but laced with sympathy. Lily looked deep into her eyes, but she saw kindness, not accusation. "He is."

"Oh, baby, I'm so sorry." Peyton hugged her close. "You got a little bit more than you bargained for in your search for blood relatives, didn't you?"

"That's one way of putting it. There's more. It's about Cyrus. Turns out he's really my father, after all." With that last bit out, she sagged against Peyton and relaxed into her strong embrace.

The last thing she remembered, before she slipped into sleep was Peyton's soft voice saying, "Everything's going to be all right."

CHAPTER TWENTY-THREE

Peyton paused with her hand on the passenger side door.
"Are you sure you don't want to stay?"

It was getting late, and she wanted to get back to Dallas, but she'd do whatever Lily needed. Bianca had brought her truck to the hospital and had caught a ride back to the office with one of the agents. Peyton had stayed at the hospital until the doctors dressed Sophia's wound and checked Lily out to make sure she was okay, and then she drove them both back to Sophia's ranch.

She had to admire Sophia. In spite of her pain and the danger posed by the fact that her other brother, Sergio, was still out there somewhere, she had insisted that she wanted to testify against Arturo and tell the feds everything she knew about her brothers.

Peyton looked around at Valencia Acres. Setting aside what had happened today in the stables, it reminded her of the relaxing atmosphere of the Circle Six. She'd understand if Lily wanted to stay here and be with the mother she'd only just found instead of driving off with her and dealing with the unresolved issues between them.

"I'm sure," Lily said. "She's says her ranch hand will check in on her. I want to get to know her, but today…today, I need to think about my future, not my past. Do you understand?"

Peyton nodded. She wanted to think about her own future as well and, as she helped Lily into her truck, she couldn't help but experience a rush of fear that she and Lily might have different visions for what lay ahead. She fastened her seat belt, put the key in the ignition, and adjusted the rearview mirror, each action a slow and deliberate attempt to delay a conversation about where they went from here.

As she started to put her hands on the steering wheel, Lily reached for her hand and hooked their fingers together. At the warmth of her touch, the fear fell away and gave her the courage to ask, "Where would you like to go?"

"Someplace safe."

Peyton wished she knew where that was. Lily's home was full of deception, and her own brought to mind her father's illness and Neil's betrayal. She drove back toward Dallas, hoping fate would guide them to the proper place.

"Do you want to talk about your father?" Peyton asked. Sophia had filled in part of the story on the ride home from the hospital. When Cyrus had found out Sophia was pregnant with his child, he'd been overjoyed. He promised to leave his wife and marry Sophia, but when Arturo and Sergio found out, they forbade Sophia from marrying Cyrus. Instead of being excited about having a niece, they were appalled at the prospect of a mongrel relative binding them to a man they didn't like. They'd agreed to allow Cyrus to keep the baby if he would agree that he would never let her have contact with her mother. If he broke that promise, they assured him both Sophia and the child would pay.

To hide the truth from Rose, Cyrus had made a generous donation to the church to concoct the adoption, and Sophia completed the information for the birth certificate, leaving the name for Lily's father blank. However, still groggy from the C-section, she'd filled out the hospital form with Cyrus's name. No one had had any reason to go looking for that telling piece of paper until Lily hired Skye to find her relatives.

As for Cyrus's business connections to the Vargases, Sophia didn't know how or when such a relationship had developed, but based on what Arturo said while he held her and Lily at gunpoint, something had gone sour between them.

"Do you mind if we don't talk about any of this tonight?" Lily asked. "I think my head might explode if I try to sort through it."

Peyton squeezed her hand and kept her focus on the road. A few minutes later, she looked over and saw that Lily had fallen asleep. Rest. That's part of what Lily needed to feel safe. Peace and rest, away from friends and family and their prying questions and demands. And that included her and her own selfish need to recapture the opportunities they'd lost. If she cared about Lily at all, she had to do what was best for her. Suddenly, she knew exactly where to take Lily to guarantee her safety and also give her the peace and rest she needed.

Lily heard the door open and struggled to open her eyes. She glanced around, hazy from her deep sleep. The driver's side seat was empty. She looked out the window and saw bellmen rushing around, pulling luggage from cars. She recognized this place. They were at the Adolphus, but where was Peyton?

A knock on her window answered the question. Peyton was standing outside the passenger door, a tentative smile on her face. Lily opened the door and asked, "What are we doing here?"

"You asked for someplace safe. This is the best I could come up with. I called ahead. They have a suite all ready for you. Since it's down the street from the office, I'll be able to check on you, but you'll have all the peace and quiet you need. What do you think?"

It sounded perfect, except for one thing. "Where will you stay?"

Peyton looked confused. "I'll probably go by the office now, but I guess I'll go to the ranch after that."

"Do you have to go to the office?"

"What do you want me to do?"

Lily looked at the doors to the hotel. She knew what she wanted. She wanted Peyton to check into the hotel with her. She wanted to order whiskey from room service and then double lock the door and lie in a bed, wrapped in Peyton's arms, safe and secure. She wanted them both to escape for as long as possible from the complicated realities that threatened to keep them apart.

But as kind and caring as Peyton had been this day, she didn't know what the future held, or even if she had the right to envision a future with Peyton. She decided to start with baby steps. "I want you to have dinner with me. In my room. Would you do that?"

Peyton smiled. "Absolutely."

When they reached the suite, Lily surveyed the large four-poster bed, couch, chair, and desk. The couch would be safest. She excused herself to the restroom where she found two robes hanging on the back of the door, and she knew exactly what would feel best. A hot shower would be the perfect solution to wash away the memories of the day. She stuck her head out. "Peyton?"

"Yes?"

"Why don't you order us something from room service? I'm going to take a quick shower."

"Okay." Peyton walked over to the bathroom door with the room service menu in her hand. "You want anything in particular?"

"If I said bourbon is the only thing I really want, would you think less of me?"

Peyton stepped closer and placed a hand on Lily's cheek. "I think you deserve a barrel of bourbon after what you went through today."

"A bottle should be sufficient." Lily leaned forward, kissed her on the cheek, and ducked back into the bathroom. "I'll be out soon," she called out as she shut the door.

Peyton stood staring at the door, both confused and aroused. *Quit acting like a teenager. She kissed you out of gratitude, and she asked you up here for comfort, nothing more.* She started to walk over to the phone on the desk, but the bathroom door opened again.

"Peyton?"

She turned and her breath caught at the sight of Lily in the hotel robe. "Yes?"

"Maybe you could join me and we could order room service together. After."

She could think of nothing she'd rather do than tug the stark white robe from Lily's beautiful body, step into the steamy shower, and run her hands over Lily's wet skin, but she heard the cautious undercurrent in Lily's voice and forced a more measured reaction. "I'd like that."

"Me too." Lily held out a robe. "You're going to need to get undressed. I'll wait."

Peyton didn't take the robe. Lily might be cautious about taking this step, but she was going ahead full force, and Peyton wanted nothing more than to meet her at every step. She kicked off her boots and reached down to remove her socks. When she stood back up, Lily was at her side and slipped an arm around her waist. "Here, let me help," Lily murmured as she started unbuttoning her shirt. Between them, they managed to wrestle through the buttons and, while Peyton pulled her arms out of the sleeves, Lily unfastened her fly and slid her hand into Peyton's bricfs. Peyton groaned and pulled Lily into a deep kiss. Her body flooded with arousal.

When Peyton broke the kiss to take a breath, Lily panted, "Shower still?"

Peyton pulled on the tie to Lily's robe, eased the fluffy fabric from Lily's shoulders, and let it drop to the floor. She gasped at the beauty of Lily's naked form. Shaking with anticipation, she stepped out of her jeans and briefs, took Lily's hand, and led them to the shower.

The water was hot and the pressure was pounding and it only magnified the swell of her desire. As the water cascaded over their bodies, she placed her leg between Lily's thighs and slid her entire body along the length of Lily's, savoring the feel of her lean muscles and soft skin and the moans of her mounting arousal.

She bent to take one of Lily's gorgeous nipples into her mouth and sucked it to a fine point while she rolled her palm over the other, turned on by the feel of it hardening in response to her touch. As she licked and played, Lily bucked against her leg and, even in the wet shower, she could feel the slick rush of her approaching orgasm.

Knowing Lily needed this release, she increased the pressure, but Lily arched away just slightly and slid her hand between Peyton's legs. Already aroused, Lily's touch set off a sharp charge to her clit that radiated throughout her entire body. Lily thrust several fingers into Peyton and kept thrusting. In and out, slow and then faster and faster until Peyton feared she'd no longer be able to stand. She placed a hand against the wall and dropped her other hand to stroke the tender folds between Lily's legs until she cried out and quaked in her arms. As the waves of orgasm roared through Lily, Peyton pulled her tighter and, through her own climax, kissed Lily's forehead, her eyelids, her cheeks until they were both limp and spent in each other's arms.

❖

Lily watched from the bed as Peyton sorted through the room service tray. "That's a lot of food."

"Seems like you might've worked up an appetite." She smiled and the glint in her eyes was impish. "I know I did."

Lily took a sip from her glass of whiskey. "I'm ravenous and I don't necessarily mean for food."

Peyton walked over to the side of the bed and held out a cracker with cheese. "We have plenty of time for that. Eat up. You're going to need your strength."

Lily opened her mouth and let Peyton slide the food in. She bit down on the sharp cheese and kissed the tips of Peyton's fingers. "Umm, I guess I was hungry for something besides you."

"Look at how quickly you've moved on. I've been replaced by a decent cheddar."

"Don't forget the cracker. It's divine." She ducked and laughed as Peyton tossed a pillow at her head. She pointed at the tray. "Don't worry. There's plenty for both of us."

Peyton slipped into the bed and placed an arm around her shoulders. "I'll eat later. Right now I just want to be close to you." Her voice was low and husky, and Lily felt the undercurrent of need.

Lily snuggled closer and slipped a hand into Peyton's robe and traced the plane of her tight stomach. She wanted her again. She wanted to be on top of her, underneath her. She wanted to taste her and she wanted to come against her lips.

She let her eyes slip closed and she imagined riding up to the house in the woods. She reached down to pat her horse and smiled when she saw it was Destiny. As she drew closer, Peyton walked out the front door of the house, and a huge smile spread across her face. "You're home," she called out. Lily climbed out of the saddle and dashed up the steps into Peyton's arms.

"What are you thinking?"

"Hmmm," Lily opened her eyes, happy to see Peyton next to her, but missing the rest of the scene she'd lost herself in. She gazed into Peyton's eyes, looking for some sign that what she dreamed could come true. The house, the future, a family. A real family, born out of love not deception. A lover who would be her partner to the end, no matter how much adversity they faced. She might not be wired for these things, but she wanted them more fiercely than she'd ever wanted anything.

Peyton was still watching her, patient and kind. Throughout the last few weeks, Peyton had only been concerned about protecting her, keeping her safe. Looking to her for a sign that they could have something more wasn't fair. She was ready to take control of her future without regard to what everyone else wanted for her. She knew with crystal clarity if she wanted a future with Peyton, she needed to take the first step. The big one. The one that would let Peyton know she was committed. She took a deep breath.

"I love you."

Peyton's eyes grew hazy and she kissed her lips. A slow, lingering kiss that warmed her soul. When Lily gasped for air, Peyton pulled back. "I love you too."

She bent down as if to deliver another kiss, but Lily pushed her chest. "Wait."

"Wait?"

"I mean I *love* you. Like house in the woods, have a pack of children, raise horses, and grow old together kind of love." She braced for Peyton's reaction to her abrupt relationship bomb. Would she run? Would she slip out in the night? Were they over before they'd even really begun?

Peyton's huge smile was just like the one in her wisp of a dream, and her words were pure magic. "Is there any other kind?"

THE END

About the Author

Carsen Taite's goal as an author is to spin tales with plot lines as interesting as the cases she encountered in her career as a criminal defense lawyer. She is the author of eleven previously released novels, *truelesbianlove.com*, *It Should be a Crime* (a Lambda Literary Award finalist), *Do Not Disturb*, *Nothing but the Truth*, *The Best Defense*, *Slingshot*, *Beyond Innocence*, *Battle Axe*, *Rush*, *Switchblade*, and *Courtship*. She is currently working on her thirteenth novel, *Reasonable Doubt*, another tale of romantic intrigue. Learn more at www.carsentaite.com.

Books Available from Bold Strokes Books

Love's Bounty by Yolanda Wallace. Lobster boat captain Jake Myers stopped living the day she cheated death, but meeting greenhorn Shy Silva stirs her back to life. (978-1-62639334-9)

Just Three Words by Melissa Brayden. Sometimes the one you want is the one you least suspect. Accountant Samantha Ennis has her ordered life disrupted when heartbreaker Hunter Blair moves into her trendy Soho loft. (978-1-62639-335-6)

Lay Down the Law by Carsen Taite. Attorney Peyton Davis returns to her Texas roots to take on big oil and the Mexican Mafia, but will her investigation thwart her chance at true love? (978-1-62639-336-3)

Playing in Shadow by Lesley Davis. Survivor's guilt threatens to keep Bryce trapped in her nightmare world unless Scarlet's love can pull her out of the darkness back into the light. (978-1-62639-337-0)

Soul Selecta by Gill McKnight. Soul mates are hell to work with. (978-1-62639-338-7)

The Revelation of Beatrice Darby by Jean Copeland. Adolescence is complicated, but Beatrice Darby is about to discover how impossible it can seem to a lesbian coming of age in conservative 1950s New England. (978-1-62639-339-4)

Twice Lucky by Mardi Alexander. For firefighter Mackenzie James and Dr. Sarah Macarthur, there's suddenly a whole lot more in life to understand, to consider, to risk…someone will need to fight for her life. (978-1-62639-325-7)

Shadow Hunt by L.L. Raand. With young to raise and her Pack under attack, Sylvan, Alpha of the wolf Weres, takes on her greatest challenge when she determines to uncover the faceless enemies known as the Shadow Lords. A Midnight Hunters novel. (978-1-62639-326-4)

Heart of the Game by Rachel Spangler. A baseball writer falls for a single mom, but can she ever love anything as much as she loves the game? (978-1-62639-327-1)

Getting Lost by Michelle Grubb. Twenty-eight days, thirteen European countries, a tour manager fighting attraction, and an accused murderer: Stella and Phoebe's journey of a lifetime begins here. (978-1-62639-328-8)

Prayer of the Handmaiden by Merry Shannon. Celibate priestess Kadrian must defend the kingdom of Ithyria from a dangerous enemy and ultimately choose between her duty to the Goddess and the love of her childhood sweetheart, Erinda. (978-1-62639-329-5)

The Witch of Stalingrad by Justine Saracen. A Soviet "night witch" pilot and American journalist meet on the Eastern Front in WW II and struggle through carnage, conflicting politics, and the deadly Russian winter. (978-1-62639-330-1)

Pedal to the Metal by Jesse J. Thoma. When unreformed thief Dubs Williams is released from prison to help Max Winters bust a car theft ring, Max learns that to catch a thief, get in bed with one. (978-1-62639-239-7)

Dragon Horse War by D. Jackson Leigh. A priestess of peace and a fiery warrior must defeat a vicious uprising that entwines their destinies and ultimately their hearts. (978-1-62639-240-3)

For the Love of Cake by Erin Dutton. When everything is on the line, and one taste can break a heart, will pastry chefs Maya and Shannon take a chance on reality? (978-1-62639-241-0)

Betting on Love by Alyssa Linn Palmer. A quiet country-girl-at-heart and a live-life-to-the-fullest biker take a risk at offering each other their hearts. (978-1-62639-242-7)

The Deadening by Yvonne Heidt. The lines between good and evil, right and wrong, have always been blurry for Shade. When Raven's actions force her to choose, which side will she come out on? (978-1-62639-243-4)

Ordinary Mayhem by Victoria A. Brownworth. Faye Blakemore has been taking photographs since she was ten, but those same photographs threaten to destroy everything she knows and everything she loves. (978-1-62639-315-8)

One Last Thing by Kim Baldwin & Xenia Alexiou. Blood is thicker than pride. The final book in the Elite Operative Series brings together foes, family, and friends to start a new order. (978-1-62639-230-4)

Songs Unfinished by Holly Stratimore. Two aspiring rock stars learn that falling in love while pursuing their dreams can be harmonious—if they can only keep their pasts from throwing them out of tune. (978-1-62639-231-1)

Beyond the Ridge by L.T. Marie. Will a contractor and a horse rancher overcome their family differences and find common ground to build a life together? (978-1-62639-232-8)

Swordfish by Andrea Bramhall. Four women battle the demons from their pasts. Will they learn to let go, or will happiness be forever beyond their grasp? (978-1-62639-233-5)

The Fiend Queen by Barbara Ann Wright. Princess Katya and her consort Starbride must turn evil against evil in order to banish Fiendish power from their kingdom, and only love will pull them back from the brink. (978-1-62639-234-2)

Up the Ante by PJ Trebelhorn. When Jordan Stryker and Ashley Noble meet again fifteen years after a short-lived affair, are either of them prepared to gamble on a chance at love? (978-1-62639-237-3)

Speakeasy by MJ Williamz. When mob leader Helen Byrne sets her sights on the girlfriend of Al Capone's right-hand man, passion and tempers flare on the streets of Chicago. (978-1-62639-238-0)

Venus in Love by Tina Michele. Morgan Blake can't afford any distractions and Ainsley Dencourt can't afford to lose control—but the beauty of life and art usually lies in the unpredictable strokes of the artist's brush. (978-1-62639-220-5)

Rules of Revenge by AJ Quinn. When a lethal operative on a collision course with her past agrees to help a CIA analyst on a critical assignment, the encounter proves explosive in ways neither woman anticipated. (978-1-62639-221-2)

The Romance Vote by Ali Vali. Chili Alexander is a sought-after campaign consultant who isn't prepared when her boss's daughter, Samantha Pellegrin, comes to work at the firm and shakes up Chili's life from the first day. (978-1-62639-222-9)

Advance: Exodus Book One by Gun Brooke. Admiral Dael Caydoc's mission to find a new homeworld for the Oconodian people is hazardous, but working with the infuriating Commander Aniwyn "Spinner" Seclan endangers her heart and soul. (978-1-62639-224-3)

UnCatholic Conduct by Stevie Mikayne. Jil Kidd goes undercover to investigate fraud at St. Marguerite's Catholic School, but life gets complicated when her student is killed—and she begins to fall for her prime target. (978-1-62639-304-2)

Season's Meetings by Amy Dunne. Catherine Birch reluctantly ventures on the festive road trip from hell with beautiful stranger Holly Daniels only to discover the road to true love has its own obstacles to maneuver. (978-1-62639-227-4)

Myth and Magic: Queer Fairy Tales edited by Radclyffe and Stacia Seaman. Myth, magic, and monsters—the stuff of childhood dreams (or nightmares) and adult fantasies. (978-1-62639-225-0)

Nine Nights on the Windy Tree by Martha Miller. Recovering drug addict, Bertha Brannon, is an attorney who is trying to stay clean when a murder sends her back to the bad end of town. (978-1-62639-179-6)

Driving Lessons by Annameekee Hesik. Dive into Abbey Brooks's sophomore year as she attempts to figure out the amazing, but sometimes complicated, life of a you-know-who girl at Gila High School. (978-1-62639-228-1)

Asher's Shot by Elizabeth Wheeler. Asher Price's candid photographs capture the truth, but when his success requires exposing an enemy, Asher discovers his only shot at happiness involves revealing secrets of his own. (978-1-62639-229-8)

Courtship by Carsen Taite. Love and justice—a lethal mix or a perfect match? (978-1-62639-210-6)

Against Doctor's Orders by Radclyffe. Corporate financier Presley Worth wants to shut down Argyle Community Hospital, but Dr. Harper Rivers will fight her every step of the way, if she can also fight their growing attraction. (978-1-62639-211-3)

A Spark of Heavenly Fire by Kathleen Knowles. Kerry and Beth are building their life together, but unexpected circumstances could destroy their happiness. (978-1-62639-212-0)

Never Too Late by Julie Blair. When Dr. Jamie Hammond is forced to hire a new office manager, she's shocked to come face to face with Carla Grant and memories from her past. (978-1-62639-213-7)

Widow by Martha Miller. Judge Bertha Brannon must solve the murder of her lover, a policewoman she thought she'd grow old with. As more bodies pile up, the murderer starts coming for her. (978-1-62639-214-4)

Twisted Echoes by Sheri Lewis Wohl. What's a woman to do when she realizes the voices in her head are real? (978-1-62639-215-1)

Criminal Gold by Ann Aptaker. Through a dangerous night in New York in 1949, Cantor Gold, dapper dyke-about-town, smuggler of fine art, is forced by a crime lord to be his instrument of vengeance. (978-1-62639-216-8)

The Melody of Light by M.L. Rice. After surviving abuse and loss, will Riley Gordon be able to navigate her first year of college and accept true love and family? (978-1-62639-219-9)

Because of You by Julie Cannon. What would you do for the woman you were forced to leave behind? (978-1-62639-199-4)

The Job by Jove Belle. Sera always dreamed that she would one day reunite with Tor. She just didn't think it would involve terrorists, firearms, and hostages. (978-1-62639-200-7)

Making Time by C.J. Harte. Two women going in different directions meet after fifteen years and struggle to reconnect in spite of the past that separated them. (978-1-62639-201-4)

Once The Clouds Have Gone by KE Payne. Overwhelmed by the dark clouds of her past, Tag Grainger is lost until the intriguing and spirited Freddie Metcalfe unexpectedly forces her to reevaluate her life. (978-1-62639-202-1)